2/08 CH 4/12

Books of Merit

MACDONALD

A NOVEL

MAC

DONALD

Roy MACSKIMMING

Thomas Allen Publishers
Toronto

Library and Archives Canada Cataloguing in Publication

MacSkimming, Roy, 1944–
    Macdonald / Roy MacSkimming.

ISBN 978-0-88762-305-9

1. Macdonald, John A. (John Alexander), 1815–1891—Fiction.
2. Pope, Joseph, 1854-1926—Fiction.
3. Canada—Politics and government—1878–1896—Fiction.
I. Title.

PS8575.S53M32 2007   C813'.54   C2007-903272-9

Editor: Patrick Crean
Jacket and text design: Gordon Robertson
Jacket image: Library and Archives Canada; C5329

Published by Thomas Allen Publishers,
a division of Thomas Allen & Son Limited,
145 Front Street East, Suite 209,
Toronto, Ontario M5A 1E3 Canada

www.thomas-allen.com

**Canada Council
for the Arts**

ONTARIO ARTS COUNCIL
CONSEIL DES ARTS DE L'ONTARIO

The publisher gratefully acknowledges the support of
the Ontario Arts Council for its publishing program.
The Ontario Arts Council is an agency of the Government of Ontario.

We acknowledge the support of the Canada Council for the Arts, which
last year invested $20.1 million in writing and publishing throughout Canada.

We acknowledge the Government of Ontario through the
Ontario Media Development Corporation's Ontario Book Initiative.

We acknowledge the financial support of the Government of Canada through the Book
Publishing Industry Development Program (BPIDP) for our publishing activities.

11 10 09 08 07   1 2 3 4 5

Printed and bound in Canada

Therefore my age is as a lusty winter,
Frosty, but kindly.

— WILLIAM SHAKESPEARE,
As You Like It, London, 1599

I feel as old Adam said, like a lusty winter,
frosty but kindly.

— SIR JOHN A. MACDONALD on his
70th birthday, Montreal, 1885

A Note on History

In the winter of 1891, Canada was in its twenty-fourth year as a nation. Sir John A. Macdonald had been Prime Minister for all but five of those years. Macdonald had negotiated the first peaceful separation from the mother country in the history of the British Empire. He had survived political defeat following a notorious scandal. After a term in Opposition, he had swept back into power and orchestrated the extraordinary completion of a national railway over the Rocky Mountains to the Pacific. He had put down two rebellions by the Metis, people of Aboriginal and European descent fighting under their revered revolutionary leader, Louis Riel.

Macdonald had met all challenges, defeated all enemies. One great battle remained.

MACDONALD

One

FEBRUARY 1891

Kingston

Suddenly awake. Expecting predawn shadows in the corners of our bedroom, Minette asleep beside me, her dark curls adrift on the pillow. But dawn has already arrived. The bed is empty, the room unrecognizable. A bulging porcelain pitcher sits by a basin. Massive curtains hang closed across a window.

I pick up my pocket watch lying on a washstand. A quarter past seven. How in Heaven's name did I sleep so late? These hectic travels and late nights. Then an acute flash of the obvious: *the British American*. Of course. The second floor of the second-finest hotel in Kingston, a suite of rooms I reserved only days ago.

He insists we stay in this shabby antique instead of the modern Windsor nearby. His preference for the British American is eccentric, but perhaps understandable—less an economy measure than an unshakeable matter of heart. It's the very place, he reminds me so often it's become a joke between us, where Lord Durham took lunch in 1838.

I was fortunate to find decent rooms anywhere on short notice. Our visit to Kingston wasn't scheduled until the day before the vote. But events, as usual, overtook us. Such is our life in recent days: perpetual reaction and response.

I must go and see how he is.

Still in my nightshirt, I part the curtains and peer outside. The brightness is startling, the gaslights along Wellington Street already extinguished. A newsboy in a cloth cap sets up his station at the corner. A streetcar halts by the Post Office to drop off passengers, the reins slack in the sleepy driver's hands.

From the look of the skies, our unsettled weather continues. Until yesterday a hard pale sun had accompanied freezing temperatures that bit us to the bone. Then came cloud and unnatural warmth, and now, beyond the limestone buildings, a gusting south wind appears to be working high above Lake Ontario, piling up banks of dark cloud pregnant with rain, threatening to melt this city into premature spring.

How did *he* pass the night? How is *he* feeling as he awakes beyond my door? More and more my life becomes his. We've coalesced, he and I, into one being, notwithstanding the decades between us.

The old man is in desperate need of rest. For days we've been living like gypsies, travelling from station to station without respite, from one five-hour rally to another, wearing the same grubby clothes and expected every time to work ourselves up to the same fever pitch as our audience. We managed to lie low during Sunday's stopover in Toronto, yet the short break failed to restore him. And from now until the vote in eight days' time our schedule is unforgiving. His wracking cough worsens with every lurch in the weather. It never leaves him now, never permits him enough sleep, even for one accustomed all his life to living on so little.

This will be his last campaign. He repeats it over and over, at every whistle stop assuring the crowds of that startling, disturbing, but inescapable fact: "I appeal to you," he implores, "to give me your united and strenuous aid in this, my last effort for the preservation of our freedom!"

Every time they loudly beseech him to change his mind, to stay on and continue leading the good fight, presumably forever. And every time I can only think what a miracle they're seeing him at all.

Wrapping myself in the blue silk dressing gown Minette gave me at Christmas, I knock softly on the door to the adjoining rooms. Ben Chilton opens immediately. Ben is already dressed for duty, his bearded face expressionless beneath his balding dome.

"Well?" I whisper.

"Sleeping like a baby."

"Excellent."

"It was the two big brandies at bedtime."

"I told you to keep them small."

"Excuse me, the two small brandies."

Ben usually stays home in Ottawa. Bringing him along this time was my idea. His judgment isn't always the best—he's a touch simple, I suspect—but as our chief's man he can attend to his personal needs. I've enough to do as it is. Hence this suite: two bedrooms, an anteroom where Ben sleeps on a cot in case anything is required in the night, and a comfortable sitting room where we can greet visitors, deal with urgent correspondence, and touch up the Speech. No matter how polished, the Speech needs embellishing at every stop. We must acknowledge local concerns, pay homage to the local candidate, flatter local worthies whose loyalty to the Conservative Party may need reinforcement.

Motioning Ben to come into my room, I close the door softly behind us.

"Was he up much in the night?"

"Twice, but only to piss. No wandering about this time." He says the word as if it's perfectly normal, even stressing the sibilants. I put it down to his stretch in the Royal Navy. "When shall I fetch his breakfast, Mr. Pope?"

"Tea will do. We have luncheon with his constituency association at noon."

"Only tea again? It's an awful poor start to the day, Mr. Pope. Starve a fever, feed a cold, me mum always said."

"I'm sure your mother had a point. All right, bring up some toast and jam."

"A bit of porridge would do him the world of good."

"Never mind porridge. You know what he always says: 'Only innocent people eat breakfast.'"

Ben looks suitably mystified, and I wave him back into the suite and shut the door. I know he calls me "the Pope" behind my back. He thinks that because I'm Catholic, all my judgments are suspect. Someday I expect to see Ben astride a white horse leading the Orangemen's parade down Rideau Street.

I pull the bell rope to order up hot water. At the Windsor they have electric bells. After shaving I'll go down to greet the newspapermen lounging about the lobby and administer their daily briefing, looking ahead to the evening rally, supplying choice quotations for those with early deadlines.

By then he'll be up and dressed, and we'll convene in the sitting room to dispatch as much correspondence as possible before lunch. He's particular to a fault about keeping his correspondence up to date. He believes it the height of discourtesy to leave any writer, no matter how humble, waiting for a reply, and always graces them with a sage and witty response. It's a fine ideal but impossible to keep to during an election campaign. I must remember to persuade him to keep his luncheon remarks brief. He needs to save his voice for this evening. Only one address is scheduled, unlike most nights, but the good burghers of Napanee will expect a long and rousing one.

It's no accident, I suppose, that our rallies take place onstage in gilded theatres. It's always a grand performance complete with brass band. Last night at the Kingston Opera House he was in fine voice, too, despite his raw throat. His convictions seized him as they always do when he needs them, tuning his pipes to perfect pitch for the duration of the Speech. Afterwards he could barely speak above a whisper. When Dr. Sullivan read his pulse and asked how he felt, he could only rasp, "I've never felt so weary in all my life."

Napanee

On the train to Napanee he nods off almost at once. He wheezes peacefully in the high wingback chair across from mine, and something about his strong, sinewy, mottled hand dangling unconsciously in the aisle, swaying to the rhythm of the train, fills me with melancholy.

He can feel well pleased with his luncheon remarks. Speaking off the cuff in the British American's private dining room over the remains of boiled halibut, mutton with caper sauce, custard pie and coffee, he spoke, if a trifle hoarsely, in his most effortlessly genial style. He charmed and amused and exhorted the gentlemen of his constituency executive so effectively that they're persuaded their efforts and theirs alone will win the day for God, Canada and the Conservative Party. And he took just one glass of claret "to keep this damned cough at bay."

Our journey to Napanee will take two hours: somewhat longer than normal. I've instructed the engineer to move at a leisurely pace. The reason isn't a raging blizzard, the usual problem at this time of year, but the hope of giving citizens along the route an opportunity to glimpse Sir John A. Macdonald himself in the window of his special Pullman car—once he wakes up. Christened the *Jamaica*, the car is placed permanently at his disposal by William

Cornelius Van Horne, the American president of the Canadian Pacific Railway. The name derives from Lady Agnes Macdonald's birthplace—that lush isle so far from here, and farther still from Van Horne's current obsession, the shipping lanes between Vancouver and Hong Kong, where he's launching the CPR's new Empress line of luxury steamships.

Luxury is the word for the *Jamaica* also. Van Horne has spared no expense in furnishing the carriage like a stateroom fit for the Czar. Ornate gold-framed mirrors reflect black walnut panelling. Shaded reading lamps with brass fittings radiate a lambent glow. Comfortable red leather sofas line both sides of the carriage, sitting at right angles to our chairs, which are upholstered in dark red velvet. Narrow tables have been designed to allow ease of movement up and down the aisle. Now those tables are obliterated by newspapers, well-thumbed copies of *Hansard*—culled by myself for damning quotations from the Opposition—and brass ashtrays overflowing with cigar butts. On occasions when Lady Macdonald accompanies us, the *Jamaica* acquires even greater elegance. Bouquets of lilies replace the ashtrays tucked discreetly out of sight along with the spittoons. Copies of *Murray's Magazine*, *Ladies' Home Journal* and *Pall Mall Gazette*, all of which publish Lady M.'s amusing and widely admired articles, are positioned artfully about the carriage.

I console myself thinking how blessed we are to have Sir John, ill or healthy, as Prime Minister. Biased as I undoubtedly am, the facts are indisputable: he not only remains clear of mind and firm of will, but Canadians know him in our bones like a long-lived relative, who happens to have been master of our national stage since colonial days. When we hear him speak, when we evaluate his promises or examine his policies, we know exactly what we're getting. Agree with him or not, vote for him or not, love him or despise him, Canadians have an honest and enduring bond with Sir John.

Americans, by contrast, are often ignorant of the man they elect to lead them. They blindly entrust the Presidency, a virtual monarchy for four years, to a man they know as through a glass darkly. Even the venerated Lincoln was practically unknown when he stood for the office—an invention of the press, a caricature— Honest Abe the rail-splitter, the backwoods lawyer from Illinois and all that. By luck more than the wisdom of the people, he proved to have the gifts to reunite the disunited States; but the voters could as easily have chosen another Buchanan, who would have made a complete botch of the Civil War, or someone like the current President Harrison, his administration under the control of his Secretary of State, James G. Blaine, certainly no friend of ours. . . .

A winter election campaign is always hard, but this weather has turned foul in a new way. The clouds have broken now, and rain inundates the countryside, driven by a south wind. As we push farther west, we pass cattle standing stoically in the downpour beside desolate barns. The snowy ground is turning to slush, forming puddles that block the bleak country roads bisecting the tracks. Needless to say, no citizens man the route to cheer us on.

Inside the *Jamaica* the atmosphere grows fuggy with cigar smoke and drying flannel. Sir John has invited reporters from the Kingston *News*, Ottawa *Evening Journal* and *Citizen* and Montreal *Gazette* to travel in the car; but while he sleeps they're just as happy to huddle around their cards at the far end, smoking and cadging drinks from Ben's tray. From their raucous conversation I gather they're desperate to recover their losses from the *Empire* man. He, stripped down to his suspenders and bowler hat, seems to be enjoying an uncanny run of luck. The *Globe* hasn't been invited on board, but we can expect their correspondent to be somewhere in the crowd at Napanee, his calumnies already written.

This election campaign is the most savage I've ever witnessed. A single issue possesses the public mind like a devil—our trade struggles with the United States—and the *Globe* itself has become directly implicated.

Opening his campaign in Toronto, Sir John shocked the country by exposing rank treason. Before thousands inside the Academy of Music, he revealed the *Globe's* Edward Farrer, tribune of the Liberals, as a traitor—the anonymous author of a pamphlet penned for a Congressional audience, which preaches not only free trade with the U.S. but outright annexation. Farrer's pamphlet alleges that Sir John's disappearance from power would trigger a movement among Canadians for union with the States. Better still, Farrer wrote this claptrap for Secretary of State Blaine, who paid him handsomely in Yankee gold.

Sir John brandished proof sheets of the document before his astonished listeners. He quoted Farrer's own words urging trade sanctions by which the U.S. can bully and starve this country into submission. And Sir John traced these ideas directly back to Liberal politicians here at home. "I say that there is a deliberate conspiracy," he intoned darkly, "in which some members of the Opposition are more or less compromised. I say that there is a deliberate conspiracy, by force, by fraud, or by both, to push Canada into the American union."

His words had an incendiary effect. The audience surged toward the stage, bellowing their fury and their loyalty. With fifteen thousand more people jamming King, York and Simcoe Streets outside the theatre, a large gas lamp was toppled, and the police feared a stampede. Sir John quickly agreed to address the mob from the ornate balcony of a neighbouring home. We approached the lady of the house to ask her permission, and I was puzzled when she replied, "Certainly, as long as you think you can trust the old gentleman with me." Later I learned the place contains one of Toronto's genteel brothels.

By raising the cry of treason Sir John lit a fire, fanned by the *Empire*, the *Mail* and other papers loyal to the Government, that has been raging ever since. No voter can now be ignorant of the Liberals' ultimate goal. The *Globe* has even published an editorial arguing that union is Canada's manifest destiny. And although I'm sure Wilfrid Laurier knew nothing of Farrer's pamphlet, the damage to his party is enormous. I suspect Laurier as Liberal leader is now spent.

Sir John's stump speech, which I helped to craft, working beside him at Earnscliffe late into the night, now echoes with redoubled force:

"To you, Canadians, I ask," he declares from every platform, "what have you to gain by surrendering what your fathers held most dear? Under the broad folds of the Union Jack, we enjoy the most ample liberty to govern ourselves as we please. We participate in the advantages that flow from association with the mightiest empire that the world has ever seen. You will shortly be called upon to determine a question that resolves itself into this: Shall we endanger our possession of the great heritage bequeathed to us by our fathers, and submit ourselves to direct taxation, for the privilege of having our tariff fixed at Washington? Shall we meekly accept the prospect of becoming part of the American union?"

It thrills me every time to hear the eruption of massed voices crying in response, "No!" and "Never!" and "God save the Queen!" and "God save Sir John!" He then throws himself into his peroration:

"As for myself, my course is clear. A British subject I was born, a British subject I will die. With my utmost effort, with my latest breath, will I oppose the veiled treason which attempts by sordid means and mercenary proffers to lure our people from their allegiance!"

Veiled treason! Uttering this battle cry, with its echo of Disraeli, Sir John summons up every last ounce of an old man's lifeblood. It always elicits thunderous roars of approval and hot tears of outrage. It brings the house down every time.

Now here he slumps beside me—insofar as such a tall man can slump—a volcano at rest.

Of course it's only temporary. The bright, moist blue eyes soon open, immediately alert. "Now Joe," comes the rich textured voice, deeper and huskier than normal, "I know you have a soft spot for Laurier. But in all honesty—how much d'you think he knew about the Farrer business?"

I'm forever astonished by his ability to read my mind. Or is it simply that my mind belongs to him?

"No doubt it embarrasses him, sir."

He straightens in his chair, clears his throat noisily. Leaning his head across the aisle close to mine, he speaks more softly. "Yes, but is it only because they were found out?" While I consider my reply, Sir John answers his own question. "Laurier of course is a thoroughly decent chap. It's my bet he's flabbergasted by that pamphlet—not just by the contents, but the *doing* of it for those Congressmen." He coughs hard and presses his handkerchief to his lips. "Laurier has his principles. He supports free trade because he thinks it's in the best interests of the farmers—the States as their 'natural market' and all that. He's wrong, but he has a right to be wrong. I don't think it would occur to him to turn free trade into annexation. Or am I just going soft?"

"As you know, sir, Minette's family and Laurier's have always been close. To her knowledge, his loyalty to the Crown is as strong as yours or mine."

"Ah, *loyalty*," he replies, punctuating the word with a lawyer's stab of the index finger, "but to what? Not to the Crown, Joe, but Canada. And why? Because he knows in his French Catholic soul that his people would never enjoy the rights in the States that they enjoy here."

The formidable nose and cleft chin thrust stubbornly toward me. "Consider the irony," he continues. "English-speaking Liberals like Farrer and Cartwright and their friends are dying to throw the country to the Americans. At bottom they want to *be* Americans—they esteem the States a better place than this. Meanwhile, the true patriot of their party is a Frenchman." He beams at me, shaking his head and making his silvery thinning hair dance in agitation, as if physically embodying the contradiction of the Liberals' position: "And *that* is why they will lose this election."

I nod vigorously in agreement. I'm delighted to see my chief in such fighting trim. But believing it's my duty to keep him on his mettle, I add a caveat: "For the country's sake, Sir John, we must hope the farmers don't agree with Laurier."

He fixes me with an unblinking stare from under his tangled eyebrows, neither agreeing nor disagreeing, simply weighing my comment, seeking its specific density. At times Sir John's imperious intellectual detachment flusters me. I find it impossible to hold his unwavering gaze for more than a few seconds. It's simply too frank, too intimate. As casually as I can, I swivel my eyes toward the window.

The passing tree trunks are black with rain. The countryside is beginning to resemble April instead of February. I remind myself that this is only a temporary illusion and the weather will revert to winter at any moment.

Signalling to Ben, Sir John summons a brandy "to lubricate the vocal cords on this vile afternoon."

I watch closely to see if Ben follows my instructions. But when the drink arrives, sloshing about in one of the bottom-heavy crystal glasses provided by Mr. Van Horne, it looks like a good three fingers. I'm upset. I wonder what to say to Ben afterwards. Yet what can he do? He takes his orders from Sir John. I simply dread a repetition of the incident when, debating a Liberal and beset by illness and brandy, Sir John vomited onto the platform at his opponent's feet. It was an appalling moment, even if redeemed by his immediate recovery to tell the audience, "Ladies and gentlemen, please forgive me, I cannot help myself—that man simply makes me sick."

But in fact drink has never harmed Sir John's prodigious memory. Indeed, he drinks far less than in his younger days, before I worked for him, and less still when accompanied by Lady M. That might be an argument for bringing her along on the campaign, except that doing so would only create other complications. At this point I hardly need to be managing her ladyship's impulsiveness.

Sir John takes a sip of brandy and smacks his lips like a schoolboy, his evident pleasure reminding me of the old saw that the voters prefer John A. drunk to George Brown sober. He sets his glass on top of his dog-eared copy of the Speech. Leaning back, he sighs and closes his eyes. He needs to rest. If the brandy helps him sleep, so much the better. I have no intention of disturbing him till Napanee.

Thinking back, the most foolish, reckless, dangerous thing I ever did in my life was at Lady M.'s instigation. The CPR was transporting the Macdonalds across the continent in the *Jamaica*, all the way to the Pacific, and Sir John had asked me to accompany them; he vows he can't do without his private secretary for more than a day. As we descended the Rocky Mountains near Hope, I accompanied Lady M.—at her insistence—onto a cushioned platform constructed for her convenience above the cowcatcher of the giant locomotive. As if that weren't preposterous enough, a family of pigs appeared on the track ahead of us. Most of the pigs broke for the safety of the ditch, but one doomed piglet absurdly chose to race the engine, sprinting straight up the track on its stubby legs. When the inevitable happened, the impact sent the creature spinning into the air backwards at lightning speed, barely shy of my right ear. I was terrified. Even the engineer was horrified—he assured me afterwards that if the direction had been a few inches to the left, it would have been like getting hit in the face by a cannonball.

As for Lady M.: "I just shut my eyes," she told me, fixing me with her long, deep, intimidating stare, not unlike her husband's, and laughing queerly. After thus putting ourselves in mortal danger, we reached the West Coast, the *ultima Thule* of Sir John's national design, and enjoyed a splendid month in the rainforests of British Columbia. . . .

Turning back to him, I see his glass is empty already. Beyond the window, red-brick homes with decorous white trim and gaunt sentinel elms announce Napanee. The light—what little there is left—is draining from the sky. The reporters are putting away their cards and climbing into their coats. I reach across the aisle to lay my hand on the forearm of the old man, who has blissfully drifted off once more.

Napanee station is symmetrically built of the local limestone, with sober Romanesque arches. An official welcoming party of two waits on the platform in the rain. The Collector of Customs for Napanee and district, a florid gentleman with abundant side-whiskers and a venerable record of service to the Conservative Party, now amply rewarded, stands under an enormous black umbrella. Beside him, without benefit of umbrella, stands a piper decked out in the Macdonald tartan. The piper is well into "Scots Wha Hae" as Charles, our Negro porter, drops the steps to let the Prime Minister descend bareheaded into the rain. I follow him, carrying his hat.

Setting foot on the platform, Sir John halts to take in the scene, which forces me to wait on the bottom step. We're getting wet alarmingly quickly. I move to his side. A gratified smile has spread across his face, deepening the grooves alongside his mouth. I know he's relieved the tune isn't "God Save the Queen"—he always says the anthem sounds ghastly on the pipes.

"Up Paisley!" he cries over the fierce whine.

The piper acknowledges the battle cry by popping his eyes and arching his brows; his distended red cheeks are streaming under his dripping bonnet. As the music snarls to a conclusion, the chief grasps him by both shoulders and thanks him devoutly. Removing the reed from his mouth, the piper replies in a thick Glaswegian brogue, "Sir John, sir, the honour's a' mine."

Sir John turns to the other man and slips nimbly under his umbrella, which hasn't room for three: "My dear Elliott! I didn't realize *you'd* be greeting us today. What a perfect surprise. How's that son of yours? Better than last time, I trust."

Elliott can't stop pumping the Prime Minister's hand. "Sir John, it's been nine years since we've met. The '82 campaign! And you still remember my Jimmy's paralysis."

"At my age, Elliott, nine years is but the blink of an eye. But of course I remember Jimmy and I hope he's long over it. He must be a man by now."

Assured that Jimmy is healthy once more and a good Conservative too, Sir John peers through the downpour to a crowd of spectators huddled in the gathering dusk. They're standing at a respectful distance under the eaves of the station and shuffling forward hesitantly, anxious for a glimpse of their Prime Minister. Sir John straightens to accentuate his height in the grey topcoat with the broad sealskin collar and cuffs. He remains hatless because he believes people want to see what their leader looks like—all his high colour and moles and wrinkles, his flowing hair softening the oversized features. With a wave and a kindly smile, he salutes them from under the umbrella, looking each in the eye, especially the children, whose faces light up at once. Everyone applauds in unison. One young man, clapping enthusiastically, leans toward his friend and remarks, "Seedy-looking old beggar, isn't he?", unaware that I, like Sir John, have learned to lip-read to detect Opposition scheming in the House.

Elliott leads us right past the crowd to two open carriages waiting alongside the station. The first carriage, decorated with soggy red, white and blue bunting, is for us; the other will carry the reporters. Ben will stay behind on the train to prepare supper.

"Well, Sir John," enthuses Elliott once the three of us are seated, "the town is positively *packed* with people. The Opera Hall wouldn't hold everyone, so we decided to move the rally to the Town Hall. I hope you won't mind?"

"Not a bit of it. How could I?"

"Splendid! And Sir John, you'll be pleased to hear this—the Town Hall is full too, but the people outside will wait patiently to hear you. We hope you'll consent to speaking twice!"

Without hesitation Sir John nods wearily. He's too exhausted to refuse, too exhausted even to wipe the rain from his face. I hand him a clean handkerchief.

Sir John

The piper was a lovely, lovely touch. How his playing took me back! The early days in Kingston, the Kirk, the St. Andrew's Society, my own amateurish efforts on the pipes.

To be in Napanee again is bittersweet. But nothing like the awe I felt on arriving here the first time, alone and scarcely a man, to open a branch office for the great George Mackenzie, Barrister-at-Law. I was so conscious of my grave responsibilities, my solemn obligations to Mackenzie, a founder of the Commercial Bank of the Midland District, no less, that I was practically dumbstruck and spoke only when spoken to, in words of one syllable.

Napanee was nothing then but a mucky crossroads. Three mills, some scattered houses, of which only one was better than a shack, a one-room schoolhouse, and Quackenbush's Tavern. There I learned to drink all night with the help of Tom Ramsay and Donal Stuart and the boys from the tannery. I shudder to think of the tricks we played! The stone wall we built and mortared all in one dark night under my preposterously drunken direction for the lunatic purpose of shutting in auld Jamie the drygoodsman— poor Jamie opening his door that morning to find his way to the world mysteriously blocked, and lamenting and entreating his God to tell him why he was being punished so. And all of us living under the imperious eye of Allan Macpherson, my distant clansman, who fancied himself Laird o' Napanee with his mills and his big hoose.

Just look at the place now: stately elms, stately homes, some almost grand public buildings. Elliott proudly points out the stone courthouse, an architectural gem set apart in a white field. But it's still a small town, so very anxious to please and make a good impression. As our carriage slops down John Street between melting snowbanks, people stand on their broad verandas and wave with loyal enthusiasm. I wave cheerily back, knowing they're too young to remember what a frontier pigsty this was—can it really be sixty years ago? Yet here I am in Napanee's present, and here they are, all of us joined together in a fleeting tableau, while Elliott rattles on in my ear about the McKinley Tariff. It's had a ruinous effect on the barley farmers hereabouts. The Congressional lash has scarred them so badly, it's understandable they'd fall for free trade.

Our destination looms through wet branches. Viewed across the square, Napanee Town Hall attempts a classical nobility but doesn't quite achieve it. It yearns to be back in the forum of some provincial Roman town in the days of Marcus Aurelius. And among the tall columns by the entrance, spilling off the portico, seethes the promised mob.

The mere sight of an election crowd fires my blood. Yet I'm also aware of the wind's impertinence, blowing clean through our open carriage with a nasty edge. It gives me the shivers. I long to pull up the buffalo robe that Elliott has spread across our knees, wrap it around myself and huddle inside its gamy warmth, but that would never do. Can't appear faint of heart before the people. Invincible, that's the spirit!

The driver delivers us up to the waiting crowd. Cheers, scattered at first, then sustained as some good party loyalist eggs them on. I cock an ear for Liberal hecklers but hear none. What's this, a town comprising only Tories? Have they run the Grits all the way to Toronto?

Elliott insists I step down ahead of him. When I pause on the rain-slick runner to salute the people, I lose my footing and nearly crash to the slushy ground, catching the sideboard just in time.

Safely on terra firma, I find myself staring into the handsome, unlined face of Joe Pope. With all the bravado and grace of youth, he has leaped nimbly down beside me. "All well, Sir John?" he asks, peering into my eyes as if he's lost something.

Pope at one shoulder and Elliott at the other, we push off into the jostling mass of bodies. Cries of "Sir John! Sir John! We're with you!" Outstretched hands emerging from dripping sleeves. I grasp as many cold wet hands as I can, gloves off, and fling phrases here and there: "Thank you kindly! So good to see you! Good of you to come on a night like this! Thank you. God bless you. Thank you for your support. Does an old heart good . . ." I tip a nonexistent hat, wondering what Pope has done with my headgear.

At last the current of our progress sweeps us between the Doric columns. We sail through the entranceway and into the bright gaslit interior; it's jammed with more people and redolent of sodden wool. Doggedly, Pope and Elliott clear a path for me up the stairs to the council chamber. Everyone, pressed body to body along the railing, is smiling and happy to be here, eager to shake hands, their faces so near I can smell the onions and whisky and rotting teeth on each man's breath.

In the chamber the gaslights hiss loudly with a bright bluish tinge. I peer over heads and shoulders to a platform erected at the far end of the room. It's draped with red, white and blue and presided over by a faded portrait, suspended from the ceiling and flanked by Union Jacks, of a practically unrecognizable Victoria, looking incomparably younger and prettier than the last time I saw her at Windsor.

On the walls, banners proclaim a variety of noble sentiments: "Hail to Our Chieftain," "No American Senators Need Apply," "Canadian Labour for the Canadians," "National Policy, Not Free Trade." Seeing three shields hung side by side, each emblazoned with a phrase from our campaign motto, "The Old Flag," "The Old Leader," "The Old Policy," I feel right at home. Indeed, my speech will be largely superfluous. These people already know what I have to say—why not simply sing "God Save the Queen" and get it over with? But applause erupts like cannon bursts followed by cheering, as different parts of the crowd realize we're here. The people crave a speech, and by God, they shall have one.

Pope steers me toward the riser leading to the platform while shouting into my ear above the racket: "Elliott will introduce you! There will be no thank-yous! No questions!" Pope relieves me of my topcoat, pushes me in the right direction, and melts into the wings. Waving to the assemblage, I make a beeline for a sturdy wooden chair set beside the speaker's rostrum. I simply must sit down.

I beam as best I can at the folk in the front row and extract my hanky from my sleeve. I've broken into a copious sweat. The damned hall is suffocatingly hot. They position more chairs near mine to accommodate the overflow, motioning to latecomers to sit on the platform. Soon there will be scarcely room for the speaker himself. Although this is standard practice at our rallies, somehow it bothers me tonight. I look about for Pope to get him to do something. He's nowhere to be seen.

As Elliott wades through the mob toward the rostrum, my heart sinks. *Something is wrong with me.*

Waves of heat are coursing up my limbs. I feel compelled to yawn, to gulp air like a landed fish. A stupid throbbing has settled behind my eyes. Impossible to concentrate. All the same I know I must, must stand now, attend to the words of the national anthem being sung so bravely and charmingly by a chorus of small schoolgirls who have somehow squeezed their way onto the edge of the platform.

Thankfully I can sit again as Elliott tries to make himself heard above the cheering. His arms flap comically in a call for silence; this only redoubles the clamour.

"Gentlemen! Ladies!" he bellows. "Loyal sons and daughters of Napanee! We are all here tonight because we admire and cherish our great Premier. We feel deeply honoured that he has journeyed through the rain to bring us his message. In this grand electoral struggle, we are confident that his Government will emerge once again victorious, for the sake of Canada and the beloved Mother Country. And since it is he you have come to hear, I will step aside and present to you without further ado, and with incomparable pride, ladies and gentlemen, the Prime Minister of Canada, the Right Honourable Sir John A. Macdonald!"

Hats, handkerchiefs, umbrellas, walking sticks and programs are waving in the air, swarming like gnats before my eyes. A pulse throbs through the hall to the rhythm of the blood pounding in my head. I remain seated while someone strikes up a chorus of "For He's a Jolly Good Fellow": a respite to will away my dizziness.

Finally I can stay seated no longer. Rising, I steady myself with both hands on the rostrum. "My friends . . ."

No one can hear me. They only want to go on singing and cheering like lunatics. What is it about elections that makes normally proper and sedate citizens mad as hatters? What upheaval in the Lord's natural order have we unleashed with our fine democratic notions? I've half a mind to nod to them all like the great Empress herself, turning to face each corner of the hall, then walk offstage to my rest, my duty done.

"Dear ladies and gentlemen, as you are obviously all Conservatives, there is no need to convert you . . ." Seeing my lips move, they finally pipe down. "I won't need to convert you this evening, ladies and gentlemen of Napanee, as you are obviously all right-thinking people in no need of salvation. That effort will be reserved for unregenerate Grits! [Cheers, catcalls.] That's right, ladies and gentlemen, our opponents persist in the error of their ways. They have as many aliases for their wrongheaded and dangerous policy as a thief has excuses for his wrongdoing. They call it 'commercial union.' [Boos.] They call it 'unrestricted reciprocity.' [More boos.] Lately they have even taken to calling it 'tariff reform.' [Jeers.] But there is another name for it, ladies and gentlemen, and one name alone, the name by which all honest Canadians know it—*annexation*!"

The howls of derision are almost frightening. If I could conjure up Laurier here and now for these people, or make Richard Cartwright materialize beside me on the stage, they'd haul them outside in an instant and hang them from the nearest tree, if they didn't tear them limb from limb first. What a beast lives in the hearts of men! For once I'm not sure I want to unleash it, even on Liberals.

I carry on with the speech, trying to remember that I'm to pay tribute to the good Tory Mayor of Napanee, who would be here with us tonight if he weren't under doctor's care in Kingston. I'm also supposed to reminisce about my days as a young lawyer in this fair town, but as I try to recall where to insert these remarks, I feel muddled. I finish one sentence and start another, but the sentences melt into a trackless waste. Did I already say that line? Or was that in Kingston last night? Or in Hamilton or Strathroy or Stratford or St. Mary's or Guelph last week? Or is the line still coming up, still waiting somewhere down the track?

The pounding in my temples and the aching behind my eyes have grown worse. Knees turning to jelly, thoughts to porridge. In my confusion I pause to check how far I've progressed in the text, then realize I've been speaking extemporaneously. I withdraw the folded speech from my breast pocket and flatten it out on the rostrum, affixing my specs to my nose to find my place, all of which takes time and delays matters further—indeed, delays them too long for comfort, and now I can't remember where I left off.

Pause for breath. Lick my parched lips. Look around for a drink. Why has nobody thought to provide so much as a glass of water?

I'm embarrassed to have left a yawning gap in the proceedings. The crowd is reacting with puzzlement and alarm. To my extreme left I detect movement. Looking in that direction, I see Pope emerging from the wings, struggling through the crowd to my rescue. At the prospect of further humiliation, my mind snaps into focus—I find the phrase I need, the bright thread of language, and weave a few turns, surging ahead, glimpsing an early conclusion. Lines come back to me automatically, so often repeated I don't need to remember them, just let them pour out of me, although they seem to be coming from someplace very far away. . . .

My usual conclusion is drowned in roars of approval.

As the audience rises in a body to applaud, I stumble. By Heaven's grace Pope catches me before I topple.

"Joe," I tell him, "get me outside." Pain clawing at the back of my throat like a wild animal, I'm close to fainting. "For the love of God, just get me out of here."

The *Jamaica*

At the back of Napanee's Town Hall, a stairway descends to a rear exit. I steer Sir John toward the stairs as rapidly as possible, threading him by the elbow through the crowd onstage, careful not to drag him. They can see he's not well. They refrain from grasping his hand as he struggles along and content themselves with calling out good wishes, kind words of encouragement.

Providentially, I told the cabman to wait in the market square behind the building. At the foot of the stairs I bundle Sir John into his topcoat. Emerging into the darkness, the frigid air welcome after the heat inside, we practically trip over a company of nervous schoolgirls waiting to shake the Prime Minister's hand—the same ones who sang "God Save the Queen" so sweetly onstage.

Sir John has been pitched forward in discomfort but immediately straightens to his full height. "Why, my dears!" he announces in a clarion tone. "How delightful to meet you again. And how splendidly you sang the anthem. May I have the honour of shaking *your* hands?"

He takes each small hand one by one, adding a few words for every child. When he comes to the smallest, who looks frightened, he bends gravely to place a kiss on her forehead. "Keep a warm spot in your heart for me, my darling," he murmurs.

We leave Elliott behind to cope with the mob. In the carriage I strain to read Sir John's face, which looked so disturbingly flushed and distracted onstage. I ask him how he's feeling, but he doesn't reply—only stirs and coughs and wipes his mouth with the back of his hand. Finally he says, "I hate letting them down, you know. I could see they were upset."

"They were worried for your sake, sir, but you finished very strongly. You had them with you. You could tell by the cheering."

"We could have set a chimpanzee before that crowd and they'd have cheered."

I instruct the driver to return to the railway station. Taking the same route as before, we pass north of the Town Hall and skirt the crowd still milling restlessly outside the building. Evidently no one has told them there will be no repeat performance. When our carriage is recognized in the lamplight, some louts aim catcalls and boos in our direction.

"Where do you think you're going?" yells one.

"What about *us*?" screams another.

Sir John sits bolt upright in his seat. "Joe! Tell the man to stop, these people want a few words."

The driver pulls up on the reins, but I surprise myself by countermanding my chief for once: "It's all right," I tell the man. "Keep going." I lower my voice apologetically: "They'll have to be patient, Sir John. They can read about it in tomorrow's papers. Your health is more important than pleasing this lot."

The temperature has dropped again, converting the rain to light snow. As we proceed up John Street, the previously crowded verandas are empty, the street deserted. All we hear are the horse's hooves. Sir John slumps into the folds of the buffalo robe.

I'm relieved he's able to walk to the *Jamaica*. He keeps a tight grip on my wrist as we step gingerly across the sodden ground and over the tracks. Charles takes his coat and, sizing up the situation, tells him his bed is made up and all ready for him.

I consider whether we should remain on the siding until morning but decide against it. Despite the heat thrown off by the cast-iron wood stove, the *Jamaica* becomes cold at night, especially in the compartments, which would only worsen his condition. In any case the journey back to Kingston isn't hard, and the suite at the British American is ours for as long as we require it.

Leaving Sir John in his compartment, I hand him out of habit a sheaf of newly arrived telegrams, still unopened. I go forward to the galley to give Ben his instructions and tell the engineer to get up steam and depart for Kingston as soon as possible.

When I return to the compartment, Sir John lies diagonally across the bed, sprawled on his back amid the open telegrams, his arms flung outwards, his eyes closed. Wisps of silver hair wreathe his temples. His skin is ashen, his features composed but lifeless. It has all, finally, been too much.

With an involuntary cry I seize his wrist. Ineptly I try to find a pulse as Dr. Powell has instructed me. Nothing. Or am I just missing the spot in my panic? As I think I detect a faint pulse, a tiny muscle under his eyelid tics involuntarily, sending a signal.

His eyes flutter open, his dry chapped lips move: "Oh, never fear, Joe. It takes more than a fever to kill this old horse."

His eyes close once more, and he snorts as he subsides into sleep.

I snatch up the nearest telegram:

LEADERS PRESENCE URGENTLY REQUIRED RALLY MONTREAL 28 FEB STOP REQUEST EARLIEST RESPONSE STOP LANGEVIN.

At random I pick another:

GRITS GAINING LANARK STOP SIR JOHN OUR ONLY BULWARK NOW PLEASE NOTIFY VISIT SOONEST STOP HAGGART.

Macdonald

I gather up all the telegrams, knowing the rest will only contain similar self-serving pleas, and stuff them roughly into my pockets.

The Professor's House

_____

Four days have elapsed since Sir John's collapse at Napanee. When we pulled in to Kingston station close to midnight, he remained asleep in his compartment. From the utter relaxation of his features, he looked content to sleep forever.

I sent Ben to fetch Dr. Sullivan, but the good doctor was away in Picton treating one of his wealthy patients. A barely bearded intern from the hospital was the only medical assistance available at that hour. He arrived bearing a black bag and an air of heightened self-importance. Waking Sir John without a hint of deference, the young Hippocrates interviewed him about his symptoms, receiving replies that were barely audible but precise. He peered into Sir John's eyes and mouth, took his pulse, prodded his neck and chest. Sir John conceded he felt pain over his left lung whenever he drew breath.

The fellow turned to me, as if I and not Sir John were in charge, and pronounced his diagnosis: bronchitis brought on by physical exhaustion, and verging on pneumonia. "The patient," he insisted, "must by no means exert himself. He must have complete bedrest for a week—absolute peace and quiet. His pulse is dangerously weak."

I begged to inform him, since it had slipped his notice, that we were in the middle of a momentous national election campaign, but "the patient" wearily waved my objections aside. Humble as a tradesman, Sir John submitted to advanced medical wisdom.

"Pneumonia is a serious illness at his age," the young man added, quite unnecessarily.

This meant scrapping our plans to return to Ottawa. It meant moving Sir John to restful surroundings somewhere in Kingston, at least until the worst of his symptoms clear up—but definitely not back to the British American Hotel, where he'd only be besieged and badgered without mercy by every fool calling himself a reporter or a politician.

But where in all of Kingston could we go?

"The Professor," Sir John muttered in a hoarse whisper. "The good old Parson Professor will put us up."

The Professor is Sir John's brother-in-law, the Reverend Doctor James Williamson. I've now heard it recounted more than once how this ancient became one of the first Scottish divines to teach at Queen's College after its founding half a century ago. Despite his doddering age, Dr. Williamson remains vice-principal of that Presbyterian institution—although how he manages to discharge his duties remains a mystery to me, since he can barely stand or move about.

Never mind. In the Professor's narrow, drafty three-storey stone house on Earl Street we temporarily reside. The place is astonishingly cluttered and cramped—thoroughly unsuitable whether as a headquarters for conducting a general election or as a nursing home. But it's Sir John's will to be here, and here we remain. Family ties bind him even more tightly than party ties.

The house is as cold and comfortless inside as its desolate outer appearance would suggest. Every room is crammed floor to ceiling with the Professor's books—theology and natural philosophy predominate, but mathematics and astronomy are also well represented—and stuffed with all manner of scientific curiosities: charts of the heavens, embalmed owls, fierce falcons, glass cases containing mineral collections with curling unreadable labels, a brown lacquered globe with the mountains bulging in bas-relief. Unswept oak leaves from last fall clutter the front entrance.

The place lacks any evidence of a woman's touch. Dr. Williamson's late wife was Sir John's older sister, Margaret, who passed to the other side many years ago. Their spinster sister, Louisa, moved here to keep her brother-in-law company, but she too has departed, leaving the Professor to carry on in Spartan isolation.

Unluckily for him and us both, the Professor had already fallen ill before we arrived, with symptoms resembling Sir John's. As a result he's been little help to us apart from opening his home. In my anxiety to settle Sir John and get more fires blazing in the rooms, I didn't discover Dr. Williamson's illness until too late— and until after Sir John, in an excess of kindness, had dismissed Ben Chilton to catch the morning train home to Ottawa. He didn't consult me before making this decision. "The poor fellow needs to be with his family," Sir John assured me, "not stuck in Kingston with a houseful of old men." No question, of course, of applying that maxim to me.

And so I find myself nursing not one but two elderly gentlemen. Worse, I've come down with a severe cold myself. My eyes throb and water, my head and throat ache like the devil, and repeated sneezing has brought on attacks of nosebleeding. Pressing a blood-stained handkerchief to my nose, I try to meet my patients' needs for boiled eggs and beef broth and tea and newspapers, all the while drafting letters for Sir John's signature and keeping at bay the journalists and party men intent only on their own immediate advantage. I'd feel utterly wretched except that the blizzard of telegrams, punctuated by uninvited callers, leaves no time for self-pity. If only the Professor's scientific interests had extended to the telephone, Mr. Bell's invention might have spared us some of the more egregious interruptions.

At times Sir John seems so weak and weary I dare not trouble him. In the absence of anyone else in authority, I can only take each hour as it comes and deal with matters as they arise, relying on my own uncertain judgment. And yet the rest of the time his manner is as stalwart in illness as in health. Although his appetite is poor and his recovery alarmingly slow, he seems content to let his body take its natural course. He may even be secretly glad of the unexpected reprieve from campaigning. He knows he's done his utmost to put the essential truths before the nation; now it's up to others to finish the job, and for Providence to decide the outcome—even though, as our latest eminent candidate in Quebec, Joseph-Israël Tarte, is fond of saying, elections aren't won by prayers alone.

Clearly sharing Tarte's viewpoint, Conservative candidates pester Sir John at all hours to help them secure their personal re-election. They burden him with written or telegraphed requests for advice or support or financial favours, obsessed with extracting every last measure of service from their chief. They seem disgracefully oblivious to his state of health. Yet none of this surprises him: "Joe," he said this morning, half-dozing in his stained white nightshirt in the Professor's study that serves as a sickroom, "if you would know the sordid depths of meanness in human nature, you've got to be a Prime Minister running a general election!"

This made me feel a guilt all my own. It was I who scheduled as many as three speaking engagements an evening for him last week, after arduous days of travelling and campaigning. If I hadn't given in to the frantic appeals for his presence pouring in from every part of the country, he might never have reached the point of exhaustion. But as Father used to say, if your aunt had been a man she'd have been your uncle. I didn't know where Sir John's limitations lay—and neither, apparently, did he.

Now he surprises me once more. In the waking hours between naps, just as we're composing the contents of his daily report to the Governor General, Sir John begins waxing nostalgic. I've seldom heard him speak much about the past; his attention is all for the present and future. His current sentiments flow, I suppose, from lying amid so many framed mementoes of his family.

He tells me that "Moll," his pet name for his late sister Margaret, was "absurdly fond of the Professor." He gestures toward an oval photograph sitting atop an old-fashioned spinet. I look more closely and see a sweet, plain elderly woman in a lace-trimmed bonnet, with a direct gaze and an expression of generous practicality.

"Moll worshipped the ground he walked on. You wouldn't think it to look at him now, but James was a great catch in his day—a *savant* with an Edinburgh degree, a rare bird in these parts. I don't think either of them had been expecting to marry. Moll was well past the marriageable age, and the Professor already a widower. They had no children of their own, of course, which was certainly a blessing for me. I was away for long stretches when the House was sitting and couldn't play father to young Hughy. The Professor served Hugh as a sort of honorary father, and Moll as a substitute mother. I dare say Hugh is more Williamson than Macdonald, to judge by his mild and gentle ways. I wonder how he likes the rough-and-tumble of electioneering."

Hugh John Macdonald is now running for Parliament, as a Conservative of course, in Winnipeg, where he's lived for years. We're all very much hoping Hugh will be elected next week.

Sir John carries on in this vein. "Did you know the Professor had a son of his own? Born to the first Mrs. Williamson, his childhood sweetheart. He brought her over from Scotland, but she died in childbirth. The baby was sent home to be raised by its grandparents. The Professor never saw him again. Now, isn't that sad? Scotch brides in our family had a terrible time of it here."

I know which other, unspoken bride he's referring to—the first Mrs. Macdonald. Isabella's portrait, I take it, is not here. I think it best to say nothing. He's speaking of events from before I was born, but to him they happened as if yesterday.

"It amazes me Isabella survived childbirth. Life itself was too much for Isa to bear, yet she could bear babies. She just couldn't raise 'em. Now, where's the Divine Plan in that?"

This isn't the first time I've felt startled by Sir John's impiety. I can't think how to reply, and fortunately it doesn't matter. He doesn't need an interlocutor, only a listener.

"Isa died just a couple of blocks from here, you know. Hughy was seven. Moll and the Professor and Louisa and dear Mother were marvellous with him. They took him in as their own. Which he was, really—poor Isa could never have raised Hugh. The opium her doctors prescribed laid her out flat."

These drear memories leave him silent, staring straight ahead. At last I find my tongue. "I can understand why you have such a fondness for Dr. Williamson, sir."

"Yes, and how *is* the good Parson today? Haven't laid eyes on him since yesterday supper."

"Resting comfortably upstairs. He sends you his regards. Which reminds me, Sir John, Mr. Haggart was here this morning, but I—"

"The old chap travelled all the way here, did he?" The old chap, the Honourable John Graham Haggart, Member for South Lanark and Postmaster General for Canada, is probably twenty years younger than his chief. "Couldn't stay away, could he? Surely it can wait till after the election."

"Indeed it could, sir. I sent Mr. Haggart packing back to Perth. Said you'd meet with him in Ottawa."

"Now, what about my own seat? Are we in any danger here in Kingston?"

"None whatsoever, sir. Your officials are working like Trojans, knowing they must campaign without you. Please don't trouble yourself on that account."

"By the way, have I ever shown you the house where little John A. lived? And died?"

"I don't believe so, sir." Suddenly he's back in the past again—now on the subject of his first-born. The rapidity of these trans-migrations is startling, even frightening. "Is the house nearby?" I ask tentatively.

"Heavens no, almost out in the country. At least it was in those days. 'Tea Caddy Castle,' I used to call it. Built by a grocer who made a fortune and wanted to own an 'Eye-talian willar'! Over-looks Lake Ontario. I was delighted to rent it, I thought the pretty views and lake air would do Isa good. We never quite knew why little John A. died—at least I didn't. Convulsions, the doctors said, brought on by a fall. He was already walking. Lovable bright wee chap. My Heavens, do you realize he'd be forty-three if he were alive today? Three years older than Hughy . . ." Sir John's eyes close suddenly. "Must show you the place someday," he murmurs. "Extraordinary house . . ."

Afraid he'll fall asleep, I broach the subject that's been weigh-ing on me since breakfast, when my kitchen preparations were interrupted by yet another telegram from Ottawa, another set of competing commands. "Sir John, Lady Macdonald wired this morning. She is strongly of the opinion that you'd be far better off at home."

"Yes? She would think that."

"And although Professor Williamson is a dear friend to you both, she fears you lack the necessary comforts here. Something about 'that museum.' Also that you should come at once under Dr. Powell's care. Lady Macdonald was quite definite on that point."

"What does old Sullivan think?"

"Dr. Sullivan's opinion is that until your condition improves, you shouldn't be moved. He's concerned about your irregular pulse—what he terms 'the weak action of your heart.' Also the congestion in your lungs."

"You haven't told Agnes, have you?"

"I've been waiting to ask your wishes."

"Good. The thing is, I must be home before voting day. I must be seen casting my ballot like any other man—not wallowing about like a sick old dog. How many days does that give us?"

"That would require our departure in four days' time."

"It's decided, then. We'll travel to Ottawa in four days. Sooner if my health improves. Tell Agnes and arrange it with the CPR."

"Yes, sir. At least that will give Lady Macdonald some certainty."

He looks up interrogatively from the pillows. His fierce bloodshot eyes and bulbous nose make a shocking contrast with the effeminate white nightshirt. "Agnes always believes it her duty to the Lord to manage me. I'll never understand why. How does she suppose I managed before I met her?"

And yet I sense from his slight smile that her worrying pleases him.

"Sir John?" Given his reflective mood, I realize this may be the opportune moment. "I wonder if you've given any thought— that is, if you'd consider it desirable—to writing your memoirs? Your own account of an exceptionally long and lustrous life in government?"

"You mean, get it all down while I can still breathe?" He cocks a shaggy eyebrow and grins rakishly up at me. "I suppose you're right, Joe. Someone will have to do it. But it can't be me, I'm still living the damned lustrous life!"

"And yet *you*, sir, are the indispensable source."

"I'm not sure about 'lustrous.' Many would say the vessel got badly tarnished with use. But there's no denying I've been Prime Minister a devil of a long time. Longer than either Gladstone or Disraeli, eh?"

"Sir, no statesman alive has greater reason to compose his memoirs."

"Now that's enough flattery. I've had various collaborators proposed to me, as you know—but you're the writer, Joe. You're as eloquent as Goldwin Smith, that old parasite. I'm just a bletherskite compared to your way with words."

"Thank you, sir."

"Oh yes, you're the man to rehabilitate my life for posterity, no doubt about it—omitting the seamier interludes, of course. No one else knows me so well, apart from Agnes. So I regret to tell you, Joe, you're it. Even old Dawson, the Queen's Printer, thinks so. Just wait, if you don't mind, till I'm out of harm's way and no longer in a position to meddle with the truth."

"Sir John," I protest, "it's you who flatter *me*. I can only hope to be worthy of the honour. And if you're quite willing," I add practically, "it would greatly facilitate my work if you'd jot down an *aide-mémoire* of the principal events as you recollect them. I entered your service just nine years ago, remember—a full generation after most events took place. I know them only indirectly."

"I suppose, I suppose. If I ever get time." And that trancelike expression steals over his face once more, the same look he had when conjuring up poor drugged Isabella and doomed little John A.

"The merest sketch, Sir John. A list. Nothing taxing. The high points, nothing more."

I exult silently.

Two

MARCH 1891

Earnscliffe

When I told Sir John I lack all memory of his early career, I wasn't being entirely accurate. At age ten I was taken by Father to greet the foreign delegations as they arrived for the Charlottetown Conference, and Sir John was one of the foreigners.

First came the Nova Scotians on their small steamer, the *Heather Belle*. I remember them disembarking, slightly the worse for wear, on a glorious late summer afternoon. After dark, well behind schedule, came the New Brunswickers aboard the *Prince of Wales*. I understood little about the conference at the time—only that its purpose was the union of Mother Britain's Maritime colonies, and that the wealthier, more remote Canadians had simply invited themselves along. I was too excited at being included for once in Father's official duties, and at staying up late, to wonder why he bothered taking me with him. Perhaps he knew it would become a memorable part of my education; perhaps he just wanted company. His fellow Ministers had chosen a more politically rewarding way to spend their time, mixing with their constituents at the first circus to visit the Island in twenty years.

Early next morning the Canadian vessel *Queen Victoria* approached, bearing delegates all the way from Quebec City. Father and I hurried down to Charlottetown harbour to meet them, sleepy from our previous night's duties, and he immediately realized the ship was too big to dock at our largest berth. Seeing a fisherman mending his nets, Father commandeered his slimy old oyster boat for half a crown. The fisherman rowed us out to the waiting vessel while we sat sweating in the stern, and the Canadian sailors lowered a rope ladder over the side. "Say, Skipper, what's the price of shellfish?" one yelled.

On deck we came face to face with a forbidding posse of grizzled, bewhiskered, sombre-suited gentlemen, Ministers of the Crown of the United Province of Canada. Out of breath and flushed from the hot sun, Father blurted out official greetings from the Town of Charlottetown and the Loyal Assembly of Her Majesty's Province of Prince Edward Island.

John A. Macdonald, not yet Sir John but already the Canadians' leader, seemed delighted by Father's greeting. He replied formally, but in such a gracious and amiable and humorous manner that he made everyone feel it was a festive occasion.

Everything about him fascinated me. He lacked a beard. He seemed, to my eyes, out of scale. I stared up at his soaring height, his naked chin, his wide mouth and bulging nose, his peculiarly thick, abundant, dark-reddish hair jutting out dramatically at right angles to his ears. And he was smilingly and unexpectedly friendly, even to insignificant me. I thought him not the least bit frightening, compared to his colleagues.

He introduced Father to his fellow statesmen. I remember taking my turn shaking hands awkwardly with Messrs. Cartier, McGee and Brown. A few days later the famous George Brown would visit our home, sit me on his knee and sternly give me sixpence, as if it were a grave responsibility to own such a sum. But it was the leader of the Canadian delegation whose presence remained fixed in my memory—right up until the moment many years later on Parliament Hill when, as a junior civil servant on a minor errand, I encountered him again in the Cabinet chamber, and he reprimanded me for being there without permission.

Twenty-seven years after seeing him on that steamer, I study the few sparse notes Sir John has made so far for his memoirs. It's mid-afternoon, and we're rocking gently back and forth in the *Jamaica* on our way up to Ottawa. Sir John has strolled to the other end of the carriage to chat with the newsmen. My understanding with the press is that he may approach them at his choosing, but they may not approach him. Still, it always makes me nervous when he speaks off the record like this. He has such an engaging way of taking even the youngest reporter into his confidence. Most of them can be trusted not to quote him, knowing it's the price of having access to Sir John, yet sometimes, especially during an election campaign, an inexperienced reporter can't resist the temptation to impress his editor by scoring a coup, even if it means betraying the Prime Minister of Canada. Intelligent editors will guard against losing the chief's trust. But how many newspaper editors are intelligent?

My cold still nags me. My nose runs. My fingers tremble holding this historic document, flimsy as it is—a mere scrap of paper, but a beginning, I tell myself. I finally admit what I'm up to: foreseeing his end, preparing for its inevitability. My practicality appalls me.

I tell myself not to be such a fool. Sir John may be full of years and down with bronchitis, but he's still too vigorous and manly and wilful, and for that matter proud, to die yet—too determined to win this election and keep his enemies out of power.

I return to his notes, mere jottings really, random words, lists. Of American Presidents, for example:

Buchanan

Lincoln

Johnson

Grant

Arthur

Cleveland

Harrison

What was he thinking when he wrote down the Presidents who have come and gone during his own years in power? (I note he omitted Hayes and Garfield. Forgetfulness, or some deeper reason?) I receive an answer of sorts when Sir John returns to the chair beside me.

He settles back with a faint grin. His brow is glistening, he's short of breath; clearly the conversation has tired him, but he just can't bring himself to stay away from people.

"It was the ever-curious young chap from the *Mail*. Somehow he knows about the Americans boarding another of our sealing vessels in the Bering Sea. He asked what we're going to do about it. I was tempted to be honest and tell him, 'Absolutely nothing.' No sense in provoking Blaine, handing him a pretext for retaliation. Instead I read the fellow a history lesson."

I should have been at Sir John's side, shielding him from such questions, instead of poring over his notes for clues to his intentions. "The *Mail* thrives on printing rumour and innuendo," I murmur, as *sotto voce* as possible. "Next thing we know, they'll have Britain sending a man-of-war."

"Yes, a prospect I dread—although I'd never say so in British Columbia. We don't need war, just some sensible settlement."

He hawks noisily and reflects for a moment.

"I didn't give anything away to the young man—just told him I have a lively recollection of how the Americans treated us at the Washington Conference twenty years ago. They refused to compensate us for damages and loss of life from the Fenian raids. Oh, said Ulysses Grant, those raids weren't authorized by *us*—though they'd done nothing to stop them. Then they demanded the freedom to fish in our waters. They used every conceivable pressure to extract a deal. But in the end they at least paid something for it.

"When the British made me sign the damned treaty, Hamilton Fish served strawberries and ice cream at the State Department. And as I took up my pen to sign, I looked Fish in the eye and told him, 'Here go the fisheries.' He shook his wattles and said, 'You're getting a good bargain.' 'Nonsense,' I retorted, with everyone looking on, 'we're *giving* them away!'"

I'm writing furiously in my journal, a fact Sir John notes with amusement. He pauses to let me get it all down. "As you point out," I manage to say, anxious to keep him going, "at least then the Americans negotiated, but now—"

"Now they won't even talk to us. They seize our sealers as if the Bering Sea were an American lake! Blaine refuses to recognize our Minister and will deal only with the British Ambassador. Some progress. And Ambassador Pauncefote is no Joseph Chamberlain: he'll keep the peace at any price. He'll give Blaine whatever he wants, just to make his posting in Washington a bit more pleasant."

"This business has been going on for years."

"Of course we thought we had an agreement in '88. Chamberlain thought so too, but then President Cleveland backed out. The problem was the Senate, as usual—the Senate demanding more, more, more. As long as the Senate runs the show, it's impossible for the American delegates to negotiate in good faith."

"Didn't Chamberlain have a telling phrase?"

"'A lot of dishonest tricksters.' But our own John Thompson went him one better: 'These Yankee politicians are the lowest race of thieves in existence.' Of course that was only in a letter to his wife, but he quoted it to me quite proudly." Sir John smiles with ineffable sweetness. "I'd never go that far myself. I'd just say the Americans have little propensity to share with their neighbours. In fact they consider the mere existence of neighbours an affront to their dignity."

He pauses. I continue making notes, and by the time I've caught up with him, he's fallen silent. We stare outside at the dull March skies, the fields laden with snow. "Only a year ago," I remind him, "you suspected American agents of opening your mail."

"I do still. How else to explain the delays in receiving Tupper's dispatches from Washington? Getting the Americans' *respect*, Joe— that's the challenge. Partly it's our being a former colony. Yet they ought to sympathize, having once been in the same position. They've completely forgotten their own colonial past. It's as if the United States had sprung fully formed from Zeus's forehead, while we're a backward tribe of Hottentots. When Canada was born, President Johnson didn't even wire congratulations. And in his first State of the Union address, Grant called Canada 'an unfriendly, irresponsible, semi-independent agent of Great Britain.' And worse in private, I shouldn't doubt. Yet what were we really? A fragile thing, a struggling infant barely three years old—scarcely a threat to the Grand Army of the Republic. Relations were off to a poor start. They haven't improved much since."

"Did you ever meet Grant, Sir John?"

"Only socially, you might say. And on one other occasion, although it was never reported. The day before the Washington Conference, Agnes and I were dining at the Arlington when an invitation arrived from the White House: an audience with the President that evening. It turned out to be brandy and cigars with yours truly as the only guest. Not a single British commissioner was present, just old Hamilton Fish. I suppose they wanted to size me up—this impudent colonial who'd arrested Americans for fishing illegally in our waters.

"Grant was glowering, as if he'd rather see anyone else. Beneath his beard he looked insignificant for such a mighty general. And *very* shabbily dressed. As Fish introduced us, I felt like a regular dandy in my checked trousers.

"It happened Grant and some of his generals had been guests

at George Pullman's fishing lodge in the Thousand Islands. The lodge being a stone's throw from Kingston, this gave us something to talk about. Grant quickly cheered up. He'd enjoyed himself there immensely. Anything to do with horses or the outdoors he loved. He admitted wanting to buy an island nearby, right on Canada's doorstep, and we began getting on like a house on fire. By the time his butler had filled our snifters a third time, I was inviting Grant to Kingston and Ottawa and Quebec, wherever his heart desired, for a festive state visit. Which was impossible, of course, without the approval of the Imperial government—I left that unsaid.

"Somewhere during our fourth glass, Fish reminded Grant about their claims against Britain over the *Alabama*. I assured them that as a government we'd taken no side in the Civil War, but in fact thousands of Canadians had fought in Union regiments— something of which Grant seemed ignorant. And I said (bending the truth a little) that I felt enormously gratified the Republic had stayed intact. Moreover, we'd tried to learn from their tragedy by not exaggerating states' rights in our own constitution.

"I could see this went completely over Grant's head. I doubt he knew or cared Canada even had a constitution. 'What about those Rebs,' he said, 'raiding into Vermont from your side of the line? None too friendly there.'

"'They were uninvited and unwelcome guests in our country,' I replied. 'Not unlike the Fenian raiders from your side.'

"'Those Irishmen? Goddamn renegades!'

"I let this pass. 'Mr. President,' said I, probably with too much self-satisfaction, 'immediately after the Confederate raid on Vermont, I set up a special police force to patrol our common border. I wanted to ensure such an outrage never happened again.'

"'I hope it did some good. We lost men in that incident,' Grant said gloomily—astonishing me, given his reputation for losing men by the thousands without batting an eye.

"'As *we* lost men in the Fenian raids,' I countered.

"'To hell with the Fenians!' he roared. Without warning he began raving in truly sulphurous language about the *Alabama* and all the damage inflicted by Confederate ships built in British dockyards. He kept pulling on his cigar, and I remembered how after the Vermont incident the Northern papers had screamed for an invasion of Canada and proudly declared Grant's initials stood for 'Unconditional Surrender.'

"When I finally got a word in, I suggested the two of us leave the *Alabama* question to the conference. It wasn't *our* quarrel after all. At that he became furious. He accused me of trying to weasel out of responsibility for the deaths of his men! Said I was a colonial flunky in the pay of the British and had no business even attending the conference. I rose saying it was time for me to go. He ordered me to sit down. When I didn't, he strode across the floor, grabbed me by the lapels with both hands—a difficult feat since he was considerably shorter than I—and shook me.

"He shouted into my face, 'Don't play the goddamn fool with me, Macdonald! Don't sit there drinking my goddamn brandy as if you don't know what the hell I'm talking about!' Then he released me and abruptly turned on his heel and left the room. Fish showed me to my carriage without a word of apology or explanation."

I've long since given up taking notes in favour of absorbing every detail of this extraordinary monologue. I'm hoping I can commit it to memory and record it later. I suspect my jaw is hanging open. Sir John grins: "It beggars belief, does it not?"

"It does, sir. It surely does."

"That's why I've never told anyone. It would have been ruinous for our relations with the U.S. Besides, it's humiliating to be treated that way by a fellow statesman. But now I've told *you*. And you may tell the world—after my death."

I understand his discretion. At the same time I must be as

accurate as possible, must get the story down faithfully in all its particulars, just as Sir John told it. But will anyone believe me?

On our arrival at the CPR station on Queen Street, dusk is settling over Ottawa. Sheets of thin hard snow drive slantwise across the tracks. Having telegraphed instructions in the morning, I expect Patrick Buckley to be waiting for us; and sure enough, old Patrick is parked under the new electric arc lamps, his horse's blanket turning white with snow. He jumps down from his seat and welcomes us home in his rough Irish way.

Sir John returns the greeting warmly. Yet he's shivering visibly inside his greatcoat; the trip has taxed him even more than I expected. Although he's rallied somewhat in the past two days, neither of us is fully recovered.

Sir John is anxious to drive up to Parliament Hill to retrieve the correspondence accumulated since our departure, and I surprise myself once again, saying, "Surely, Sir John, the letters can wait. Tomorrow is election day—no one will expect a reply till after the vote."

To my great relief he agrees. "Very well, Joe. Sensible as ever."

We sit strangely silent throughout the canter along Sussex Street. Normally this is the time when he speaks his mind most freely, commenting during the drive on whatever passes our gaze or enters his thoughts, on politics or the strange conduct of men, even on the droll habits of Rosie, Buckley's flatulent chestnut mare.

I watch Earnscliffe approach, its Gothic stone profile standing proudly apart as if still in the countryside, even though Lower Town spreads ever closer. From its perch on the bluff, the house oversees the broad Ottawa River and the lights winking fitfully from the Quebec shore. Earnscliffe's own windows glow through the snowy dusk. No other carriage passes. All sounds are muffled save Sir John's laboured breathing.

We sweep through the iron gates kept open for our arrival and into the circular drive. The peaked gables loom above us. Lanterns are lit on the pillared portico.

Even before Buckley brings Rosie to a halt, the front door swings inward and a tall stately figure emerges onto the step, white hair and russet dress framed in light. Braving the cold and snow, Lady Macdonald strides with arms crossed toward us.

I assist Sir John down from the carriage by his left arm. Lady M. grasps his right in both hands, as if hauling in a drowning man.

"Ah, my dear," he murmurs, "I've been too long away."

"That you have," she replies tenderly. Her emotion lends her voice a deep vibrato. She threads her arm through his and turns at once to escort him to the house. Buckley hurries on ahead with Sir John's portmanteau and deposits it inside the entrance. "Thank you, Joseph," Lady M. throws back at me over her shoulder, "and good evening. Good night to you, Mr. Buckley."

"Good evening, Ma'am," we reply in unison.

Buckley climbs onto his seat without a glance at me. His loyalty is reserved for Sir John. He snuffles gruffly, wiping his nose with the back of a fingerless woollen glove.

Sir John pauses in the light from the open doorway and looks back. "For Heaven's sake, Joe, won't you come in for a sherry? Minette and the children can wait another half-hour."

"I'll let you settle in, Sir John," I call. "I must go arrange the special wire for tomorrow night. They'll be closing soon. Then I'm off to bed!"

The plan is that I'll join him in the morning, election day, at noon. That will leave me a few hours to meet with my assistant and begin catching up on my paperwork. And it will allow him a few extra hours to sleep, and to submit to Lady M.'s ministrations.

We both have our crosses to bear.

Sir John

I've always cast my ballot in every blessed election for which I was eligible—national, provincial, municipal, ecclesiastical, or filling the Rideau Club executive with loyal Tories. But not today. On the culmination of this, my last and greatest campaign, the seventh general election of our good young Dominion, I stay home in bed.

Yet I feel as on any election day before the returns begin. In this brief and precious interval, I become wondrously detached and contented, my spirits light, my mind serene in the knowledge that no matter what the people's will, I've done my utmost. For the moment the struggle is over. I'm no longer different from any other citizen. The outcome is entirely out of my hands, and I can let go for the remains of the day and enjoy a good book or a sound nap. Fleeting as it must be, this is always the time I savour most.

Agnes was right: I'm far better off at home. I should have returned from the Professor's house days ago.

At dawn this morning she entered my bedroom in a blaze of glory, the sun just topping the trees to pour through my window and catch her ivory hair, already put up for the day, in a noose of light. When she stooped to kiss me, her warm beloved scent filled my nostrils. She waited patiently as I struggled out of the covers, and I could sense her self-restraint, refraining from saying I should remain strictly abed as commanded by Dr. Powell. Instead her smile broadened as I rose creakily to my feet, trying not to cough too much, and embraced her, grateful for her unyielding softness, her tender solidity.

Arm in arm we walked to the great window. In the sun's warmth, the panes were barely frosted over. Agnes threw the drapes open and together we surveyed the expanse of fresh sparkling snow stretching unbroken across the front lawn to the gates—closed, I noticed, to tell visitors they aren't welcome today. I recited:

"And Winter, slumbering in the open air,
"Wears on his smiling face a dream of spring."

Agnes squeezed my upper arm so hard it hurt. Normally I spout these lines by Coleridge in our drawing room as we gaze across the river north toward the Gatineau Hills.

"Coleridge is apt in either direction, don't you think, my dear?"

She made a low murmur of assent. "And did you hear me come in during the night to listen to your breathing?" she asked.

"I did not, my darling. I heard the grate rattle and thought it was only Ben stoking the fire."

"Your snoring drowned out my steps. You seemed to be enjoying your sleep."

"I was dreaming of stupendous Tory majorities."

"Your dream will come true tonight."

"We'll see. I must ensure it by voting in our own riding."

"You'll do nothing of the sort. You heard Dr. Powell."

"Has Dr. Powell become the arbiter of all truths?"

"In this house, at any rate."

I didn't oppose her, any more than I did last evening. After bidding Pope farewell, I found I could scarcely mount the stairs to my bedroom, much less carry off the usual entertainments—an amusing chat with wee Mary, followed by regaling her and Agnes with the latest exploits over dinner, then a bit of reading aloud by the fire. I had no appetite for food or anything else. I allowed myself to be put to bed straightaway, and in bed I've remained ever since, bouts of hard dry coughing succeeded by bouts of sleep. My throat feels like a coal scuttle.

Agnes proceeded to rub a vile-smelling mixture prescribed by Powell on my chest and back. Apparently it consists of ammonia and bark. Her devotion to my care never ceases to amaze me. At times it can be too much for her own good, or mine; but this isn't one of them.

My current indisposition calls up memories of twenty-odd years ago. Agnes saved my life at a time when others, including my own Cabinet, had given me up as a goner. Even the public thought John A. would no longer be theirs—an impression abetted by the same newspapers that were always calling attention to my financial troubles or fondness for port at midday.

You wouldn't think a gallstone attack could cause such an uproar. It *was* excruciatingly painful and debilitating, and it kept me prisoner in my office on Parliament Hill until Dr. Grant considered it safe to move me—and even then only as far as the Speaker's chambers. All Grant would permit me to eat was half an oyster. He insisted it would be dangerous to indulge me in my plea for more: "Remember, Sir John, the hopes of Canada are depending on you!" I told him it was strange Canada's hopes depended on half an oyster.

But to tell the truth, the fevers and convulsions frightened even me. I'm told my face resembled a death mask. Only Agnes believed I'd recover. She sat by my side the whole time, rubbing my chest with whisky, the one cure that seemed to do any good, and vexing Dr. Grant with demands to try everything possible, while confiding to her diary that the medical men might have abandoned hope but she hadn't. My brave darling.

When she finally got me home from the Hill, Ottawa's stifling summer heat had set in. Agnes booked us on the train to Montreal and bundled me aboard the sublimely named *Druid* for my first voyage to Prince Edward Island since the Charlottetown meetings. In the Island's cool healing airs, in a big old house falling apart even faster than I, generously donated for my convalescence, she nursed me through the rest of it—just as, she said, I'd nursed her through the long and painful wait for Mary's arrival. Every day we'd sit side by side on the lawn beside the river, and I'd consume Bagehot's *The English Constitution* and stirring eyewitness accounts of the Franco-Prussian War in the *Pall Mall Gazette*, while Agnes read her novels and *The Invalid's Cook Book* purchased from Durie's bookshop on Sparks Street. She fed me recipes from that tome until I felt strong again; we agreed how thankful we were that even in desolate, filthy, unhealthy Ottawa, one could still obtain modern scientific literature.

So it was love that pulled me through. By the time we were back home in September, I was good as new—or as near to new as one gets at my age. To all who'd wished me gone, it must have seemed I'd risen from the dead, a Canadian Lazarus. As much as I hate to disappoint them, they'll think the same again tomorrow. All I have to do is win an election.

After a brisk knock, Robert Wynyard Powell, M.D., strides in. His deep bluff voice gives out with, "Good morning, Sir John! And how did we spend the night?" Of course he already knows from speaking with Agnes. Dr. Powell has acquired the complacent, omniscient air of all medical men, despite being still shy of forty.

He examines the fire before examining me. "Shall we throw more coal on? Must make sure you stay warm."

Powell seldom has anything new to tell me. Perhaps it's just the nature of my case: an old man with the boring old man's complaints. He has me take deep breaths, which I find uncomfortable, taps my chest and back, listens to my pulse. He'd rather talk politics anyway. He's already voted, he tells me, having arrived at his polling place early to avoid the crowds.

"And how did this McGreevy business go down on the hustings?" Powell asks, peering down my inflamed gullet. As a good Conservative he's rightly worried about the public outrage brewing over allegations brought by Joseph-Israël Tarte against Thomas McGreevy, one of our less esteemed MPs. Sir Hector Langevin is widely assumed to be mixed up in McGreevy's kickback scheme—inadvertently, I'm sure, and against Hector's better judgment, no doubt—in consequence of being both Minister of Public Works and McGreevy's brother-in-law.

I make light of the matter. No point in getting people talking, or more especially thinking, even at this late stage of the campaign. I assure the good doctor that in any case the voters are too exercised about trade threats from the Americans to pay attention to the sordid details of a petty scandal in Quebec. If only this were true!

Powell assures me in turn that Langevin will have to defend himself in the days ahead, rather than relying on his Prime Minister for protection. I must remain in bed, he says, if I'm to recover from bronchitis and possibly pleurisy. Ministers will have to manage their own problems for the time being.

These are strong words. I listen to him politely, inclining my head. "Thank you, Doctor. I will certainly heed your excellent advice, as far as circumstances permit. But I must attend to my work if I am at all able."

Powell leaves. He seems unhappy. His worries, it seems, aren't confined to the outcome of the election.

My next visitor is infinitely cheerier. "Papa, it's me! It's me, I'm here!" As soon as Powell's gloomy coattails disappear through the doorway, Agnes steers Mary's wheelchair into the room. Sweet Mary has been patiently waiting all morning in her alcove down the hall, Agnes tells me, and thoughtfully leaves the two of us alone to chat.

"And how is my little Baboo this morning?" I pull myself high up onto the big down pillows and reach for both her wee hands.

Leaning forward in the wheelchair and tightly gripping my fingers, she replies, "Very well, Papa, thank you. But you're not."

"Oh, my darling, no need to be sad. Papa will be up and about in no time."

She brightens and abruptly exclaims, "You look like Mr. Bedford-Jones!"

"Ah yes—all in white. But the Reverend Bedford-Jones is far too proper to preach at St. Alban's in his nightshirt."

She giggles. "And Papa, your nose is bigger!"

I ask Mary what she's been doing this fine morning. She tells me in fairly precise detail. Helping Mama to do her hair. Helping Alice to shell walnuts for a cake. She likes her big new chair with the padded seat, which she finds very comfy. She's also been "reading" the newspapers. I've no idea how much of them she can puzzle out, but she's overheard enough of our conversations to know that the *Empire* and the *Journal* and sometimes the *Mail* say nice things about Papa, but the *Globe* says horrid things, and this makes her so angry she refuses to "read" it.

She's wearing the "swell blue frock" Agnes brought her from Harris and Tom's in Cavendish Square on our last trip to London. I tell Mary the colour matches her pretty eyes. Then she produces a piece of paper stuffed between the folds of her dress and the side of her chair.

"Here's your speech, Papa. I know you don't like the typewriter for letters. But it does fine for speeches."

Pope has been showing Mary how to type, letting her have some old remarks of mine to copy on the typewriter in his office downstairs. This one consists of a few notes I made to welcome a speaker at the Albany Club in Toronto. She holds it out eagerly, and I take it with expressions of gratitude. As I run my eyes over the page, I'm astonished.

My Mary has made enormous strides—I can scarcely believe it. Instead of the cross-hatchings and strikeouts and very approximate spellings she's always produced before, I see a tolerably clean, almost accurate text. She must have practised endlessly and taken enormous pains to produce such a fair copy.

"My darling," I tell her, "you've done a splendid job! Did Mama or Joe help you?"

"No, Papa, they don't need to anymore. I do it all by myself. But please show me where I've made mistakes. I want to do better."

We chat happily until Agnes comes back to fetch her with pointed reminders that I must get my rest if I'm to recover. I lean close to Mary so she can kiss me on the cheek, and she wishes me sweet dreams.

Agnes and I exchange sad smiles as she pushes the chair out the door. After all our dashed hopes and anguish during Mary's infancy, the special shoes and braces that didn't work, the Swedish masseuse recommended by Princess Louise, the journeys to New York to consult orthopaedic specialists and investigate the latest treatments, the stays in Banff to try the waters, we both take encouragement from any sign of progress, however small. Improvements, nonetheless, seem to be coming more rapidly lately. It's strange they didn't occur sooner, since Mary is twenty-two now. She expects to be treated as a grown-up, and it takes an effort of will to remind ourselves she's an adult after all, albeit one with the diminutive stature, features and mind of a charming child.

I try to sleep but can't; I'm too elated by Mary's progress. My thoughts wander to what others call the McGreevy affair but I call, in the privacy of my thoughts, the Langevin affair. It's the sort of needless, stupid, greedy business that could lose us seats, even the country. Why has Hector put up with that moral imbecile for so long?

The allegations against McGreevy have been making the rounds for months. The *Grip* cartoonists have had a field day. The trouble is, the possibilities for graft at Public Works are literally endless, and the department has been Langevin's for so long he'll end up taking the blame, even if his hands are lily-white. But how could they be? How could he be plausibly ignorant of a scheme that must have been going on for years, if not decades? It galls me that Hector persisted in tolerating these games long after I gave him Cartier's mantle as my lieutenant in Quebec. Silly old ass. And yet as I've known from the start, Langevin is no Cartier.

It's obvious where all this is going. Joseph-Israël Tarte, despite being elected tonight by my supporters, will use his new Parliamentary platform to bring his evidence before the House. He clearly intends to destroy and eventually supplant Langevin. The Liberals will leap on his testimony like hyenas on fresh kill: McGreevy must be condemned, Langevin must be discredited, the Government must resign, and the great issues on which I've waged this campaign will be forgotten, instantly displaced in the public mind by the wretched details of a scandal nobody will remember in ten years' time because it will be followed by some other, more wretched one.

Meanwhile, what of the nation? What of our sovereignty? What of the great national scheme of western settlement?

It's all too familiar—similar to the last election in '87, when we risked defeat not because of our policy of protecting domestic producers and jobs, or because of our stewardship of the public interest, or anything we'd done or left undone, but for entirely extraneous causes: in Quebec, because in the ordinary course of justice a rebel was hanged for treason; and in Ontario, because the British government refused to grant Home Rule to Ireland. What an impossible country to govern!

And so the next few weeks will unfold as they must. After our well-deserved victory tonight, however slim, I'll sit down with the list of elected Members that Pope will have assiduously typed up, province by province, each victor's name followed by his riding.

In red pencil I'll strike through the names I know to be hopelessly Liberal and hostile to our cause. In blue I'll tick off our known Conservative friends and allies. And alongside the loose fish, those whose views, temperament and allegiance are uncertain or un- known, I'll place a large blue question mark. To those gentlemen I'll pay close and occasionally flattering attention. Pope will invite them to Earnscliffe for dinner as early in the session as possible. If one or two decline on grounds of neutrality or concern for Mr. Laurier's good opinion of them, Pope will assure them on my behalf that I'll understand, but that even Mr. Laurier accepts the occasional invitation to Earnscliffe. And I'll hope in time to add a blue tick beside their names too. The Speech from the Throne, which I'll construct with Pope's inestimable help, will contain irresistible bits of fish bait.

But somehow it's all become quite wearying. Foreseeing how these scenes will unfold is gratifying, in a way, but not edifying. As I visualize myself performing the same rituals I've performed after every election for thirty years, I wonder why I bother—it's as if I've performed them already. And whether I do or not, the world will carry on the same. It's just so with the McGreevy business. I can picture its outcome in photographic detail. Is it then neces- sary to live it out?

A discreet knock interrupts these peculiar thoughts. Pope's familiar signal: time for our appointed visit. His impeccably groomed head appears, then the rest of him, attired in a Savile Row suit after my own taste.

"Ah, Sir John, you're awake. I thought you'd want to know— the telegraph wire is successfully installed. It comes downstairs into my office. Ahearn's men have tested it, and it works without a hitch."

"So we'll get all the returns tonight?"

"Yes, all the latest news, right here—practically as it happens!"

"How splendid. I won't even have to leave my bed."

The Returns

Much restored after a night's sleep in my own bed, I'd assumed Sir John would feel the same. Alas. When I popped into his room at noon, I found him still *hors de combat*. I asked how he was feeling, and he repeated his words from early in the campaign—"tolerably well for an old chap"—but without an ounce of his former conviction. He looks as grey and weary as a week ago at Professor Williamson's. And his cough is worse.

I'd expected him to demand we dive into the mountains of unopened correspondence awaiting us downstairs: not a word. He simply couldn't face it. He lacks a young man's constitution, after all. How much of his renowned resilience and fighting spirit is left? Impossible to tell.

It troubles me that I can't be more useful to him. I don't know what to do beyond following doctor's orders and letting him rest, and as a result I'm feeling unmoored. The only reason Sir John keeps an office for me in the bosom of his household is that so much of his correspondence comes here, and proximity allows us to work together uninterrupted, into the night when necessary. But without serious work to do, I'm an interloper trespassing on the family's privacy. I can't even entertain Mary with any of the childish games that once amused her when she was far easier to amuse. She's grown remarkably serious and ladylike, and one must treat her accordingly. Are she and I fated to become confidants? Sharing sly, knowing observations about the parents, like a brother and sister?

I must reorder my afternoon. There's plenty of work to tackle back on Parliament Hill, yet something—the novelty of an election day, I suppose—makes me restless. I find it exciting that all across the land, people are voting either to replace a government or to confirm it in office. It offers a sense, however illusory, that the country may be on the brink of change and could be a very different place this time tomorrow.

On Sussex I try riding for the first time on the Ottawa Electric Company's brand-new horseless streetcar. Its speed and silence on the straightaway are impressive, the screeching of its wheels at stops and turns distressing. I suppose I'll get used to it, though it seems a highly unnatural mode of transport. I don't miss the horse smells.

I step off the tram near my polling place on Rideau Street, and after standing in line to vote, stroll home for lunch in the mild March sunshine. I find myself relishing the sight and sound of melting snow dripping off the roofs of Sandy Hill: a delicious hint of spring. Perhaps I'll surprise Minette.

Surprise indeed. Letting myself in, I find her at her bath, the children all off at school, and we pass the time most agreeably, as we haven't for ages. After a shockingly belated lunch, I walk to the Hill, accomplish a few small but essential tasks and return to Earnscliffe. Once again I board the electric tram, a spring in my step as I alight and approach my private entrance.

I find a telegrapher sitting at my desk. Nervously the man explains that his employer's instructions are to remain here until the returns are complete or the Prime Minister instructs him to leave, whichever comes first. I assure him that's perfectly fine, but the first returns from the Maritime provinces won't begin for another two hours, so he should stand down for a bit. I show him to the kitchen where he can get some supper. I also ask Alice the cook to inform her mistress of my return: Sir John must know I'm available if he needs me.

Presently Lady M. comes downstairs. She wonders if we might have a little chat—most unusual. She lingers in the doorway to my office, hesitating to seat herself in the old cracked leather arm-chair, and invites me to join her in the drawing room. There we perch at right angles on upholstered chairs and converse idly about the children's progress in school, about Minette's health—"In the pink," I assure her knowledgeably—and the ever-so-gradual approach of spring. This is a subject of some anxiety for Lady M.; her tropical upbringing has instilled lingering doubts that the long Ottawa winter will ever end. She's also bored, she confesses. She was off again to Banff in the Rockies in November: "Compared to the wonderful air and exhilarating atmosphere out West," she declares, "Ottawa seems so dull and tame and stupid and *old*." Meanwhile my limbs are tensing; I wonder what she's leading up to.

Alice brings us tea and petits fours on a silver service. As Lady M. pours ever so studiously, I steal a glance at her face. Not for the first time, I notice her unusually large, well-shaped but rather masculine ears, both completely exposed by her severe coiffure. I wonder if she displays them on purpose, flaunting their size. I'm surprised she never softens her appearance by covering them with some of her abundant white hair. Perhaps Sir John prefers it this way—fancies the sight of those ears in public. Her wide mouth and jaw are set as firmly as ever, but her cheeks have become fleshy lately, a bit puffy, creating a misleading impression of gentleness.

With one hand she extends a full teacup, with the other a plate. "Do help yourself, Joseph," she murmurs. Sir John has confided to me that his wife has never felt comfortable serving tea; she fears she doesn't do it gracefully.

She tells me he's been dozing most of the afternoon—very unlike him. Her face is drawn with anxiety. I'd like to be able to soothe away her worries, but it would be presumptuous to try. What are my words beside Dr. Powell's? And in her eyes, who am I but the instrument of her affliction? I'm Sir John's henchman on his late nights and hard travels away from her, the unco-operative fellow who didn't bring him home soon enough from the Professor's house.

But for the moment Lady M. betrays no such feelings. And surely she understands in her heart of hearts that all decisions, in the end, are Sir John's.

"Joseph, I would like to make a request of you." She says this rather stiffly, as if she'd prefer not to have to, looking away toward the French doors facing the river. "I hope I'm not presuming. You've been so *marvellously* helpful to Sir John, so indispensable to him, that he—and I—can scarcely repay you. So I hope what I'm asking won't add to your burdens."

I'm taken aback by her tentativeness, her girlish modesty. And her flattery. Yet she seems utterly sincere, sitting there holding herself in, and I abandon my suspicions.

"I assure you, Lady Macdonald, I'm always happy to be of service. As much to you as to Sir John."

"Thank you, Joseph. Well, it's thus. With Sir John as he now is—or as he at the moment appears to be—that is . . . Let me be blunt. Let me ask you if, in the event it becomes necessary, I may count on your assistance—your good, solid, sensible advice—no matter what? May I simply turn to you for counsel in my moment of need? Whatever happens? May I? Would that be an imposition?"

She looks imploringly at me. I've never seen her in anything other than complete command of a situation or herself. Now liquid is welling up in her eyes. Her mouth remains pinched and stern, but her tears contradict it.

"Lady Macdonald, of course! It goes without saying. I can't claim I'll always have the answer or know exactly what to do, but I'll try to be helpful. However I can."

To my surprise and embarrassment, tears are inching up behind my eyeballs, too. I blink rapidly to dispel them. I can't imagine why I have such feeling for the woman.

And so I appear to have entered into some amorphous yet binding pact. Lady M. and I are both loyally committed, in our different ways, to Sir John, both dedicated to serving his needs and interests. Now we're committed to each other, too. Or at least I'm committed to her. Meaning what? Looking after her in her old age? Hardly—she's still vigorous and twenty-one years younger than her husband and, if it comes to that, remarriageable. I'm not at all sure what I've gotten myself into. My only fear is that it could affect how I serve *him*. I may have unwittingly compromised myself: become a servant of two masters.

The returns have begun coming in. Seated at my desk with a big pad of yellow paper in front of him and a stubby pencil between his fingers, the telegrapher translates the Morse signals into concrete electoral numbers. So far the results are heartening. In Nova Scotia and New Brunswick, the Government actually appears to be gaining seats. In my home province of Prince Edward Island, the Conservatives are ahead in all four ridings, which would mean a gain of two.

I tear the sheets off the telegrapher's pad and run them upstairs to Sir John. He's sitting up in bed looking quite composed in his nightshirt, hands clasped in his lap, a touch drowsy after his supper. Lady M. is seated beside him. Dr. Powell paces before the fireplace, with a good blaze going. They all turn to me, and I smile to signal that the news is good, waving the pages gaily above my head.

Sir John holds up his hand.

"Before you tell us your tidings, Joe, let me make some predictions. We have faced a grave crisis. We have shown the Americans we prize our country as much as they do theirs and we'll fight for our existence as a nation. Having seen this, Canadians have had little choice but to vote for the Government. Some have been seduced and traduced by our opponents' cry for commercial union and have voted accordingly, but they remain a minority. There now. Am I right so far?"

"You are, sir."

Cheers go up from Lady M. and Dr. P.

Then Sir John again: "One more truth: an election is like a horse race—you can tell more about it the next day."

We all laugh, and Lady M. and I glance wordlessly at each other. She's clearly relieved to see him so animated. Sir John simply grins at us, then yawns and sinks his head back into the down pillow.

An hour later I return with a sheaf of more conclusive results from the Maritimes, as well as the early returns from all-important Ontario and Quebec. This time the prospects look less promising. Although the Government will apparently gain two seats in Nova Scotia, two on the Island, and as many as three in New Brunswick, it's running behind Liberal candidates in many Quebec and Ontario ridings, including some previously held by Conservatives.

Listening to me rhyme off the vote totals riding by riding, Sir John purses his lips and raises his eyebrows, as if he were a detached, disinterested, scholarly observer.

"Quebec I can understand," he murmurs when I finish. "Hard for the French to resist the appeal of a native son. But don't tell me my own province has been bought with Yankee gold." Sir John is certain that U.S. industrialists have contributed to the Liberals' war chest. The *Globe* itself, he insists, has been the conduit for big money from Cleveland and Chicago.

Patterns are emerging. The Quebec constituencies deserting us for Laurier are the same ones that fled to Mercier, the province's fiery Liberal Premier, in the recent provincial election. In Ontario it's the rural ridings: the McKinley Tariff has terrified the farmers into embracing free trade as their only salvation, no matter what the consequences.

Sir John observes matter-of-factly, "If I'd postponed the election until after another harvest, we'd have lost Ontario for sure."

He's philosophical about both gains and losses. Some Liberal margins are still thin, only a matter of a few votes, and Conservative candidates may yet make up the difference later in the night. Three of his key ministers, Thompson in Antigonish, Langevin in Trois-Rivières, and Bowell in North Hastings, have already been returned. And then there are the imponderables. Such as Mr. Blake.

Edward Blake was no free trader back when he was Liberal leader, and to judge from his recent words and actions, he's even less enthusiastic about the idea now. Because of his party's slavish commitment to commercial union, Blake retired from active politics; yet he remains influential in Ontario Liberal circles. Rumour has it that he's written an open letter to his former constituents in West Durham, to be published in the *Globe*, denouncing free trade and dissociating himself completely from his party's espousal of it—and that Laurier was barely able to persuade him to hold off publication of the letter until after the election. If Blake speaks for many Liberals, and if they were willing to sit on their hands today, or even vote Conservative, Ontario could stay with the Government after all. This notion, however speculative, seems to raise Sir John's spirits. Meanwhile his personal lead in Kingston is substantial and continues to grow.

On my next trip upstairs, after the arrival of a great many more telegrams requiring considerable collating and cross-tabulation, the grandfather clock in the front hall shows nearly ten o'clock. Dr. Powell has gone home. Lady M. is trying to read her novel but

nodding off. Sir John raises his puffy eyes to mine, and I summarize the overall results to spare them both unnecessary suspense.

Encouraging results from the West have begun arriving. Nonetheless, outcomes have been decided in only half the constituencies
across the country. Sir John's Kingston seat is more than secure,
his margin of victory the greatest ever in his political career. And
Hugh John Macdonald is decisively defeating his opponent in
Winnipeg!

At this news, an enormous, beatific grin transforms Sir John's
face. He nods his head repeatedly as he savours the prospect of
his son entering Parliament. He turns to his wife, his voice hoarse
and trembling with pleasure, yet tinged with some indefinable regret: "Of course, of course, I knew he'd win, I knew it."

I wait for the moment to pass before stating the obvious: at
this point in the evening, a decisive outcome remains some hours
away. The Government's fate, and the nation's, still hangs in the
balance.

"In any case," Sir John says dreamily, "I think that will do for
tonight." And without looking at either Lady M. or me, he turns
over and goes to sleep.

Visitors

Outside my office window the morning is grey, soft, indetermi-
nate: no longer winter, not yet spring. Large irregular patches of
grass show through the crust of gritty snow on Earnscliffe's lawn,
but snowbanks still rear up along the drive.

I've slid closed my tall pocket doors, hoping to remain undis-
turbed for an hour to finish drafting Sir John's memorandum to
the Governor General, Lord Stanley. The Colonial Secretary in
London, Lord Knutsford, has asked the Governor General, who
has asked Sir John, for a detailed explanation of Canada's position
on the Bering Sea. It's not that we haven't thoroughly briefed London on the matter; but the civil servants in the Colonial Office
keep changing—as do their political masters—and we must start
all over again persuading them not to sacrifice Canada's interests
on the altar of peace with Washington.

From his bed upstairs Sir John has sketched out what he wishes
the memorandum to say and has asked me to try my hand at a
draft. The Canadian position remains unequivocal: these are open
waters under international law; British Columbia sealers have
worked them for decades; there is no historical or legal basis for
the United States to police them as if they were American territory; accordingly Canada has a strong case for damages. Yet there

are so many legal ramifications, in addition to political ones—so many references required to the Anglo-American Convention of 1818 and the Washington Treaty and the stillborn Chamberlain–Bayard Treaty—that I keep having to run around the corner to Sir John's study to consult the published authorities in support of our argument. I'm no lawyer. Although he and I both left school at sixteen, Sir John went on to article under the great George Mackenzie, as he still refers to his mentor, and I went to work in a bank.

Congratulatory messages have been pouring in from the great and the ingratiating. The Queen, Lord Stanley informs us, has wired him "her gratification at the result of the general election." Cables have arrived from Lord Salisbury at 10 Downing Street, from the previous two Governors General—Lord Lorne wiring from Scotland, Lord Lansdowne from India—and from Sir George Stephen of the CPR, now residing in England. Letters are piling up from every loyal and not so loyal Conservative in the land requesting a government job. On election night, writes Professor Williamson from Earl Street, bonfires of celebration illuminated the centre of Kingston.

It grieves Sir John to see his Parliamentary majority reduced—and turned into a minority of eleven in Quebec. Yet across the nation he's won a fourth consecutive victory. At Earnscliffe the outcome is already an accepted fact of life; we've moved on to other emergencies.

The day after the election, Edward Blake's letter to his former constituents appeared in the *Globe*. The letter argued sonorously, as only Mr. Blake can, that free trade with the United States would be a fatal mistake, since it would inevitably lead sooner or later to absorption into the Union. Although too late to bolster Government forces in the House, the letter has severely embarrassed the Liberals and in particular Laurier, Blake's protegé and hand-picked successor.

Three days later Sir John ventured downstairs for the first time. He got as far as his study—"my workshop," as he calls it—and settled himself comfortably at his desk as if returning from a long voyage. As always I'd opened all his letters, answered the ones I could without overstepping my authority, and arranged the rest in folders in order of importance. What most animated him was reading Sir Richard Cartwright's extraordinary comment about the election in the *Globe*. Cartwright calls Sir John's majority "a thing of shreds and patches, made up of the ragged remnants from half a dozen minor provinces, the great majority of whom do not even pretend to be actuated by any principle save that of securing a good slice of booty for themselves." *Minor* provinces indeed! Sir John could only shake his head with delight at such self-defeating intemperance; it will further alienate the Maritimes and the West from the Liberals.

The next day dawned sunny and bracing. Despite Lady M.'s strenuous objections, Sir John decided to drive to Parliament Hill, and as a result I'm in her bad books. But does she really expect me to dissuade her husband from doing what comes as naturally to him as breathing? He insisted on presiding over the first meeting of his new Cabinet—largely a reconstituting of the old—and long before the agenda was complete, he felt so drained and over-whelmed by exhaustion that he had to beg his Ministers' pardon. I walked him slowly to the East Block exit, steadying him by the arm and helping him into Buckley's cab for the drive home. Langevin and other Ministers were clearly upset by his weakened condition. I could scarcely credit their distress—as if they hadn't the slightest remembrance of the severity of his illness during the last days of the campaign.

Naturally Sir John feels disappointed about having to leave the Cabinet meeting early. He'd assumed he could master his weakness by progressive acts of will and is disturbed to find he can't. Since then he's tried to conduct as much business as possible from his bed. It isn't easy. I feel the weight of his depressed spirits. His colour too is bad—the same ashen hue I observed that night in the *Jamaica*. Only acts of menace and bullying from Washington, it seems, are enough to revive him.

"You can tell," he told me this morning, "when an American election year is coming up. The Yankees will do anything under the stress of politics. Now they threaten us as a surrogate for Great Britain. It helps carry the Irish vote."

Before any more dangerous provocations break out—any more revenue cutters seizing our ships, or fretful London Ministers wondering if they should dispatch the Royal Navy—he wants to herd the British and Americans toward negotiations on the Bering Sea. He fumes inwardly over James Blaine's evasiveness and disingenuousness, yet exercises all the patience of a saint. Never mind that the Secretary of State refuses to renounce the American claim to a closed sea, on the grounds that they've never asserted such a claim—all the while acting as if a *mare clausum* is an established fact. Never mind that Washington's pretensions of supremacy over those waters are based on an ancient Russian claim, which the U.S. renounced when it bought Alaska from the Czar. We still must settle matters by treaty. And we must have the British at the table, since we aren't yet sovereign enough to sign international agreements on our own. It's an exasperating dilemma; yet somehow Sir John never despairs of resolving it.

Of course he recognizes a far greater game is afoot. Blaine, after all, isn't merely interested in the revenues of the American Alaska Fur Co. Sir John produces a ragged, two-year-old newspaper clipping reporting one of Blaine's speeches. He keeps it handy at all times, often quoting it to telling effect. Blaine expressed himself with remarkable candour: "Canada is like an apple on a tree just beyond reach. We may strive to grasp it, but the bough recedes from our hold just in proportion to our effort to catch it. Let it alone, and in due time it will fall into our hands."

Sir John fully expects Blaine to make our life difficult for years to come. "Were Blaine in power," he says, "he'd do everything disagreeable short of war, and perhaps, if England had trouble elsewhere, go even further."

Sir John thinks, as do many in the States, that Blaine is working toward a presidential nomination next term. "To win it," Sir John predicts, "he'll throw himself headlong into the arms of the Irish-Americans."

These baleful thoughts provide further inspiration for the memorandum. Just as I'm beginning to believe I can finish it before noon, there's a loud knocking at the main entrance. Assuming it's a tradesman who can't read, I carry on writing, but the knocking persists. Alice answers, and I faintly hear her explaining that Sir John remains indisposed. A peremptory reply comes in a strident voice that's all too familiar.

I ought to intervene but simply haven't the time to entertain the self-serving monologues of the Honourable John Graham Haggart. The Member for South Lanark is capable of going on for hours.

A silence follows; but no such luck that Haggart is retreating. The next voice belongs to Lady M., unmistakably indignant as she sweeps down the staircase. She can't abide the man.

I station myself behind the pocket doors, putting my ear to the crack. I can easily picture Haggart's bulk filling up the front hall, slush melting down his overshoes into Lady M.'s prized Persian carpet. Prussian in his self-importance, Haggart doesn't wait for her to wish him good day: "Lady Macdonald, good morning! I trust you'll forgive the intrusion. I simply must have a moment with Sir John. I—"

She stops him dead in his tracks: "Mr. Haggart, do you realize you have reduced my housekeeper to tears?"

"Why, no, I—"

"Indeed you have. Now if you would be kind enough to state your business."

I hold my breath. Knowing Haggart well, I suspect he's furious at being spoken to this way by any woman, no matter how elevated. Like the master of a particularly ill-bred dog, he'll be struggling to keep his temper leashed.

"I assure you, Lady Macdonald," he begins, "it was never my intention—"

"What *was* your intention, Mr. Haggart?"

"Simply to—"

"Mr. Haggart, do you realize Sir John is *simply* too ill to receive callers? That his recovery is far from complete? That Dr. Powell has forbidden visitors? And you have apparently forgotten that persons calling at Earnscliffe on public business are to use Mr. Pope's entrance. Mr. Pope keeps Sir John's agenda. The only exceptions are persons sufficiently important that Sir John *must* see them, and even they give notice in advance. I don't recall seeing your name on the list for today."

For a moment Haggart has no comeback. Imagining him fumbling for a reply, I almost pity him. He's beginning some lame effort when I pull open the doors and emerge innocently into the hallway, rounding the corner as if on my way somewhere else. "Ah, good morning, Lady Macdonald. And to you, Mr. Haggart."

They face each other like prizefighters, several feet apart in the middle of the hall. Seeing me approach, Haggart stops speaking, strokes his moustaches, and brightens. He brushes past Lady M. to reach eagerly for my hand. "Why, Joseph, grand to see you. I'm sure it will be all right with Sir John. I was just telling Lady Macdonald here—"

"To her face, if you please!" she commands.

I try to intercede. "Perhaps Lady Macdonald will consent—"

"No, no question of perhaps, Mr. Pope. If Mr. Haggart wishes to meet with my husband, he will await his turn like everyone else. He will wait until Sir John is up and about and ready to receive. If Mr. Haggart insists on pressing his candidacy for Minister of Railways and Canals with you, Mr. Pope, he is entirely free to do so. But not in my home!"

Lady M.'s dark eyes blaze beneath her tawny brow. I've never seen such a fit of animal rage. She begins to stride across the hallway, making for the front door, but Haggart, with astonishing agility for a large man, springs backwards to the entrance, bows, and lets himself out.

Suddenly the house is silent as a stone.

"My goodness," says Lady M., staring at the closed door, barely suppressing a giggle. "Why do you suppose he left so suddenly?"

I grin in spite of myself. "Perhaps he thought you were making for the umbrella stand," I murmur, "to select a weapon."

Her face falls. "I must try to keep my temper in check, Joseph. But really, everything has been so trying lately. When men are so nakedly self-seeking, without a moment's compassion for him to whom they owe everything, I lose all patience. Why, not so long ago I was even furious with *you*—" ah, here it comes, one of Lady M.'s moments of unnecessary frankness "—with your stubbornness, Joe, your obstinacy. You can be so dreadfully stubborn at times."

"Yes, Ma'am."

"It's not that Professor Williamson isn't a fine and well-meaning brother-in-law. I'm immensely fond of him. It's not his fault he has no practical common sense. But what sort of place was that for a great national Premier to convalesce?"

"It was doctor's orders, Lady Macdonald. I didn't feel I had the authority to decide—"

"No, no, of course not. And I'm sure you did what you thought best for Sir John. Believe me, I'm grateful, Joe. Please forgive an old woman's anxiety."

Abruptly she turns her back to return upstairs. Something makes me blurt out, "Oh, Lady Macdonald, *you're* not old."

She pauses on the first stair. "Why, thank you, Joseph," she pronounces, softly but firmly. She turns around to face me, hand still gripping the railing, and seems to arrive at some conclusion: "Do you know, Joseph, when I went into his room this morning, I found him not asleep—not reading or signing letters either—but playing with toys. They were the familiar, peculiar, old-fashioned ones. The broken rattle, the little cart, the wooden animals with the paint coming off. He'd pulled them out of their wooden box. He's kept that box hidden under his bed ever since we moved here."

Visualizing the scene, she shuts her eyes: "He had them spread about the counterpane. A little of his old colour had come back. There was light in his eyes. 'Ah, my dear,' he said—his voice still weak but bearing up bravely—'I was just thinking about little John A. I wonder if he still watches us?'"

Her eyes reopen and she continues on her way upstairs.

Returning to the clutter in my office, I feel strangely agitated. I try to concentrate on captivating the dry minds in the Colonial Office. I stare out the window. There's so much to do, I wish I could remain here around the clock, perhaps set up a cot in the corner. But Minette has already begun to protest I never see the children during the week; they're asleep when I leave in the morning, asleep when I return home at night. Her concern puzzles me. When ever *have* I seen them, except on Sundays and holidays?

Wretched Haggart. I can never forget he owes his Cabinet post entirely to a moment of anger on Sir John's part. Sir John had taken a scunner to George Kirkpatrick, whose loyalty to his chief and party was questionable. Kirkpatrick pressed relentlessly to be awarded the Cabinet seat for eastern Ontario, even threatening Sir John with dire consequences if his demand wasn't met, and for reply, Sir John filled the vacancy with John Graham Haggart—

showing his followers how he deals with blackmail. It was the only way Haggart could ever have attained such a distinction.

Meanwhile the voters of South Lanark have returned Haggart to Parliament for the fifth time. In my early days with Sir John, I cited something Haggart had said in the 1882 election campaign as reported by the *Mail*, thinking the quotation downright clever. "My dear Pope," Sir John admonished me, "apart from his ability to hold his seat, I can detect no virtue in the man, no matter what the *Mail* may claim he said." Sir John asked rhetorically why, when Haggart was already notorious for his taste in plump and accessible lady typists, he found it necessary to carry on with the first female librarian in the history of Parliament, setting back an admirable experiment in employment practices.

At Cabinet meetings Haggart acts as if he's earned his place. Yet lately he's made no secret of the fact he isn't satisfied with the Post Office. His motive for wanting Railways and Canals is well known to Sir John and me, if to no one else. Before the last campaign Haggart managed to lay his hands on some unspent public funds and have them applied to rebuilding the Tay Canal—sometimes known as "Haggart's Ditch"—connecting Perth with Lower Rideau Lake. He plans to spend these funds on digging yet another branch of the canal, so that Haggart's Ditch can be extended from the Tay River Basin to Haggart's Island, permitting the steamer *John Haggart* to travel to and from Haggart's Mill. When word of this boondoggle gets out, there will be no end of outrage in the House and the press—unless, of course, Haggart becomes Minister of Railways and Canals, in a position to bury the expenditure deep in the departmental estimates.

My early days with Sir John now seem like an innocent dream. Back then it was enough simply to take dictation from his lips, feeling glad of my timely decision to learn shorthand; and to transcribe my notations into flowing lines for his signature and manage his daily schedule. I worked long hours, my universe bounded by the trinity of Earnscliffe, Parliament Hill and Rideau Hall, and I was happy. I didn't have to *think*—aside from practical suggestions to help Sir John achieve certain elementary goals—or arrive at complex judgments. Now it's altogether different. Now I must weigh the demands of Honourable Members and Deputy Ministers, Justices and Senators, party and constituency, and decide which should take precedence. Although I don't consider myself incapable of such judgments, there are times when I'm staggered to realize I'm actually thinking for the Prime Minister.

Perhaps I overstate the case. But every day I take the measure of political events and present them to Sir John in a synthesis, during those precious minutes when I have his full attention. We're always being interrupted by Lady M. or Dr. Powell or some other person whose intrusion into our presence is unavoidable—persons who can't be privy to what I have to share with him. And so in our moments *en petit comité*, I compress my knowledge into compact, uncluttered, unambiguous sentences, containing only such information that's vital for him to know, and offer him an array of choices for making decisions that only he can make.

These labours have always been meat and drink to him. Yet his capacious mind—and I would never for a moment admit this to another—may no longer be entirely equal to the task. I can't remember a time since leaving home to make my way in the world, unschooled, unheralded and unknown, when I've felt more alone.

But in fact I'm not. A rapid knocking on my outer door recalls me to the present. I open up and behold the pointed beard and knowing wintry gaze of Joseph-Israël Tarte.

At least M. Tarte uses the proper entrance. I bow in the French-Canadian manner, inviting him inside. Tarte enters uttering pleasantries, his short wiry frame in constant, writhing motion. I always have the feeling his busy mind is off somewhere else, winning arguments. Gesturing toward the leather chair with a rueful glance at my unfinished memorandum, I station myself behind my desk.

Tarte has an annoying habit of beginning a conversation in French and then, remembering my limitations in his language, switching into English after only a sentence or two. There is something both obsequious and insulting about this: condescension masquerading as courtesy. I wish he'd stick to one language or the other. At the same time he's unfailingly polite. Recently *The Week* termed him "the mildest mannered man that ever scuttled a ship or cut a throat."

But as Sir John's gatekeeper I can't be cut or evaded by M. Tarte—not for him the clumsy tactics of a John Graham Haggart. I must be gotten around with as much tact and guile as possible. Tarte has the advantage of knowing even better than I the family I married into. The Taschereaus are everywhere in Quebec society, and inevitably Tarte has attacked some of them, including Minette's father, the Chief Justice, in his columns in *Le Canadien*. And so he invariably asks after my dear wife and our *enfants adorables*.

When I've satisfied his enquiries and congratulated him on his election in Montmorency, Tarte gets down to business. He realizes Sir John is unwell. He wishes only a few minutes of private conversation with the Prime Minister. It is a matter, he assures me, of the utmost importance to the country.

Conscious of the fact that my memorandum is sitting in full view, also mindful that an old journalist can read upside down, I abruptly ask him which matter that would be. Of course it's *l'affaire McGreevy*. Tarte has spilled copious ink on the subject in *Le Canadien* and is now launching his Parliamentary career on that same ocean of scandal. Perhaps, I enquire, he wishes to discuss with the Prime Minister his intentions when the House opens next month?

"I cannot deny I will make public the informations I have," he says, tilting his beard upwards with an air of noble indignation. "The whole country must know the injustice of what I have elsewhere called *McGreevéisme*."

"And if that brings down the Government?"

"I remind you, M. Pope, that although I am a Tory, I ran in Montmorency as an Independent. If the Government should fall, it will be because of others. My duty is only to bring their *malfaisance* to light."

I remember Sir John telling me that power means more to Tarte than money. If his idea of power is to pull the temple down upon his head, he'll assuredly be powerful. He seems to believe implicitly in the righteousness of his cause—the challenge lying, as ever, in knowing exactly what that cause is. Tarte has changed positions more often than a . . . however that scabrous joke goes.

"I see you hesitating," he says. "Let me explain. Sir Hector Langevin was once a great man. He believed, as I do, in a strong Québec within a united Canada. And he believed, as I do, that the Conservative Party is the best means to achieve that end. At that time I was happy to follow Sir Hector. But he is no longer worthy to lead our party in French Canada. He has forgotten his roots, just as he has forgotten his principles. He has breathed too long the air of *McGreevéisme*. His politics are unclean. He is now entirely useless as Sir John's man in Québec."

"I see. So you would bring *Sir Hector* down."

"There are better men to serve as our Québec leader."

"But as I'm sure you'll agree, Sir John has done more than anyone to unite French and English in this country. If he falls along with Langevin, how does that serve Quebec? Or a united Canada?"

Tarte shifts uncomfortably in the chair. He fixes his eyes on me with a stare to set the curtains afire. "That simply need not happen. One year ago, I took my *dossier* on Langevin and McGreevy to Sir John. He refused to read it. He even refused to hear me out. Sir John still believes in Sir Hector. He prefers to leave Québec politics and patronage to the French. Well, M. Pope, I am French, and now I am a Member of Parliament too and a supporter of Sir

John's Government, and he must listen to me this time. This scandal need not destroy him. We Conservatives can settle it among ourselves. But Sir John must do it soon, and properly, or I cannot speak for the consequences."

"I see. You have a proposition for him."

"I have a solution. I believe he deserves a second chance to do the right thing."

"All right, then." I rise, my temperature rising also. I shuffle the pages of my memorandum together and place them into a file, which I tuck firmly under my arm. "I'll go up and tell Sir John you're here, M. Tarte. Please feel free to read the newspapers on the table. They're today's."

On my way upstairs I decide to relate the conversation verbatim to Sir John, without allowing my personal feelings to colour the issue. Only he in his wisdom can know what's to be done with M. Tarte.

I knock softly and open. Sir John appears to be awake but unmoving; he's leaning back against the pillows, facing the door. I see no sign of little John A.'s toys. Presumably they're back in their box under the bed.

I repeat the gist of my conversation with Tarte, without adding a single gloss. Sir John listens intently, taking it all in without a show of feeling one way or the other.

When I finish, silence. He moistens his lips with his tongue. He swallows with some difficulty and a sound like paper crumpling.

"I won't see him," he says finally, turning his face slowly to the wall. "It is too late."

Sir John

This isn't what Pope meant when he asked me to recall my years in power: "Just a sketch, mind you, Sir John. Nothing taxing."

He wasn't proposing I record my dreams. Oh no, nothing as feckless as that. Joe has a more auspicious, more public project in mind. And of course I'm all for it—in principle.

He's also testing me. He wants to discover how much of my faculties I retain. I can't say I blame him; I'm not entirely sure myself. But for the moment the infernal dream is all I can think about. It keeps running through my head like an escaped dog.

In this morning's version, the hairy fellow had the gall to be wearing a *kilt*. It suited him, too. He was an impressive-looking man, hair and all. He was striding about, declaiming something or other. Riel was always posturing and declaiming, sanctifying his preposterous notions of changing the world with appeals to Scripture, like any man educated by Jesuits, or Sulpicians, or whoever his teachers were, raising their armies of seminarians in the glooms of old Montreal. De'il tak' their black conspiratorial hides! They try to win by being the last man standing after everyone else is talked to death, complete with Biblical citations.

Riel had his own peculiar version of the disease. It came complete with visions, delivered to him and him alone by the

Almighty Himself. But in any case, the kilt is unforgivable.

The next thing I know, I'm engaging him in imagined debate. Once again I fall for his provocations. I can't seem to help myself. We take up right where we left off, at our last and only meeting: an incident nobody knows about, not even Agnes. Now, there's a revelation for Pope's wee book!

At the end of March '74, a month equally miserable for its weather and its politics, we were just beginning our exile from government. Riel had been skulking about Montreal all that bitter winter, hiding in two-faced Desjardins' mansion on Dorchester Street, behind Bishop Bourget's palace—all with the Bishop's knowledge and connivance. Few knew this but me. The intelligence came from a trustworthy source, and I kept it to myself; I didn't even tell Langevin. No point in wasting it. I could have used it to expose Riel, not to mention the disloyalty of the Catholic leadership in Quebec, but what would have been the good? I'd never subvert my pact with Cartier to keep friendly relations with the French, dead though the poor fellow was by then.

The people of Red River had re-elected Riel to Parliament, but he still had a price on his head for executing Thomas Scott. Though Scott wasn't worth the rope to hang him, rebellion against the Crown must come at a cost.

Rumours were flying that Riel was travelling to Ottawa escorted by Metis sharpshooters. Utter madness. The Orangemen in Alexander Mackenzie's Government—even in my own party— were beside themselves, howling for his blood. But I'll give Riel credit: though every policeman and private detective in Ottawa was prowling the streets for him, armed to the teeth and desperate to claim the reward, he slipped through their fingers. He eluded every damned one of them, mingling with his fellow MPs and their wives and officials at the opening of Parliament. By then he'd sprouted a heavy beard; he'd been provided with elegant new clothes by his protectors in Montreal, and not one of us, not our eagle-eyed policemen or worldly MPs, nor all-knowing journalists nor deputy ministers nor sergeants-at-arms, realized we were rubbing shoulders in the Parliamentary lobby with the most wanted man in Canada. He was one clever Halfbreed.

Consuming a magnificent lunch at public expense, Riel was ushered down the corridor to the Chief Clerk's office. His fellow sectarian and MP, Jean-Baptiste Fiset, told the Clerk he had a new Member with him who wished to take the oath of allegiance. The Clerk was old Alfred Patrick. Not identifying himself to Alfred, who was no doubt distracted by more urgent matters, Riel swore fidelity to Her Majesty and signed the Members' roll. When Alfred thought to examine the signature, inscribed *Louis David Riel* in a large brazen hand, his sidewhiskers stood on end. He looked up in astonishment, but the room was empty. Rushing into the corridor, he saw Fiset turning a distant corner with the bearded man beside him, and Riel offered a low bow before he disappeared.

Alfred lumbered straight to my office, burst in without knocking, and sputtered, "Sir John, Sir John, the devil's been here and he *bowed* to me!"

That evening the House was electric. News of Riel's escapade was flying everywhere. The spectators packing the galleries, including Lady Dufferin and her dinner guests, were agog with speculation, hoping to see the devil himself enter the chamber to claim his rightful place—on our Opposition benches, no less. But they were deprived of their thrill. Such an act of defiance would have got him arrested the moment he left the House; constables were stationed at every exit. In those days Riel was too canny to risk capture. He hadn't begun seeing God's footprint in the burning clouds and hearing the Divine voice and abandoning himself to his mad destiny. Instead he sensibly hightailed it across the river to Hull to spend the night safe in the bosom of his cronies.

In his absence that evening, his Parliamentary admirers rose to plead his cause with passion and eloquence. But when they moved a full amnesty for all the Metis rebels at Red River, Riel included, most of the French-speaking Members were easily defeated by most of the English-speaking ones. For myself, I voted my conscience and walked home. A nasty blizzard was getting up steam. Having been demoted by the people to Leader of Her Majesty's Loyal Opposition, I'd lost my appetite for lingering on the Hill till dawn.

I let myself in to our house on Chapel Street. The rest of the household was asleep. Most nights throughout our marriage, Agnes has waited up for me till all hours, but not in those days. Little Mary still needed too much care, and Agnes went to bed by nine, thoroughly exhausted.

Arming myself with a bottle of *porto fino* and stoking the fire, I settled down comfortably in my study. I took a reviving sip or two, picked up my Trollope, and immersed myself by the light of my reading lamp in the quaint doings of the pink-cheeked vicars and genteel ladies of Puddingdale and Plumstead, while the wind peppered the French doors with icy grapeshot.

After a chapter or two the storm seemed to grow louder. I looked up to see how bad it was getting and was startled to make out through the frosted panes the dim outlines of a man. Without being conscious of it, I'd heard his rapping on the glass. He was standing in our little yard and wearing a square fur hat. I knew instantly who he was. Despite a mild sense of shock, I didn't think twice about admitting him.

Riel hesitated as I flung the doors open, clearly alarmed that I was inviting him inside. Perhaps he suspected North-west Mounted Policemen lying in wait behind the bookshelves. He stepped across the threshold in a gust of snow, gave me a swift nervous glance, and removed his ice-crusted hat, revealing a great deal of wavy, dark brown hair. His eyebrows and dense beard were frozen white, and he pulled out a hanky to wipe his face. Although his nose was hooked like a hawk's beak, his full lips were pink and smooth as a baby's. He was still a young man.

"Forgive my intrusion, Sir John." His accent was marked but his English rapid and correct. "I wish only a brief word."

"As brief or as long as you like," I replied. "I am in for the night!"

He either didn't notice or wouldn't acknowledge the intended humour. I held out both hands to receive his wet, heavy buffalo coat. With a certain diffidence he struggled out of it and allowed me to hang it on the rack. I poured him a glass of port, which he accepted reluctantly and eyed with deep suspicion.

"We're quite alone," I began. "You've nothing to fear. Congratulations, by the way, on your visit to Parliament today. You astonished many."

His sombre expression didn't change, but he permitted himself to inch closer to the fire. His pant cuffs were turning dark with melted snow.

"It is not easy, coming to Ottawa," he said. "But the people of Red River have twice voted me in. It is their right to have me here."

"Ah, still. It took great courage."

We remained standing, gripping our glasses like weapons. Riel's eyes avoided mine but continually roamed about the room, taking in the burgundy drapes, the globe in its gleaming mahogany cradle, the law books in their black buckram bindings, the framed photographs of Agnes and Mary and Hugh John and little John A. He seemed startled to realize I had a family. His gaze lingered longest on my old secretary desk, its pigeonholes crammed with letters and bills, until you'd have thought he was searching for something kept there expressly for him.

It didn't seem quite the thing to invite him to sit, like any normal visitor. We both knew he was taking an enormous risk.

"I understand you've been staying with Alphonse Desjardins," I resumed blandly, letting him know I could have had him arrested if I'd wanted to.

"I've stayed in other places too."

"The United States?"

"I have many friends in New York State."

"A pity they can't vote for you."

"It is God's blessing to have friends in many places."

"Quite true."

"Having to travel all the time, Sir John, to keep moving, is very hard. The worst part is the travelling. I want nothing more than to go back home to Red River. But as you know," he said, looking me in the eye for the first time, "I cannot."

I nodded briefly.

He seemed encouraged, his voice quickening. "That is why I've come here tonight—to your home, your place of refuge. Forgive me, but I had no choice."

"No choice but to come here?"

"About the pardon." He set his untouched glass on the table between us. His voice took on an edge. "Why did you not declare it?"

"There was no—"

"You promised, Sir John. More than once. Ask Bishop Taché. Ask Père Ritchot."

"Tell me, why do you need to be *pardoned* too?" I caught myself raising my voice and hurriedly lowered it so as not to wake the house. "I sent you a thousand dollars, for God's sake, through Taché. You had the means to escape, Riel, to go and live in peace somewhere else. All you had to do was disappear. Leave Red River for a while. Take the grand tour. Vamoose. A little exile does a man good. Return in a few years and everything is forgiven—no one gives a tinker's damn anymore. Look at Cartier—he did exactly that after the '37 rebellion, then returned to Montreal to become a great statesman beloved by all. Especially by me."

"Of course," Riel responded. "And like Cartier I did go away. To Minnesota."

"And gladly took our cash. But you didn't *stay* away, Riel. You came back too soon, far too soon."

I had him dead to rights, and he knew it. His big, bearded melodramatic face flushed with anger.

"Do you think exile is pleasant, Sir John? With Orangemen searching for me in St. Paul, trying to hunt me down like a wild animal to collect the reward? My life was abominable. And besides . . ."

"Besides?"

"You'd given your word."

"Ah."

"Amnesty." He said it in a hushed tone, like a lover's name.

"Well? What of it?"

"I expected you to keep your promise."

His self-righteous piety made my gorge rise. "Good Heavens above, man, I'm not even Prime Minister anymore! You'll have to speak to Mackenzie about that."

He remained calm. "Not I. *You* must speak to Prime Minister Mackenzie on my behalf. His party would like nothing better than to try me and string me up. Or just shoot me on sight, it would save the expense of a trial. No, Sir John, only you can persuade them they are bound, *Canada* is bound, by your word of honour. Sent to me through Bishop Taché, a man of God."

"Hell's teeth, that was four years ago. Everything has changed now. How for the love of God do you expect me to persuade my worst political enemy of the very thing he's least able to do?"

"Because it is the only way I can live as a human being."

"And if I can't persuade him?"

"Sir John, please—do not betray me again."

That was Riel, damn him, always insisting on the last word. I wouldn't give it to him.

"There's something you don't know," I said. "A division was held in the House tonight. Parliament voted against pardoning you. It's settled, I'm afraid—once and for all."

I wish to Heaven I hadn't been the one to tell him. I wish I hadn't seen his collapsing face, the wretched crushed expression of a man hearing his mother has died. It's the face I still see in sleeping and waking dreams, in imaginary arguments—a victim's face, twisted by martyrdom and grief into justifying rebellion and murder. And it's still his peculiar deep accented voice echoing in my mind, interrogating, accusing:

You never troubled to consult us, Sir John. Nor even consider us. Not once. The Metis were a free people. A simple people with simple needs, but proud. We knew we deserved the same right as any other people, the right to a homeland. We were no threat to your dream of a Canada stretching from ocean to ocean, but we had a right to be where we were. We belonged there. We were God's children, patriots, not rebels. You never troubled to visit the banks of the Saskatchewan to see our farms running down through prairie grass to the wide river. You didn't see our little general stores, our white parish church, our cemetery where our fathers and mothers lay. You didn't see we were simply defending our birthright and our children's future. You didn't see because you didn't want to see.

What do you mean "we" and "our," Riel? You'd never lived in the Saskatchewan valley in your life!

Where my people go, I am there. I share their fate.

I can say the same about my people.

Our sin, then, was to lie in the path of your people's destiny.

We could hardly build a new country interrupted by another country in our midst, now, could we? It had to be one nation indivisible or nothing.

Spoken like an Englishman, Sir John. Don't you see? The Scots were an obstacle to King Edward and his armies in exactly the same way! They too had to be annihilated. But William Wallace and Robert Bruce rallied their people and fought and defended their homeland. I was the Metis Wallace!

Rubbish.

If only you had left your seat of power in Ottawa and all your eastern comforts to travel west, to witness my people living peacefully out on our land, you'd never have crushed us. You'd have respected our right to exist.

I did travel west, Riel. Five years ago. I crossed the Prairies on the CPR and saw pastures and farmhouses. I saw settlements. I saw thousands of acres under fresh cultivation by sunburnt settlers from Ontario and sweating Maritimers and immigrants speaking every language of Europe. I saw raw new towns that someday will grow into great modern cities, engines of industry and commerce and wealth. And I saw shiftless Indians and Metis too, sitting on the burnt prairie grass, gazing listlessly at our passing train. So yes, Riel, I did visit your homeland. But by then you were dead, executed by the blind hand of Justice. By then your day was done. As mine will be too, at any moment. Isn't that the way of the indifferent world?

I've got him there, damn his eyes.

Three

APRIL 1891

The Russell House

On Saturday morning I leave work early, startling my assistant. Minette's mother has arrived from Quebec City; she's gracing us with her semi-annual visit and has astonished me by offering, for once, to mind the children while we go shopping.

I rendezvous with my darling on the East Block steps at eleven. Under her bonnet her face is carefree, her dark eyes sparkling: a radiant sight, unfamiliar too long. Chatting brightly in the cool sunny air, we stroll past crocuses erupting yellow and white from the lawns of Parliament. At last, a truly springlike day, the kind that inspires us with the promise of warm months to come. It won't be long before we're planning our annual summer visit to Rivière-du-Loup, where we'll stay alongside the Macdonalds for several weeks among the pines by the St. Lawrence. This morning our plans are as mundane as shopping and lunch, but I feel on holiday already.

We cross Dufferin Bridge over the Rideau Canal. A small steamer sits chuffing in the locks below, sending up puffs of oily smoke as it waits to be lowered to the next level. The bridge is thick with traffic. Our nostrils are assailed by one of the delights of spring in the capital, streets churned to fetid mud-and-manure soup by hooves and carriage wheels. We're forced to walk single file, with me in front, keeping to the inner sidewalk, to avoid being splashed with filth.

Crossing Sussex, Minette hikes her skirts as high as decency allows and forges ahead to the planks of the far shore. Our destination is Charles Ogilvy's new dry-goods shop on Rideau Street—new to me, at least, since I seldom have time or inclination for shopping. "You're a little out of touch," Minette informs me. "The store has been open for three years." She likes it because it provides a less expensive alternative to Bryson & Graham's or Murphy Gamble's. She wants to buy muslin to make curtains for little Maurice's room and some fancier stuff for the front parlour.

Ogilvy's small store is tidy and uncluttered compared to his competition. I fall in behind Minette as she inspects swatches of fabric and bolts of cloth, escorted by Mr. Ogilvy himself, a gaunt, laconic young Scotsman. My role is simply to pay once Minette is satisfied she's found good value. Ogilvy's goods appear to be of high quality, but his tastes are dreadfully sober and sedate, nothing too pretty or frilly or French—another dour Presbyterian to keep us from getting fancy ideas!

After much gloved fingering of the merchandise, Minette is satisfied with her choices. "For a little extra we can have them delivered," she remarks offhandedly, and I immediately arrange it with Ogilvy. We then retrace our steps to the Canal, this time taking Sappers Bridge over to Sparks and Elgin Streets and not bothering with the tram, since we're only going as far as the Russell House.

It's a relief to reach Sparks, still the only thoroughfare in this city to be paved. Visitors must find Ottawa a dismally one-horse town, hardly auspicious enough to be the nation's capital once you're off the Hill. But the Russell House is another matter. Those who have visited Washington say it rivals Willard's as a political crossroads and unofficial arm of government. Under the hotel's striped red-and-white awnings, we discreetly stamp the muck off our shoes onto the pavement and enter the large electrified lobby.

Feeling ravenous, I escort Minette so briskly across the mosaic tile floor, beneath the dome decorated with pastel nymphs, that I almost miss Wilfrid Laurier passing the other way. That would be an unfortunate *faux pas*, an unintended snub, all the worse in light of his election defeat. It wouldn't do to appear spiteful or vindictive, notwithstanding his heated battles with Sir John. Laurier keeps a suite in the hotel where he lives a bachelor existence during the week, his wife Zoë remaining home in Arthabaskaville.

I stop and hail him over the heads of several people. He's just descended the marble staircase and is heading directly outside, and I notice he's not alone.

Imperially tall and graceful in his grey frock coat and white gloves, Laurier wheels about in search of my voice. In the crook of one arm he cradles his silk top hat, in the other the arm of a lady I've never seen. "Why, Pope! And my dear Minette! What a lovely surprise! Allow me to present an old friend, Madame Lavergne."

His companion is slim and extremely well turned out, though far from pretty. Her face is dominated by a prominent jaw and large, overly dramatic eyes that lend her from a certain angle a touch of the grotesque. But as we exchange pleasantries I'm struck by Madame Lavergne's vivacity, her supreme self-confidence. In elegance and fragrance she exudes Paris.

Laurier explains at unnecessary length that Madame Lavergne is the wife of his law partner back home in Quebec, has just arrived to visit Ottawa, and has graciously accepted his offer to conduct her on a brief walking tour. She simply insists on staying at the Russell, since she's heard so much about it—from whom, one wonders?—and hopes to find it as interesting as its reputation. Laurier pauses to catch his breath. He looks pale, his full lips trembling faintly, his wavy chestnut hair receding farther than ever from that noble brow.

I ask Madame whether the hotel measures up to expectations. "Ah yes, Mr. Pope," she replies in a melodious accent, her strange eyes darting from me to Minette and back again, "it does indeed! Even more splendidly than I had hoped."

Laurier mentions that they're on their way to Parliament Hill to visit the chambers before touring Notre-Dame and the By Ward Market. I remark that Notre-Dame is our parish church, and we trust Madame Lavergne will find it as beautiful and inspiring as we do.

She's certain she will. And makes a point of smiling intently at Minette.

"How is Sir John?" Laurier inquires gravely. "You know," he says, dropping his voice and looking about to see who might overhear, "I haven't been well myself since the election. But I'm deeply saddened to hear he is sinking. It's like the ship of state going down. He is a giant, after all. We will never see his like."

I reply a touch defiantly that Sir John will be pleased to know Laurier was asking for him, and sorry to hear he's been feeling poorly, but that he himself feels much better now—in fact grows stronger every day. I exaggerate only slightly. When I left Earnscliffe yesterday afternoon, Sir John was strolling slowly with Lady M. in her rose garden, his first outing in a month.

Laurier beams, pronouncing himself delighted by the news; he hopes Sir John will soon be completely restored to health. The animation of his impossibly romantic features suggests he's sincere, even relieved. There's a popular view that Laurier's easygoing nature makes him leery of taking on the burdens of power, and that he'd gladly give up the Liberal leadership if only he could find someone foolish enough to take it off his hands.

We say our goodbyes, and Laurier escorts Madame Lavergne outside.

As Minette and I carry on to the café, I notice she's blushing. "Goodness, my dear, what is it?" I ask. "Don't you think Laurier meant what he said about Sir John?"

She refuses to answer until the maître d' has seated us at a table for two, sufficiently far from the other guests. "You don't remember?" she demands severely.

"About?"

"Emilie Lavergne!"

"Oh, that petty gossip."

Flushing more deeply, Minette speaks rapidly under her breath. "How can you call it *petty*? Everyone at home knows about them. And she knows *I* know—how couldn't she? Didn't you see her staring at me?"

"She was simply acknowledging you, my dear."

"And now here they are in Ottawa, flaunting themselves in full public view. They simply don't care! Imagine how awful poor Madame Laurier must feel."

"If there's any truth to the gossip, wouldn't poor Madame Laurier have put an end to it by now?"

Minette gives me a withering stare that suggests I'm either an idiot or an aspiring philanderer.

"That's how it would *look*," I admit, "if it were anyone else. But a man in his position, escorting his law partner's wife on a little walk—it's hardly a capital offence. The very fact he does it publicly proves their innocence. He's telling the world, '*Honi soit qui mal y pense.*'"

Minette sighs with exasperation; she's clearly disappointed in me. I think how exquisitely pretty she looks, and how I hate to see our little Saturday outing clouded by argument.

But what if Laurier and Madame Lavergne really *are* more than friends? What if the purported resemblance between Laurier and her son Armand is no coincidence? It seems to me that after devoting the prime of his life to serving his party and his nation,

Laurier has earned the right to live as he pleases, and the devil take his detractors. Of course I'd never utter such thoughts out loud.

"Really, Joseph, you can be a dreadful *naïf* at times," Minette murmurs, directing her eyes to the café's excellent luncheon menu. "I hope all English Canadians don't think like you."

I take this as closing the topic and feel grateful when the Russell's manager, M. St-Jacques, a fastidiously *soigné* gentleman who knows me well, arrives at our table to wish us a pleasant day and inquire solicitously after Sir John. I accept his offer of a chilled bottle of champagne on the house. Champagne always puts Minette in a generous frame of mind.

Rideau Hall

Sir John has added a few pages to my precious folder of notes for the "life." Nonetheless, it's still pathetically thin. I wonder when we'll ever find time to add to it. There are always so many more pressing demands: if not correspondence and Cabinet making, then the Bering Sea business, complicated by Sir John's slow recovery from his illness—and now the fast-approaching deadline for the Speech from the Throne, to be delivered next week by Lord Stanley. The message must be got right, containing just enough substance to show the Government has a program to put before the people, but not so much as to provide plump targets for the Opposition. Not that they'll have any difficulty inventing their own.

Sir John and I have been poring over the draft text. He's summoned certain Ministers to Earnscliffe to review it, after which I go back and take another run. Just when I can't imagine how the draft could be improved, Sir John detects some deficiency invisible to me, some insensitivity to one group or another, which requires that comfort be added for the merchants of Quebec, or the manufacturers in Ontario, or the Maritime commercial interests. His constant political vigilance reminds me of the description of Sir

John by Principal Grant of Queen's: "His mind has windows in it all around."

Sir John is enjoying himself again. Speechwriting and the political conjuring act that goes into it seem to have buoyed his spirits. When I allude to his historical reminiscences, he laughs merrily: "My dear Pope, don't you see? I'm busy writing your final chapter!"

The whole of Earnscliffe is busy with preparations for yet another reason—the imminent arrival of Hugh John Macdonald and his family from Winnipeg. They plan to stop here a few days while Hugh looks for permanent lodgings in Ottawa. I've met Sir John's surviving son just once, and only briefly, during a stopover on our westward journey on the CPR. Hugh moved out there nine years ago, leaving behind his junior partnership in Macdonald and Macdonald to join twenty thousand other Ontarians in the brave and risky enterprise of settling the Prairies. By all accounts he's made a great success of himself far from his father's looming shadow, and now he's built on that success to get himself elected. It will be fascinating for me, feeling in relation to Sir John almost as a son, to see his true son at close quarters.

As usual Sir John takes his first meal of the day in the Earnscliffe dining room. Popping into my office on the way from his study, he invites me to join him. I never take my presence at lunch for granted but always wait for his spoken invitation, even when we have work to dispatch over the meal, as we always do.

Alice serves us with silent efficiency. Lady M. is off at a bazaar at St. Alban's. Sir John downs a whole bowl of chicken broth with vegetables before tucking into his marrow bone. This is more than he's digested for some time, he tells me, gratified to be enjoying his food again. He sits erect as he eats, one arm akimbo, head cocked to one side to hear a comment or question. We sip strong coffee with plenty of cream from the Jersey cow that Lady M. keeps at the rear of the house, and precisely on schedule at one o'clock, Sir Charles Tupper arrives.

Bustling, burly, gruffly benevolent Sir Charles has come to say farewell before sailing for England and resuming his duties as High Commissioner. Given his close relations with the Colonial Office, he'll cast his eye over our latest version of the Throne Speech, to ensure it contains nothing that would disturb Whitehall or Downing Street.

Sir Charles still has the fleshy jowls of a handsome bulldog—a face framed, despite his years, by flourishing sideburns and a full head of hair. He's also a medical doctor who has sometimes attended Sir John; I observe him noting the chief's improved condition whenever he glances up from the text. Ignoring me, Sir Charles drains his coffee cup and pencils suggestions into the margins. He points silently with a blunt fingertip to draw Sir John's attention, and Sir John leans forward to examine the notes, murmuring noncommittally but otherwise keeping his counsel. There will be, in the end, only one arbiter.

Watching them, I think what battles these two political warriors have fought together: what blood they've spilled in the three decades since Tupper, leading the Nova Scotians, echoed Sir John's toast to Colonial Union in Charlottetown. Their comfort with each other would be the envy of any married couple.

Pushing away from the table, Sir Charles regrets he must be off soon to Montreal, thence to Boston to sail to Liverpool on the *Polynesian*. But first he wants to alert Sir John to political tempests he sees on the horizon.

Sir John frowns. "Not Tarte and his everlasting Langevin dossier."

"Attacks from a more accustomed quarter," Sir Charles replies.

"Richard Cartwright? He's been attacking me for as long as I can remember. You'd think he'd weary of flogging the same old horse."

"Our friend has set his sights on me this time—my not-so-secret trip to Washington to visit Blaine. He plans to denounce me as a hypocritical scoundrel and the visit as a hopeless failure. He's also going to condemn my stumping for you in Kingston when you were ill. Most improper for a diplomat, you know."

"But entirely proper for an old friend and comrade-in-arms."

"And for a fellow Father of Confederation, as they're calling us."

"Good Lord, I've always assumed *I* was the little lad's father!"

"Then I'm his Dutch uncle. Anyway, forewarned is forearmed, John. I've discussed both matters with young Charlie too."

"Thank you. It's a comfort having your son in Cabinet—even if he's a trifle idealistic yet. But that's part of his boyish charm."

"Of course it is. And he admires you greatly. Never forget that when he's making your life difficult."

Sir John sighs. He looks up from the draft speech, which he shunts off to the side with an elbow. "You know, Charles, I wish to God you were sitting in my place."

Tupper replies fervently: "Thank God I am not."

One of Lord Stanley's aides-de-camp telephones my office from Rideau Hall. His Excellency wishes to discuss the Throne Speech today, as he must travel to Toronto tomorrow. This means we're down to the final draft at last. Retyping the blasted thing one more time, I find its lofty turns of phrase, especially those I wrote myself, begin to stick in my craw.

At a quarter past three Sir John and I leave Earnscliffe in Buckley's cab. We breeze along Sussex, dangerously downwind from Rosie's massive rear, and Sir John remarks on the first subtle greening of the trees. The sense that spring is crouching everywhere, ready to erupt from hedges and woods, is powerful as we drive between the great budding elms along the winding approach to Rideau Hall. The afternoon is warm enough that we've left our topcoats behind.

Lord Stanley receives us in the Small Drawing Room. "It's brighter here in the afternoon," he offers, as if some explanation were required. His Excellency is a self-contained, soft-spoken gentleman, with a voice that dips at the end of each utterance, like his beard. Not yet elderly, a former Colonial Secretary himself and the son of a Prime Minister, he shows a high, even deferential regard for Sir John.

They sit facing each other across a small inlaid table. While Lord Stanley scans the text, I stand alongside Sir John. His Excellency's ADC, young Lord Kilcoursie, stands at ease opposite me in his regimental uniform. We're like a pair of seconds, breathing in, breathing out, our duty to wait in silence while our masters dispose. When I look out the tall windows, I can see great drifts of yellow daffodils filling the lower terrace and, beyond that, unbloomed lilies and irises thrusting through the soil.

"Well done, well done," the Governor General says at last, abruptly handing the papers back to Sir John. "I shan't have any difficulty reading that."

"No errors or omissions?" Sir John asks lightly.

"Well, you know my views on the militia question. The defence monies would be spent to better purpose if directed more efficiently and . . . prudently."

"We're certainly in agreement on that, Your Excellency. I feel sure we can make administrative adjustments to the militia's budget without calling attention to it in the Speech from the Throne."

"Oh quite. No need to draw people's notice. And I don't presume to advise you on political tactics, Sir John. You've shown your judgment to be impeccable—the Farrer pamphlet being the latest case in point. Using it as a weapon of political warfare turned the tide in the Government's favour, and thank Heaven for that. Good thing you didn't listen to me!"

"Now, Your Excellency, you know I always listen. Being a deaf old bird, I just don't always hear."

"Indeed, indeed." Lord Stanley gives a grimace meant as a grin, and the tea tray arrives. "Before you go, Sir John, have some tea and listen to a proposition I have for you."

I sense Sir John's defences going up. "By all means, Your Excellency."

"I'm not sure I've told you of the great pleasure I derive from watching the Rebels."

"Rebels?" Sir John looks alarmed. "Now I'm *not* hearing properly."

"The Rideau Hall Rebels? Surely you've heard of them—Arthur and Algernon's team. Ice hockey."

"Ah, of course." Unlike the Governor General's sons and aides-de-camp, who maintain the outdoor skating rink at Rideau Hall, Sir John is no sportsman. "Not curling, then?"

"No, that was Lansdowne's sport. He put up the curling rink. We use it mostly for dinner parties now. No, ice hockey's our game these days, and we adore it. Especially Arthur and Algy. You must come and see a match next winter, Sir John. The Rebels wear splendid red sweaters. Very dashing."

"Make a note of that, Joseph," Sir John says dryly, turning aside to me and restraining the impulse to wink. "Would that be the proposition you mentioned?"

"Not precisely. You see, the Rebels have been touring about a good deal. Playing against sides from Kingston and Montreal and so on. They even played a team of Parliamentarians last year—won, of course, being younger and faster. But as Arthur tells me, there doesn't appear to be any method of determining which team is best. Considering the great public interest that hockey matches now elicit, I think there ought to be. Canadians ought to be proud of their prowess at hockey. Put it on display, if you ask me. And so I'm prepared to do something about it. I'm willing to donate a cup."

"Really, Your Excellency? What sort of cup?"

"A challenge cup. To be held by the winning side until somebody beats them. If a club thinks it's good enough, it can make a challenge. Like prizefighters."

"Prizefighters," Sir John repeats.

"But not for money, of course—for the glory of it."

"So the cup would be a sort of drinking cup. A goblet."

"Bigger. More the size of a soup tureen, I should think. Silver, with room around the bottom to engrave the players' names. Now, *that* would give the lads something to shoot for."

"I dare say. And are you suggesting the Dominion Government present this trophy?"

"No, no need, Sir John, I'll give it myself. Get it made in London by a silversmith I know. I've already given one for curling. But ice hockey is far more exciting, *and* more popular. I like the idea of leaving things behind."

"That's admirable, Your Excellency, if I may say. Canada is already fortunate to have Stanley House, Stanley Park . . ."

"I take it you have no objection then, Sir John? I *always* seek the advice of my First Minister!"

On our drive back to Earnscliffe, the old man shakes his head. "What is it about winter sports that makes our aristocrats so delirious? It's not exactly riding to hounds, is it? Next thing you know, they'll want to give out a trophy for snowshoeing. Or skiing! They make a great cult out of winter. You're too young to remember Lord and Lady Dufferin—they started it all. Ice castles and toboggan runs and winter at-homes. The Lansdownes went even further—very big on skating parties by torchlight. Every blessed Governor wants to outdo his predecessor."

"Perhaps it's the novelty of snow, sir," I venture.

"Yes, and I'd far rather they amuse themselves that way than by meddling in politics. Most of them know better by now. Especially this one."

"Yet in a way, sir, this is politics too. They hope winter sports will get them closer to the people."

Sir John allows I may be right. Even so, he believes our Governors General "cheapen themselves" by stooping to everyone else's level. Aristocrats, in his view, ought to remain aristocrats.

On our arrival at Earnscliffe, the welcoming of the Hugh John Macdonalds has just begun. Sir John becomes agitated when he sees their carriage standing in the drive. He begins to clamber down even before Buckley has brought Rosie to a standstill. "Hughy!" he cries, hurrying toward the entrance. "We should've ordered a piper!"

In the front hall, family and servants mill about as Ben Chilton conducts luggage upstairs. Ben has already carried Mary down and left her sitting in the entrance to the drawing room, where she can survey the comings and goings. Sir John's grandson, Jack, yet another John Alexander Macdonald, is examining both Mary and her wheelchair with innocent curiosity and loudly asking how the contraption works, which she explains in her halting way. Jack looks about six—a pale ethereal lad with unnaturally large eyes. I understand his parents take him to Banff every summer for the mountain air. The boy's mother, Gertrude, a pleasantly plump young woman wearing a flowered hat, chats animatedly with Lady M., who looks delighted with all the activity swirling about her.

Sir John greets his son with a shout and a fierce handshake and continues to grip Hugh's hand in both of his as they talk. I take in Hugh John Macdonald's ramrod military posture, his embarrassed stiffness before his father. His manner is hesitant and apologetic. He looks only a little like Sir John; the strongest resemblance lies in the long and elaborate nose. Hugh's moustaches droop over his mouth but don't conceal a decent, kind face. I can see where little Jack gets his eyes—Hugh's are both staring and sad.

"We had an uneventful trip on the CPR," he's telling Sir John. "I suppose we'll eventually get used to this travelling back and forth."

Tea is in the drawing room—a real English tea with watercress sandwiches and little cakes—and Alice receives assistance with serving it from the kitchen help, decked out in their finery. Lady M. invites me to join the family. Much regret is expressed that fourteen-year-old Daisy, Hugh's daughter by his late first wife, and Lady M.'s great favourite, can't be here. Daisy is off studying at the Sacred Heart convent near Montreal, but has received permission to travel on the weekend to be present for her father's entry into Parliament.

Mary beams at the news that Daisy will be coming. Her pinched little face becomes enlivened and almost pretty. I overhear her telling Lady M., "Daisy is my niece, but really she's my best friend."

After a decent interval and a bit of cake, I take my leave. Sir John insists on accompanying me to my office to review tomorrow's schedule, and I realize that in the mad rush of things I've completely forgotten to tell him about bumping into Laurier last Saturday. I feel mortified; it's the sort of lapse I'd never have made in the past.

Sir John listens with amusement, head on one side, as I recount the episode at the Russell House with as much piquant detail as I can muster.

"Madame Lavergne turning up in Ottawa, eh? The plot thickens. And I'd have thought she'd be a great beauty. Ah well, to each his own." Sir John is much less apt to criticize or moralize than most. He accepts men and their ways, as long as they don't do each other serious harm. He'd never use Laurier's personal life against him for political gain, although the Grits have been doing it to him for thirty years.

Sir John turns thoughtful. "Now, Joe, let me tell you something. Don't be shy about your and Minette's acquaintance with Laurier. This may sound odd coming from me, but I'm glad you're friends with him." He pauses before saying good night, his eyes regarding me earnestly. "Laurier will look after you, should you need a friend when I am gone."

Sir John

I find Hugh John much changed—and all for the better. His move out West has done him the world of good. He's a man now. He has gravity. He has purpose. A natural pride has replaced vanity and posing. This time he's chosen a wife whom I can more than tolerate, whom I can talk to and joke with and embrace wholeheartedly into the family. Gertie, or Gay, as she calls herself, seems a loving mother to Jack and an attentive, if stern, stepmother to Daisy. Above all, she's a wholesome and devoted companion for Hugh. She's a Vankoughnet from Kingston. I've known the family for decades.

Gertie carries none of the burdens of the unfortunate Jean King, God rest her soul. Poor Jeannie was a choice of wife I simply could not commend or comprehend: a fact I made all too clear to Hugh, to the point of rupture between us. She wasn't merely a widow with another man's child, but a Catholic. Hence Daisy's current sentence to a convent, in accordance with her mother's dying wish. Ah well, what's past can't be helped. Hughy will surely spring the lass free before long.

I ask him about this on Sunday morning before Agnes drags us all off to St. Alban's. I'm reading the Saturday papers when Hugh strays into my study for no apparent reason. "To be honest,

Father, the convent doesn't trouble me in the least," he replies. He has great respect for the Sisters. They've been very kind to Daisy, knowing she's lonely so far from home. She already speaks French like a native. "You said yourself that Sacred Heart is one of the best schools."

"Of its type." But I won't let this become another bone of contention between us. "I'm glad your mind is at ease, my boy. You're too much like your father to place undue emphasis on creed."

"Thank you, sir. I take that as a compliment."

"For Heaven's sake, Hughy, there's no need to 'sir' me! You're not in the army anymore."

I regret this outburst at once. Yet Hugh's face betrays no emotion—as if he chooses simply not to hear. We both think it best to pursue other topics, and he beats me to the punch.

"I know Gertie has written you on the subject, but I do want to thank you for the handsome ring you sent her at Christmas. She's utterly charmed by it. Loves to show it off."

"Well, thank your mother. Agnes, I should say. She picked it out."

"It's helped Gertie feel truly one of us."

"Has it? A full-fledged member of our little patched-together family? Good! We manage pretty well, don't we?"

"Yes, Father. We do."

Hugh's mouth and heavy-lidded eyes retain their air of melancholy and disappointment that I remember from his youth. I've always believed Hugh has a perfect right to his melancholy, yet to my great discredit it never ceases to irritate me—as if he's nobly enduring some undeserved ill treatment.

No doubt I'm haunted by a bad conscience. There were the frightful alarms and incessant loneliness of his early years, Isabella's perpetual state of collapse, the unavoidable neglect and displacement. Hugh was forever being parcelled out to others who took him into their homes. In Toronto our friends treated him as kindly as they could, a small boy awkwardly and unexpectedly underfoot, while raising their own bairns. Hugh was afflicted with a father who was much absent and a mother scarcely aware of his existence, much less his boyish needs and wants. Although Isa and I both loved him dearly, it was chiefly *in absentia*. Sad to say, he was far better off when she died, finally; he could lodge permanently in Kingston with Moll and the Professor and Mother and Loo, who gave him his first proper home. From such sorry scraps of childhood, he's constructed a life. And now a nest in the Wild West.

Hell's teeth, what am I talking about? He grew up in highly favoured circumstances. His has been a life of inestimable advantages—not the least of them being his father's son! He had a Shetland pony. He attended university. He was a man-about-town in wicked, wicked Toronto. He enjoyed a hundred privileges I never had.

"So now we're to be a political family too," I tell him. "Your triumph at the polls gave me great pleasure, you know. A whopping victory. Are you looking forward to taking your seat?"

"Very much." Hugh doesn't elaborate. He glances nervously about the study and out to the front hall, but there's no one there. "I hope by being in the House of Commons I can put the Rykert affair behind us."

I'm surprised he'd bring this up: a minor scandal I haven't thought about in a year. "But my boy, you were completely exonerated. Even the Liberals admitted there was no evidence against you."

"People assume where there's smoke there's fire."

"To hell with them."

"I find politics daunting, Father. I didn't plan a political life, as you know, any more than I planned a life in law."

"You'd have preferred the army."

"Army life gave me my most memorable experiences, I admit—my adventures. But we've been through that before. I simply feel I owe it to you to sit in Parliament."

"Owe it! How?"

"The way my financial dealings came up in the last session, and you rose to defend my character . . . I can never repay you."

"Nonsense! No need for amends. I testified to your character and honesty, and it was the simple truth. But now you'll have the chance to show them yourself. You'll *prove* what kind of man you are. It's a far more persuasive argument."

He blinks rapidly. "Quite frankly, the prospect of speaking in the House fills me with the same dread as addressing the court."

I find this dismaying. "Surely you've got over that by now."

"I'm afraid not. Probably I never will. Fortunately my anxiety comes over me only when I begin speaking. It passes after I've been on my feet for a time."

"You'll find the same thing in the House, my boy. It's nothing but a bigger and more self-important courtroom."

Hugh smiles a little. He stares almost happily at his shoes. Why the devil must he always act so solemn and repentant? "Perhaps you could give me a few pointers about addressing the House," he says. "After all, you've been doing it since before I was born."

"There's really not much to it. Know your facts, and your point of view on the facts. . . . Scribble a few notes on the back of an envelope. . . . That's all the preparation you really need. Try not to lose the envelope, as I usually do! And stand proudly by your desk with your hands firmly in your vest pockets. Then you don't need to think what to do with them."

"I could never get by with so little preparation. I'd freeze up."

"If that happens, remind yourself of some occasion when you showed courage."

He hesitates. "Oddly enough, there *was* a time—I'd expected to be terrified but wasn't. I was volunteering with the Winnipeg Rifles and marched with General Middleton to Fish Creek."

"As I well remember."

"Dumont had his sharpshooters hidden in the coulee. They were deeply dug in and we didn't dare charge them, so we tried to draw them out by outflanking them. I led the movement on the right. My men were falling near me, and I just kept advancing and was completely exposed out in the open but didn't receive so much as a scratch." He grins faintly. "I was very pleased with myself that day—happy to find I was cool under fire and able to—to lead my command."

My heart brims for him. "I wish I could have been there to see it."

"It's a good thing you weren't!"

"When you stand to deliver your maiden speech, remember that day. The Grits are a tame lot compared to Riel and his rebels."

Hugh looks anxious again. "I'm beginning to realize, Father, that politics is far more than giving speeches and shaking hands. I thought I was doing well at New Year's when I paid fifteen visits in one day. I congratulated myself for coming out of my shell. But ever since my election, my office has been absolutely jammed with people, total strangers, wanting favours, jobs—even money! They're there from morning till night. I can't complete one straight hour of legal work. If that sort of thing keeps on, I don't see how I'll ever earn my living."

"Did I ever mention the sacrifices one has to make in public life?"

"If you did, I didn't take any notice. To me you just seemed completely successful in every way."

"Successful at avoiding bankruptcy by the skin of my teeth."

"I've no stomach for bankruptcy either! I may not even make a politician in the long run. It won't surprise you that I was reluctant to stand in the first place. I only agreed after a great deal of pressure. And in the end it was only the popular cry for a railway to Hudson Bay that swept me in."

"What of it? You took advantage of the local political conditions, and you won. That's normal."

Hugh nods, but impatiently. "I'm obliged to sit for the term of this Parliament, Father, but the way I feel now, nothing could induce me to stand in another election. The life of a politician is distasteful to me. I'm already longing to resume the even tenor of my ways."

"Good Heavens above. Then why did you run at all?"

"I've already told you." He sets his jaw. "It's obvious to anyone that your Cabinet is deplorably weak. There's practically no Conservative Party to speak of anymore—only a John A. Party. Your Ministers are shaky on their feet, all depleted and mutually resentful. Not a new idea among them. What in Heaven's name will they do when you're gone? If ill health should remove you, God forbid, I see nothing but chaos and ruin ahead. And the Grits will take us, directly or indirectly, to annexation."

I'm impressed by his clear-sighted view of my situation. "I wake half the night worrying about that."

"I can well imagine. Who can wear your mantle if it falls from your shoulders? Much as I admire him, Sir Charles Tupper has abandoned active politics. Langevin has disappeared into the devil of a fog, never to return. John Thompson seems the only one possessed of any first-rate abilities, yet they say he's more Nova Scotian than Canadian, and not only a Roman Catholic but a convert. The Orangemen despise him for it."

With renewed interest I search Hugh's eyes. I haven't heard him speak so forcefully since he was a young man playing at soldiers, fresh home from Red River, and insisting on smoking a cigar in our dining room. He isn't finished: "You might wish to hand the reins to a Frenchman, of course, but they already have Defence and Public Works. Apart from Thompson—and maybe Foster and young Charlie Tupper—there isn't an English-speaking Member worth his salt."

"Sad but true. Which is why you must stay in Ottawa and stick with politics, Hugh, not run from it. There's such a thing as duty. Not merely to party or family, but Queen and country."

He resumes in a softer voice: "I've no need to board a train to Ottawa to serve my country. But it's the only way I can serve *you*."

After examining the wool stretched tightly across my knee, I glance back at him. He maintains an expectant frown, a mask of allegiance mixed with defiance.

"Tell me more about Fish Creek," I say. "I was just thinking, that wasn't the first time you'd chased Riel. Do you realize you may be the only man to have fought in both rebellions? Besides Riel, of course." He nods rapidly. Evidently the thought has occurred to him too. "Did you actually lay eyes on him? Was he carrying his white cross?"

"Not at Fish Creek. Some of his men retreated homeward to Batoche, and Riel went with them."

It comes back to me now. I no longer remember how I heard it—whether it was part of Riel's testimony at his trial, or if Middleton described it for me in one of his dispatches—but Riel was said to have spent the Battle of Fish Creek praying with the women at Batoche. Apparently he locked his arms before his face in the shape of the Cross and when he became exhausted, he told the women to hold him upright and fix his arms crossways so he could continue praying. They took turns at this until their husbands and fathers returned home from the battle, bringing the astonishing news that they'd defeated the Canadian Army. The Metis had lost only a few men. Their loss in horses was worse. Riel swore that victory had resulted from God's hearing his prayers, and that the animals' deaths had been punishment for the Metis' wickedness in gambling on horse races.

There was a man of faith: twisted and misplaced, to be sure, but faith nonetheless. Once I understand him, I'll explain to Hugh the true nature of the man we tried, in our different ways, to destroy.

"I only saw him in the flesh once," Hugh goes on. "It was after he'd given himself up. He was sitting on a box of ammunition outside General Middleton's tent, writing in his journal. I thought what a peculiar duck he was—writing poetry and such, when his people's homes had just been destroyed."

"Destroyed? Now, that I never heard."

"Oh, absolutely. Completely demolished. Our boys looted, smashed and burned everything in Batoche—everything except the church and the graveyard. We were no better than Grant's armies at the end of the Civil War. Not much better than the rebels themselves, to be honest."

Astounding. Why didn't anyone tell me?

Ceremony

A day of glory for Sir John. It begins quietly enough this morning. We rendezvous in his Hill office to review the order of business for the opening of Parliament and to ensure I've assembled all the necessary documents. His manner is calm, judicious, practical; he's been through these rituals many times before. Yet for all his attention to detail, his nose and mouth fairly quiver with anticipation.

At times like these I'm mindful of his admonition that "forms are things"—that every social usage, from a person's proper title to the correct spelling of his name to the accurate observance and enactment of public ceremonies, conveys a significance beyond itself. I've consulted closely with the Clerk of the House of Commons, the literary Mr. Bourinot, to ensure that proceedings to open the Seventh Parliament of the Dominion of Canada run in accordance with British precedent and custom.

By the time the Clerk and his commissioners take their places in the noisy House, I'm moving about nervously behind the still-unoccupied Speaker's chair. From the floor I scan the packed, chattering galleries. Lady Macdonald occupies her customary seat in the middle of the front row, which ushers know to keep free at all times, lest she find it occupied by some unwary usurper. Confident of her place as *prima inter pares*, Lady M. fans herself decorously, her piled ivory hair supporting a modest tiara. To her right sit her daughter-in-law, Gertrude, little Jack wearing his sailor suit, and fourteen-year-old Daisy, newly arrived from Sault-au-Récollet and looking, in her maidenly white dress, as pure and innocent as her name. How dear Mary would love to be here beside her niece!

With the conspicuous exception of Sir John, most Members have occupied their seats when Bourinot rises at one end of the long heavy table. He's holding, as tenderly as if it were a baby, the Protestant Bible. At the other end his assistant Rouleau also rises, cradling the Catholic Bible. Bourinot's opening words are inaudible until silence overtakes the gallery, the spectators shushed by Lady M. herself. As the commissioners read out their names, each Member of Parliament approaches the appropriate end of the table to take his turn pressing the Holy Book to his lips and reciting, "I do swear that I will be loyal and bear true allegiance to Her Majesty Queen Victoria, so help me God."

Just as the hands of the Commons clock point exactly to the half-hour, applause and shouting erupt from the Conservative benches: Sir John has entered the chamber. Strikingly elegant in stovepipe hat, black frock coat, red necktie and grey trousers, he marches proudly up the aisle escorting by the arm the newly elected Member for Winnipeg. Sir John responds to the acclaim by nodding formally to his front bench. Hugh looks as startled as a racehorse. The applause broadens into a salvo of sustained desk-thumping, followed by wave after wave of heartfelt guttural cheering, as father and son reach the long table arm in arm. Sir John halts, Hugh halting a half-step behind him. The severity of Sir John's composure gives way to a smile of sheer delight as the other side begins to join in the cheering. Sir John turns to acknowledge his opponents' grand gesture, and Hugh turns with him, lips compressed below his wobbling moustaches.

First the father takes his oath, lightly kissing the Bible in Bourinot's grasp, then the son. Sir John signs his name on the parchment, and Hugh signs directly below him. Members from both sides of the aisle then rush forward to shake their hands, slap their backs, offer gruff words of welcome. Even Sir Richard Cartwright extends a hand to Hugh.

Once everyone is settled, Sir John rises to put the first motion before the House. In a fainter, weaker voice than usual, but with his customary ease of manner, he extols the qualities of the Member for Renfrew North, Peter White, enumerating his virtues and qualifications for the position of Speaker. Bringing his exposition to a close, Sir John glances up at the gallery toward Lady M., who returns his smile as if they were the only two in the chamber. He looks challengingly across the aisle at Laurier, flips the skirts of his coat like a young buck, and sits down.

Laurier rises, nodding gravely to Sir John and assuming an air of humorous reproach. He wishes to remind his Right Honourable friend that British Parliamentary precedent would dictate the reappointment as Speaker of the incumbent from the last Parliament, the Member for Laval: "Nonetheless, I am disposed to say on behalf of the Opposition—of the Loyal Opposition of Her Majesty; loyal, sir, in every sense of the word; loyal to the Crown, loyal to the People, loyal to this House; even loyal to the majority of this House, and ever ready to accept a good suggestion from the majority, when on the few and rare occasions a good suggestion comes from them—I am disposed to agree with everything that has been said by my Right Honourable friend about the Honourable Member for North Renfrew."

Sir John grins, acknowledging Laurier's sally with a dip of his chin. Laurier addresses a few words of advice to the nominee, who sits at his desk on the back benches with a humble expression, evincing, as custom demands, an awareness of his complete unworthiness for the office:

"My Honourable friend will pardon me, I hope," says Laurier, "if I remind him that perfection is not of this world. He would not be of the human race if he did not allow me to tell with perfect candour that he cannot be altogether free from fault. I must say, however, that the only fault I have ever found with the Member for Renfrew North is that I believe he is imbued, nay saturated, with a certain political heresy which at one time was very prevalent in this country, but which under the lessons of sad experience is now fast disappearing, and which will be long remembered by a long-suffering people as the National Policy. I am sure that this heresy will not affect him at all when he is sitting in the Speaker's chair."

With that, Laurier seconds the motion, which is carried unanimously. Somehow Laurier's sunny ways—his unforced eloquence, his mellifluous French accent graced with unmistakably Scottish notes, his ability to sting lightly without inflicting pain—win everyone over. Laurier has already stolen the show, and this Parliament is only two hours old.

Accepting his opponent's little coup, Sir John beams. He's never prided himself on being the greatest orator in the House; and in any case he's eager to adjourn, so that he and everyone else can rush off to dress for His Excellency's arrival this afternoon.

Luncheon at home is a brief affair, after which I discover my frock coat has become tighter under the arms. I'm afraid it will rip at the seams if I move too strenuously, but there's no time for repairs. Returning hurriedly on foot, accompanied by Minette, whose milliner has outdone herself, I reach the Hill through a mob of gawkers and sightseers. Both sides of Wellington Street, as well as the Parliamentary precinct, are thronged. The bright colours of the ladies' dresses contrast with the sombre attire of their companions and the rich scarlet of the military men.

We have the advantage of being able to cut through the East Block's empty corridors and out the north exit. Clambering onto a stone parapet near the Centre Block, Minette in her voluminous gown gripping my arm for dear life, we're in time to watch the cavalry of the Princess Louise Dragoon Guards escort Lord and Lady Stanley's carriage through the gates. At that precise moment, the Ottawa Field Battery thunders a twenty-one-gun salute from Nepean Point overlooking the log booms on the great river.

With a fine sense of occasion, the sun slips out from behind the clouds. It glitters on the polished steel held by a hundred Governor General's Foot Guards massed before the Gothic arches of the Victoria Tower and on the brass instruments of the regimental band alongside. As His Excellency and Lady Stanley step down from the carriage, the band strikes up "God Save the Queen." I'd feel embarrassed to be standing so conspicuously on our high perch, except that so many others have crowded up beside us. Lord Stanley inspects his honour guard, then links arms with Lady Stanley, who looks stunning in her black court gown trimmed with diamonds, and turns with her up the steps of Parliament.

This is the cue for Minette and me to scurry inside. We use a basement entrance where the duty constable knows me, climb the stairs, and find a spot in the mob outside the Senate doors. MPs have already been summoned from the Commons by Black Rod. Craning my neck above the familiar heads of Dewdney and Davin, Caron and Chapleau, Foster and Langevin, picking up the sweetness of pomade from Chapleau's flowing wavy hair, I can just glimpse Sir John standing inside the Red Chamber. He appears calm as he waits in his Imperial Privy Councillor's uniform with its swirling gold braid and tasselled sword, which he's been entitled to wear since the Queen swore him in to her Privy Council years ago. Even his Ministers look rather splendid in their navy blue Windsor uniforms. All this dressing up makes us giddy as children at a garden party.

The Stanleys approach surrounded by their entourage, advancing up the corridor with measured strides. The Commoners part gracefully like the Red Sea. Sir John steps forward to greet Their Excellencies as they enter the Senate chamber, Lady M. right behind him. As she heaves into view through the doorway, I can scarcely credit the sight: her gown is rich crimson silk, flowing in one direction into a crimson train and rising in the other into a bodice ornamented with white blossoms encircling several sizable diamonds. Minette looks at me, her eyes widening. It's obvious Lady M. has dressed purposely to outshine Lady Stanley, whom she persists in seeing as her rival in prestige and influence. Lady Stanley in her black brocade now looks almost dowdy by comparison.

Sir John and Lady M. follow the Stanleys up the aisle at a respectful distance. The Governor General settles himself onto the Throne, Lady Stanley on his left and the Macdonalds on his right, and the Throne Speech that emerged so recently from my typewriter reappears between His Excellency's manicured hands. He begins to read.

By now it sounds flat to my ears, especially after all the spectacle and pageantry. Still, the banal words are elevated in significance by Lord Stanley's distinguished accent: "Let us hope that the people's labours may be crowned with fruitful returns from land and sea, and that the great resources of Canada may continue to reward the toil and enterprise of its inhabitants. . . ."

Pushing closer for a better view, while urging Minette forward with a hand in the small of her back, I stare about the chamber. The Senators are as drab as penguins, but the ladies up in the gallery more than compensate. Together they comprise an impressive spectacle. Madame Chapleau, who shares her husband's flare for the dramatic, sets off her raven tresses with a dress of ivory satin adorned with gold. Mrs. Dewdney in her black satin gown pulsates in prisms of colour thrown off by her diamonds. Beside her shimmers Mrs. Van Horne in pale blue silk—certainly her husband can afford the gown, as well as the ornate and vulgar jewels. Not to be outdone, Mrs. Hugh John Macdonald is startlingly mature-looking in a dress that Minette whispers is made of pink chiffon; it's decorated with clusters and loops of pink velvet ribbon, the substantial bodice pleasingly but redundantly surmounted by an enormous white corsage. My word.

"... in making efforts for the extension and development of the trade between the United States and the Dominion, as well as for the friendly adjustment of those matters of an international character that remain unsettled," Lord Stanley intones. "Revisions of the laws governing the Courts of Maritime Jurisdiction ... Measures relating to the Dominion of Canada foreshores and obstructions of her navigable waters ... Amendments to Acts relating to the official language of the North-west ..."

We've saved the disputed language measure for last. And indeed, the Government's intent—to let the elected representatives of the North-west choose their own language of official discourse in that vast empty landscape between Manitoba and the Rocky Mountains, rather than impose from Ottawa either English or bilingualism—dominates discussion during the reception afterwards in the great vaulted lobby. Never mind that the Government has secured Washington's consent to a conference in October to negotiate the long-standing trade and fisheries disputes. Never mind about our national sovereignty. It's language and religion that fire our blood in this country, setting it raging and screaming in our veins! The question of whether a few words of French will be tolerated in the legislature of the Territories, or whether Roman Catholics in Manitoba will be allowed to keep their legal right to their own schools, once magnanimously guaranteed by Ottawa, is enough to inflame Orange passions. If Dalton McCarthy and his fanatics have their way, these rights will be crushed to powder, abandoned as if they'd never been, sacrificed on the sacred altar of English Protestant supremacy. And McCarthy a Conservative too.

Reconciling warring factions within his own party will present Sir John with another trial in the weeks ahead; but for now gentler sentiments prevail. At the reception, Lord and Lady Stanley having returned to Rideau Hall, he accepts hearty congratulations on every hand—compliments on his health, on the jaunty spring in his step, on Hugh John's election or his own, as if it had happened only yesterday. Standing erect with his hands in his pockets like a schoolboy on holiday, he rears his head back and laughs at some broad Irish joke of Davin's. He rocks back and forth on his heels beaming with energy, betraying no sign of fatigue or infirmity. The champagne punch is flowing. The afternoon is young. The season is spring.

Lady M. arrives under full sail, docking directly in front of Minette. "My dear," she pronounces, "you look superb. It's about time your husband let you out of the house so the rest of us can feast our eyes on you."

At this moment the Liberals' James Edgar passes by, his gleaming round dome a beacon of light, accompanied by his wife, Matilda. They say Tillie Edgar, with her high ideals and literary aspirations, has become quite the bluestocking. I catch her and Edgar rolling their eyes as they pass within earshot of Lady M., who is going on about her theories of child rearing; no doubt her views are sententious and old-fashioned. Lady M. is quite oblivious to being overheard, and to the sad fact that she isn't universally admired in this city—especially not by ambitious and scheming Liberals.

Keeping half an ear on her monologue, I observe the Edgars' progress through the crush. Although I must credit him with broad-mindedness and principle on questions of race and religion, despite coming from Toronto, James Edgar has a keen nose for scandal, as long as it's Conservative scandal. And sure enough, he veers off to exchange words with Joseph-Israël Tarte, who stands watching the festivities conspicuously alone beside a stone pillar.

"Joe," Lady M. commands, calling me back to her presence, "wasn't that a fine moment when Sir John entered the House with Hughy? I hope," she adds, lowering her voice, "you do it justice in that book you're writing."

I'm taken aback that she imagines I'm already in the throes of composition. I've scarcely even begun my research, much less mentioned the project to Minette, who looks inquisitively at me but says nothing. "I'll try my best, Lady Macdonald. Isn't it grand to see Sir John in such capital spirits?" I nod to where he's standing fifteen feet away, clinking punch glasses and blithely recounting one of his favourite stories—the one about the Washington reception where the Senator's wife, unaware who he is, asks him why Canadians keep electing such a rascal for Prime Minister—with a grin from ear to ear.

"Among ourselves," confides Lady M., leaning intimately toward Minette and me, lavender water and not champagne perfuming her every word (she no longer drinks, as an example to her husband), "I haven't seen him so happy in ages. It does him a world of good to have Hughy near him in the House. Isn't it remarkable, the power of the son to rejuvenate the father?"

I suspect she's describing her own happiness. And why not? Her affection and gratitude toward Hugh are clearly genuine.

I keep my eye on Tarte. It's said he won't let his documents incriminating McGreevy and Langevin out of his sight; he carries them in his coat wherever he goes, locked in a little satchel attached to his person, and stores them every night in a safe in Hull. I notice him patting the side panel of his coat as he converses with Edgar.

Not for the first time, I wonder if Tarte even belongs in the Conservative Party. A deep darkness runs in him. Would it dissipate if dipped in Liberal red? Is that party his natural home? He has an obvious affinity with Laurier, who has agreed to defend him in court against libel charges. Or is Tarte's self-appointed mission in life simply to bring down whoever sits in authority above him? We'll find out soon enough. He's made it known he plans to introduce his charges in the House at the first opportunity. The Liberals will be only too glad to give it to him.

Four

MAY 1891

Warfare

This new Parliament brings an immediate resumption of hostilities. Instead of settling the issues by verdict of the people, the election merely provided a lull in bitter party warfare. I find both sides' intransigent rage and insatiable thirst for vengeance repellent. These violent appetites! Tempered for a day by pomp, circumstance and civility, they're now indulged with greater ferocity than ever.

All eyes are once more on the Commons. Unless Sir John signals to me from his seat, I'm free to linger behind the curtain on the Government side of the House and watch the battle rejoined. It's a bizarre and fascinating ritual: a medieval joust, lances unsheathed, visors down. Sir John has cannily chosen two unbloodied backbenchers to move and second the Speech from the Throne. This youthful pair represent ridings from the farthest ends of the nation, from coasts three thousand miles apart: Hazen from Saint John, New Brunswick, and Corbould from New Westminster, British Columbia. Sir John reckons their maidenly virtue will protect them somewhat from ravaging by the Liberal elders.

Hazen is brief, correct and circumspect in introducing the motion. But in seconding it, Corbould delivers one of those paeans to British Columbia that citizens of the place seem unable to resist. They believe other Canadians are completely ignorant of their province, yet deserve to be pitied for this rather than scorned: "I would dearly love to see every member of this House," Corbould proclaims, an ecstatic smile spreading over his face, "pay a visit to British Columbia ere long. It requires a personal acquaintance with our province to properly realize its beauties and its richness, to fully understand what a prize the Dominion of Canada secured when B.C. came into Confederation . . ." etc., etc.

The formalities completed, Laurier is first to rise in reply to the Speech from the Throne. As even the Conservative Montreal *Gazette* was saying yesterday, "the Opposition are fit for battle and in fighting humour." Laurier now stands at the head of a visibly enlarged contingent of troops. The crowded Liberal benches seem to puff him up physically, making him appear even taller than normal, more square shouldered and substantial. Before uttering a syllable he's cheered to the rafters by his supporters.

Laurier's Quebec ranks especially have swollen, which can only bolster his confidence in his political base and personal authority. Several of his Ontario members are also new to me. To Laurier's immediate right, however, sits a very familiar face—Sir John's real nemesis, and a man once close to him politically—the Member for Oxford South. Sir Richard Cartwright's implacable hatred for everything Sir John stands for is legend, suiting him only for perpetual opposition. It's impossible to think he could ever have been a Conservative.

As Laurier begins to speak, Cartwright stares across the aisle in furious anticipation, his upper body pitched forward across his desk, his walrus moustache literally twitching. He appears to be grinding his incisors in expectation of raw meat. Yet his little round spectacles suggest a venerable schoolmaster or divine, the kind who refuses to let experience dim his moral indignation. It's easy to forget Cartwright sits atop three generations of wealth and influence in Kingston. As a schoolboy, I understand, he lorded it mercilessly over Sir John, whose father was a struggling immigrant. But Sir John chooses to ignore the difference in their origins; he's convinced Cartwright's hatred for him arises solely from being denied the Finance portfolio in his first Cabinet.

Laurier's voice remains as golden and his deportment as courtly as ever, but his delivery has acquired a sardonic, even pugnacious quality. Complimenting the mover and seconder of the Throne Speech on "the manner in which they contrived to build upon such slender material," he takes immediate aim at the Speech in general—"dry bones, a very dry skeleton indeed"—and John Graham Haggart in particular. Laurier singles out the Postmaster General's decision to ship Canada's mail to Great Britain by way of the port of New York.

"For the last forty years," Laurier booms, "our mails have been carried to the motherland in *Canadian* bottoms. Two years ago the Government told us that this system was antiquated, and it was about to provide us with a better one. But would the House believe it?" he asks in mock disbelief. "The Postmaster General is today sending the mails of this loyal country, this country positively bristling with sentiments of loyalty, through *the United States*! And so I denounce the Postmaster General as a traitor—whether veiled or unveiled I cannot say, for I am not sufficiently posted in the ethics of loyalty as understood by the Conservative Party. But in my blunt judgment, the Postmaster General is a barefaced traitor, whom I denounce to the indignation of the loyal men and true who sit around him."

Seeing their leader has got Haggart's goat, the Liberals hoot and jeer with delight. They're just warming up for choruses to come. Even some Conservatives are openly amused. Sir John appears to be ignoring the badinage, listening intently as Langevin speaks into his left ear. As for Haggart, he can't decide whether Laurier is serious or merely poking fun at him and becomes impotently red-faced, turning this way and that to his seatmates for support. No doubt Laurier's play on "veiled treason" has gone right over his head. Thankfully Haggart decides against rising on a point of privilege.

Laurier does Haggart the kindness of smiling at him to signal no serious offence was meant. Then his expression darkens. Rather than making even token acknowledgment of the Government's victory at the polls, Laurier immediately turns to the attack; he proceeds to paint Sir John's administration as losing, not winning, the confidence of the people.

"When this House last met," Laurier declaims with a broad sweep of his arm, "the Ministerial ranks were not only filled up on the opposite side, but also on this side of the aisle, so as hardly to leave us a small corner. But where are now the serried ranks of the Ministerial party? Battered, shattered and crushed, simply from their contact with the will, the mind and the heart of the people. Why, it seemed to me, when I heard the Honourable mover of the Address praise the Conservative triumph, that he must have felt as did King Pyrrhus when congratulated on a victory over the legions of Rome, and could only say with him: 'Another such victory and we are undone.'"

Mocking howls erupt from the Conservative benches. The shouts of derision from Laurier's French-speaking opponents are particularly loud. Chapleau shouts something in French that I can't catch, stinging Laurier for a moment. But he has Sir John's full attention now. He directs his remarks straight across the aisle, ignoring all others, placing his palms squarely on his hips and rearing back:

"Why, not one supporter of this Government would *dare* to lay its policy—that hazy, misty, undulating, fluctuating, shifting mass of contradiction which constitutes the policy of the Conservative Party—before the people, unless they had been gagged in advance—as gagged they were in the last election."

The Conservatives' bellowing protests fuel Laurier's purpose, egging him on to adopt a harder, more indignant tone of voice: "Yes, Mr. Speaker, gagged! Shackled and manacled! Gagged, shackled and manacled by iniquitous laws—laws which have mutilated the boundaries of counties so as to swamp the voice of the people, laws which have left the preparation of the voters' lists in the hands of the Government, laws which have allowed the Government to appoint the revising officers of those lists, laws which have allowed the Government to appoint unblushing partisans to that office, laws which allowed them to perpetrate the most disgraceful frauds. The Honourable Gentlemen speak of 'the continued confidence of the people' in the Government. That confidence is only obtained by aid of the iniquitous measures to which I refer, Mr. Speaker, supplemented by other iniquitous modes of bribing constituencies, worse than ever known in any country!"

Laurier pauses as his supporters pound their desks to drown out the cries opposite. Standing directly opposite him, yet invisible behind the curtain, I study Laurier closely. Amid the tumult he sips delicately from a glass of water. Perspiration has broken out on his bare upper lip and broad forehead. Whether out of vanity or some more fastidious motive, Laurier forgoes the facial hair under which most public men hide their emotions; in that regard, as in many others, he's like Sir John.

Laurier appears shaky, however, swaying slightly on his feet. I doubt he's overcome the illness that has kept him out of public view for much of the time since election day. How much longer can he keep up the feverish pace of his diatribe?

He asks why the previous Parliament was ever dissolved in the first place, when the Government still had a year to run. He demands to know the reasons Sir John gave His Excellency in advising dissolution. Sir John, who has turned aside to converse with his seatmate, George Foster, smiles faintly and settles back to listen, as if now thoroughly absorbed in his opponent's argument.

Essentially Laurier posits that Sir John is guilty of treachery toward the electorate and even toward the Governor General. First, according to Laurier, Sir John advised Lord Stanley that he needed a fresh mandate to negotiate free trade with Washington. Then he went to the country to advocate the exact opposite: continued protection for home industry under the National Policy, while accusing the Liberals of treason for espousing free trade. "The Government appealed to the people on their prejudices," Laurier charges: "the worst prejudices that could possibly be used against an Opposition."

It's a pithy argument, and Laurier seems to mean every word of it. He dresses it up in a mixture of allusions both homely and historical. He recalls the fable of the bat who falls one day among the birds and the next among the rats. "When he fell among the birds," Laurier chants in a singsong voice, as if instructing his congregation, "the bat said: 'Look at my wings, I am one of your tribe.' When he fell among the rats, he said: 'Look at my claws, I am one of your tribe.' So the Right Honourable Gentleman says, when he is among the farmers: 'I want to soar like the birds to reciprocity.' But when he gets among the manufacturers, and particularly among the monopolists, he says: 'Look at my claws, I am one of your tribe; and like you, I still have the people of this country to prey upon.'"

Sir John jerks his head defiantly. From my position behind him, I can't tell whether his expression is mirthful, mocking or angry: possibly all three.

Laurier rejects the charge of treason: "The Right Honourable Gentleman's only argument was to say that the policy of the Opposition was disloyal, and hostile to Great Britain. Loyalty! I am reminded of the words of Madame Rolland when she was led to the scaffold. She was one who had contributed to the French Revolution, of course, and fell victim to the passions she had aroused but could not control. When on the scaffold she was compelled to bow to the statue of Liberty, she exclaimed: 'O Liberty! How many crimes are committed in thy name?' We in Canada now have to ask, How many crimes are committed in the name of Loyalty?"

Laurier's most shocking argument is one that does in fact smack of disloyalty. In alleging that Sir John asked Lord Stanley to dissolve Parliament on the pretext of negotiating free trade, he quotes what purports to be a telegram from His Excellency to the Colonial Office, in which Lord Stanley advises the Colonial Secretary as follows: "My Lord, the Government of Canada is desirous to propose a joint commission to prepare a treaty with the United States renewing the Reciprocity Treaty of 1854 . . ."

How did Laurier get his hands on such a telegram, and from whom? Who from behind the scenes wants to embarrass Sir John? Surely not Whitehall. Obviously not Rideau Hall: Lord Stanley himself is painfully exposed by the Liberals' manoeuvre. I'm astonished Laurier would exploit the vice-regal office for political gain.

Leaving my questions unanswered, Laurier claims the Government compounded its hypocrisy by sending Sir Charles Tupper to Washington last month, accompanied by George Foster, the Minister of Finance, and John Thompson, Minister of Justice, for the sole purpose of reopening trade negotiations with Secretary Blaine. According to Laurier, they were rebuffed and humiliated: "Like Caesar they went, they saw; but unlike Caesar, they did not conquer. They came back without having achieved a thing."

Of course Laurier has a point; but again he goes too far. He says the Canadian delegation actually deserved ill treatment at the hands of Blaine and his officials because of a widely reported speech Sir John made in Halifax last fall.

In the speech Sir John simply adumbrated the social and philosophical differences between Canada and the States. He came down, naturally enough, in favour of our own way of ordering national existence. He spoke admiringly of America's greatness, her undoubted ability to overcome someday "the struggles of a fierce and discordant democracy"—yet pronounced Canada the more fortunate of the two countries, having created for her citizens a society based on the principles of peace, order and good government.

In Laurier's version of events, you'd think Sir John's speech had handed Washington a cause for commercial war. As happens so often, the Liberals are all too ready to construe any criticism of the United States, however justified, as unwarranted and dangerous, even disloyal—anti-American, one might say.

"Nothing could be more contrary," Laurier claims, "to the friendship that we owe the neighbouring Republic. There was hostility in that speech, as there was hostility by the Canadian Government towards American authorities during their Civil War."

At this, Sir John bristles and throws up his hands in exasperation. Laurier has revived an old canard. "At that time also," Laurier persists, "we 'looked with philosophic eyes at the struggles of a fierce and discordant democracy,' and the result was that we lost the Reciprocity Treaty of 1854. And now we can only pray that the Government's similar imprudence will not cost us another trade treaty."

Sir John is itching to rebut these allegations but he'll have to wait; Laurier isn't about to surrender the floor. Now Laurier demands to know exactly what the Throne Speech meant by announcing our commissioners will negotiate with Washington this fall. Will they treat for complete or partial free trade? Or solely settlement of the fisheries disputes in the Atlantic and Bering Seas? The Government doesn't say, because the Government doesn't know its own mind. The Liberals, of course, know theirs: "We of the Liberal Party maintain that the policy of this country must be based not upon sentiment but upon business principles. As fresh as we come from the people, I say this: the only policy which will benefit this country is unrestricted reciprocity and continental freedom of trade."

Well, nothing could be clearer, I'll grant him that. What I find breathtaking is that Laurier attempts to justify such a cold-blooded, hard-headed policy with an argument based on the most dubious sort of patriotism. First he insists free trade can't be such a terrible thing if the Conservatives themselves are courting some measure of reciprocity: "Have the pure fallen from grace? Here is treason rampant! And who is to indict the traitors when the Minister of Justice himself connives at treason?"

Having wound up and thrown his pitch, Laurier runs to the plate, picks up a bat, and tries to hit his own ball for a home run. The entire purpose of his opening address is now clear: to destroy, at the very outset of this Parliament, the fundamental argument on which Sir John constructed his election victory.

"Mr. Speaker, I know very well that there are men in this country who honestly believe unrestricted reciprocity would be the first step towards annexation. I do not dispute any man's conviction. But I ask these men to exert their reason: if we have reciprocity, as we shall have it, I believe, before very long, these men will have the right to vote against annexation, if annexation be proposed. But shall we be so diffident of our manhood that we dare not do what is best for our interests, because someone might be dragged away from his allegiance in favour of American citizenship?

"Whatever may be the fears of the Conservative Party on this question, I have no fears for the Liberals of Canada. We do not boast of our loyalty, but we have it in our hearts—not upon our lips, as the Honourable Gentlemen opposite have it—and we do not fear that we shall be seduced away from what we believe right in principle."

Taking a deep breath and looking triumphantly about him, Laurier drives to his conclusion:

"The Right Honourable Gentleman opposite said that our policy was hostile to Great Britain. Again, I deny it. But Sir, I am free to admit that I, for one, when I made up my mind in favour of this policy, looked first and last to the interests of Canada, and not to those of England. I am a British subject and I never forget it. Yet I remember that I am also a Canadian, and I sit in the Canadian Parliament. Let the British subject who sits in the British Parliament look after the interest of England.

"When this Confederation was organized—and no one knows it better than the Right Honourable Gentleman himself—it was organized to form a new nation. The Fathers of Confederation must have foreseen that some day or other its interests would come into conflict with the interests of the motherland. It is absurd to suppose that, situated as we are, the interests of Canada will always be identical with the interests of Great Britain. Some day must come when these interests will clash. And for my part, whenever it comes to that, and however much I must regret the necessity, I will stand by my native land.

"Let me ask, Sir, why did your ancestors, and why did my ancestors, leave *their* native land? Did your ancestors leave Great Britain and Ireland, and did my ancestors leave France, because they loved their motherland less? No, Sir: the truth is they were not satisfied with the condition of their own country. And therefore, to make their lives better, and for the comfort and happiness of their families, they parted from their native land—not because they loved it less, but because they loved Canada more.

"Now, Sir, we are agitating for this policy of unrestricted reciprocity because we believe it is in the best interests of this country. For my part, I have again and again affirmed that I am as fondly attached to British institutions as any man of English blood. But I have never hesitated to say that, whether for ill or for good, whether for my condemnation or my justification, whether for right or for wrong, as long as there is in me the breath of life, my guiding star, and my only guiding star, shall be Canada first, Canada last, and Canada forever."

The entire House is perfectly still. Laurier remains standing, head erect, body immobile, until he breaks the silence by sitting down, and the Opposition benches explode with a roar of awe, admiration and tearful relief.

Despite my attempts to resist Laurier's remorseless logic, I find I'm a little breathless—almost, I have to admit, persuaded. I'm grateful when Sir John stands in his place, bows to the Speaker, and restores order to the House and my brain.

The measured cadences of Sir John's reply make me see how dangerous are the emotional appeals of demagoguery. Having sketched on the back of an envelope Laurier's arguments during the past hour and a half, he coolly and systematically demolishes them one by one.

First he disarms with praise. His compliments are all the more devastating because, as I'm well aware, they're perfectly genuine: I've often heard my chief say in private how much he admires Laurier's gifts of mind and speech, his firmness and tenacity. He considers Laurier, more than anyone since George Brown, his most formidable foe.

"I have listened with enormous interest to the speech of my Honourable Friend," Sir John begins. "It has much of his eloquence, much of his facility of language, much of his happiness of expression." He pauses to glance benignly in all directions, as if daring either side of the House to contradict him. "It has, as well, a tone of exasperation—and, indeed, bitterness, which is not usual in his speeches. I can, however, quite pardon the feeling which has induced and prompted that tone."

An anticipatory stirring rustles the Conservative benches, countered by barely audible mutterings from the Liberals. I glance up at the spectator galleries. Lady M. is at her post, soberly dressed today, smiling at her husband, seeming even more confident than he of the compelling and irrefutable arguments about to issue from his mouth. His voice is still strained from his illness, and this makes the Members lean forward in their seats to listen more attentively.

"If ever there was a party disappointed," Sir John remarks with apparent compassion, "if ever a public man was disappointed in an election result, it is my Honourable Friend opposite. The certainty that he had in his own breast, his confidence that the country was with him—a confidence in which all his party joined—was so great, that the ensuing disappointment must have been dreadful. The Honourable Gentleman went to bed on the night of the fourth of March confidently believing that he would be sent for in a few days to form a Government. But the illusion disappeared by nine o'clock the following morning. I can pardon, therefore, the feeling the Honourable Gentleman has. And the only thing that I feel personally aggrieved at is his assertion that there was, on the part of this Government, some dishonourable action on the subject of dissolution."

Sir John detours to pick up Laurier's jibe at Haggart. He makes a disquisition on the antiquated state of the railway lines running from the St. Lawrence and the Maritimes to Halifax, and the similar condition of the steamships running from there to Glasgow, Liverpool and Southampton. The Government chose not to waste public money, he explains, by continuing to pay the Allan Line to perform the transatlantic mail delivery service; but it does plan to invest in a new all-Canadian service once the English money market offers reasonable rates of borrowing. Thus, "We shall have a line of which we may be proud, and which will relieve us of the charge of disloyalty brought by the Honourable Gentleman."

Sir John refuses to let a factual error in Laurier's speech slip past. Laurier alleged that the Government has a majority in the House without a majority of seats in either of the two largest

provinces. That is incorrect, Sir John points out: the Conservatives still command the most members from Ontario.

Laurier sits slumped in his seat with one hand shading his
brow. Exhausted after his long address, he coughs softly into a
handkerchief grasped in his other hand. He can only look up and
call in a weak voice, "Not much to boast of." But of course it is.

Warming to his task, Sir John recalls how the Liberals "from
every hustings, on every platform, on every stump they could find
to stand upon," declared that only unrestricted trade with the
U.S. could save the country from penury. And yet they failed to
bring even their own followers to that position: "The Honourable
Gentleman denied that unrestricted reciprocity would cause any
political change in Canada. He therein differs from his late, great
leader, Mr. Blake, the gentleman whom he followed most—
I was going to say 'blindly'—but most completely and without
any shadow of dissent, without any variance of opinion, until that
gentleman resigned the leadership. Mr. Blake holds a different
opinion and consequently has deserted the party. He has retired
from public life, of which he was an ornament, retired apparently
forever into private life, because he could not follow a course
which he believed, in its logical consequence, must lead to annexation to the United States."

The Liberals' catcalls sound half-hearted to my ears; the steam
has gone out of them.

Sir John smiles at the sound, as if its harmlessness pleases
him. He's on comfortable ground now—so comfortable that he
actually turns his back on the Opposition benches to address his
own followers directly. With a contemptuous shrug and a shrewd
smile playing across his face, he rings the variations played by the
Liberals on their main policy plank—"continental free trade,"
"unrestricted reciprocity," "commercial union"—and finds them
nothing but aliases for annexation. This may be an old refrain, but
it's an argument that found much favour at the polls. It leads him

straight into a defence of his Halifax speech, and he turns back to face his opponents:

"The Honourable Gentleman has stated that my language at Halifax was unfriendly and impolitic with reference to the United States. I said then, as I say now, that the United States is a great nation and will be a greater nation; that there is no limit to its future greatness. But I spoke in the same sense as the best and the ablest and the most patriotic citizens of the United States now speak. Look at any of the writings of their political men, look at the writings of their literati, and you will find they make the same cry about the approaching dangers to the United States. . . .Why should we who are free from those dangers, why should we who have not the same causes of apprehension as the people of the United States, why should we who are as yet free not only from the cause of socialism brought from Europe, anarchy brought from Europe, atheism brought from Europe, mix ourselves up in these questions? Why, above all, should we mix ourselves up in the consequences of the Negro question? All their writers agree that the United States is in great danger, and they are using their best intellects to see how they are to overcome the great dangers which are so imminent, and from which we, under the flag of England, have been free. . . ."

Visibly beginning to tire, Sir John pauses for water. He rallies his strength to repel the argument that I'm sure troubles him most. It's a matter of verifiable fact and personal honour: Sir John himself headed the Colonial Government at the time of the American Civil War, long before his opponent even entered politics. From that vantage point, he condemns as baseless Laurier's claim that Canada was hostile to the Union.

"There is no *evidence*," he cries, "none at all, of hostility to the United States. This is proved by the fact that from twenty thousand at the minimum to, as some say, forty thousand men went from Canada to fight for the Union side. Some few men, some way or other, got through the Northern lines and joined the South. But twenty to forty thousand Canadians joined the ranks and fought and fell and died in the ranks of the Northern army. And I will undertake, now that the statement has been made, to bring down to this House and show to Parliament the repeated thanks which the United States Government gave for the way in which Canada behaved."

When the desk-thumping dies down, Sir John recalls Secretary of State Seward's statement at the time—all the more remarkable because of Seward's well-known position in favour of annexing Canada and Mexico—that he wished Great Britain had behaved half as well as Canada in adopting neutrality in the Civil War. In fact, Sir John reminds the House, Canada went well beyond the obligations of neutrality. She spent her own scarce cash, even scarcer in those narrow Colonial days, to ensure the Confederacy didn't use our territory as a base of operations against the Union.

Remembering his tale of meeting President Grant, I pull my notebook and pencil out of my coat pocket and scribble down Sir John's exact words in shorthand: "We had ten thousand volunteers watching the frontier in warlike array, men taken from their homes for months and months, and we cannot be charged with having been neglectful of our duties. We, members of the Government, were determined that by no action or sympathy of Canada's should the mother country be brought into a conflict, or into a hostile or semi-hostile position, with regard to the United States. That I avow, and that I can prove."

Sir John's face is set as grimly and vehemently as I've ever seen it. No one on the Opposition benches gainsays him.

His expression quickly grows cheerful again. A burden has been lifted. He returns to the present.

"Mr. Speaker, my Honourable friend says we have achieved a Pyrrhic victory. If so, it is a victory that will last five years. I am satisfied with it. I ought to be, because at the end of this present

Parliament, if it lives, I shall be some eighty-one years of age.
[Hurrahs.] I tell my friends, and I tell my foes: *J'y suis, j'y reste*. We
are going to stay here, and it will take more than the power of the
Honourable Gentleman, with all the phalanx behind him, to disturb or shove us from our pedestal."

As Sir John sits down, his supporters rise to a man around him.
If there existed some magical machine that could measure his
ovation's volume and compare it to Laurier's, it would tell a fascinating tale. To my ears, in all honesty, the result is a draw.

Inquiry

Laurier is laid up at the Russell House, too weak from an attack of bronchitis to attend debates in the Commons. Madame Zoë is staying here to nurse him instead of returning home to Arthabaskaville—or leaving the task to someone else. Sir John jokes that he's doing better than either Laurier or Professor Williamson, who writes to inform us of his diarrhea. Yet it's obvious Sir John's strength isn't gaining either. His colour is bad, the skin grey and slack with fatigue around his mouth. More than once at the close of day, he complains of feeling weak.

The younger Macdonalds have moved into the Bodega Hotel on Wellington Street, but Hugh John visits Earnscliffe, and he and I join forces to reassure Lady M. about her husband's fitness to attend Parliament. We all know a week's rest would do him the world of good, but we haven't the slightest chance of inducing him to stay home. This has meant a return to my familiar long working days and evenings. Sir John has more than once apologized for this, even expressing his gratitude, but the fact is, he says, he can't spare me: "I'm an old man now and don't like changes."

In Laurier's absence, Sir Richard Cartwright tears into Sir John unfettered. The Conservatives are so wasteful, venal and corrupt that it must be a sorry electorate that elected them yet again. Sir

John is accountable not to the people but to "his taskmasters and paymasters in the Red Parlour"—Cartwright's epithet for the billiard room of the Queen's Hotel in Toronto, where Sir John occasionally meets leading businessmen. Even Sir John's loyalty to the Crown is specious: "His is the loyalty that pays, and as long as it pays, Her Majesty will have no more faithful subject."

Contrary to Cartwright's fulminations, good legislation is coming from the Government. The most ambitious bill will be John Thompson's effort to systematize the scattered bits and pieces of the criminal law within a single Criminal Code. It's a mammoth undertaking, and Thompson has emerged as the most thoughtful, constructive, far-sighted and useful of Sir John's Ministers—the only one with the talents to make an effective successor. "What a shame he's a pervert," I keep hearing, a reference to Thompson's conversion from Methodism to Mother Church—a history he and I have in common. If I allow myself to think about it, I can imagine serving under Thompson with enthusiasm. Although he doesn't suffer fools, he has wit as well as learning; if he wished, he could charm to his side the very Orangemen who detest him. Not to mention the fact that we're both Maritimers.

Dalton McCarthy, however, is about to poison Parliamentary life by re-introducing his divisive bill on the North-west. This will inevitably distract attention from the Criminal Code legislation, adding insult to injury for Thompson by casting scorn on his choice of faith. McCarthy proposes to abolish the separate schools for Manitoba's Catholics and repeal the dual-language provision in the Territories. Debate is sure to be heated and acrimonious. McCarthy's real aim, as everyone knows, is a nation that speaks only English: a goal that Sir John has denounced as impossible to achieve and "foolish and wicked if it were possible."

I've always been puzzled by the bitterness of McCarthy's attacks against the French and Catholic communities; as far as I know, neither has ever done him any harm. And he seems such a courteous and tolerant fellow in private life. I ask Sir John how he accounts for this apparent contradiction. "My dear Pope," he replies mildly, "it's in his blood. His father was just the same."

Sir John resumes his long-established custom of Saturday evening dinner parties at Earnscliffe. Typically he invites each of his supporters from both Houses twice a session, trying for a mixture of old and new hands, MPs and Senators, accompanied by wives if resident in the capital, and I look after the invitations. Sir John is assuredly the prince of entertainers; his invitations are greatly prized, especially by new Members, who are flattered by his attentions and desirous of observing him at home. The younger MPs are so jealous of each other that I have to reassure those who aren't invited that their turn will soon come.

It doesn't occur to Sir John to give himself a rest and risk dashing his followers' expectations by postponing the first dinner party of the session. Or to forgo at dinner the presence of his personal secretary.

On Monday, after a morning plowing through correspondence with Sir John, I nip home for a bite of lunch. Minette seems mildly amused and gratified by my presence.

Much refreshed, I carry on to Sparks Street. Sir John wants me to pick up a copy of Goldwin Smith's new book, *Canada and the Canadian Question*, from Durie's. At two dollars it's not as good a buy as Bryce's *American Commonwealth*, which old Mr. Durie will part with at three dollars for the two volumes. He also has stock of the new Sara Jeannette Duncan novel, *An American Girl in Paris*, which I buy for Minette. But it's the Goldwin Smith Sir John wants to read, the latest effusion from the Sage of the Grange, in which Professor Smith apparently makes his most elaborate defence yet of his political Utopia of a greater North America.

What compels a rich old Englishman who taught at Oxford and Cornell to lecture Canadians that our destiny lies with the

States? Years ago Smith termed Canada "a lost cause"—yet here we remain, persisting in our folly, and still he pours forth articles and speeches and essays and books arguing why this country ought not to exist in the first place. I'd have thought Sir John had better things to read, but he always insists on being up to date in literary matters, prepared for the day when someone, in or out of Parliament, will ask him what he thinks of the latest volume by that clever Smith fellow.

Back outside the bookshop, my purchases wrapped in brown paper and string and tucked under my arm, I pause on the sidewalk to let a streetcar rumble past. The temptation to play hooky in this warm dusty sunlight is irresistible. Perhaps just the briefest stroll down Sparks, since Sir John isn't due in the House till three. . . .

For some time I've been considering a bowler hat from R. J. Devlin's. Minette thinks it would put me right in fashion, but I'm not so sure; Sir John detests them. Heading in the direction of Devlin's store, I know very well I'll just stare at the array of headgear in the window without going inside, but this gives me a destination.

Outside the Canadian Pacific Railway office, I halt in front of a poster offering to take one "Around the World for $600." Reading the fine print, I discover this is a slight exaggeration—it's necessary to pay one's own passage to Liverpool first—yet from there, Van Horne's *Empress of China* will sweep one away on an exotic and magical voyage: a tour of Gibraltar, Naples, Port Saïd, Suez, Colombo, Penang, Singapore, Hong Kong, Shanghai, Kobe and Yokohama, and thence to Vancouver, returning home in the splendour of a private berth on a CPR Pullman. Ah, the romance of the East! Someday, my dear, someday.

This fantasy seems to spawn a fantastic apparition as lovely as it's unexpected. The approaching rattle of roller skates on the pavement announces a fetching young woman wearing an outlandish costume. She's decked out in shocking shades of pink: high-collared pink satin dress open at the throat, two rows of deeper pink buttons, flaring balloon sleeves, skirt decorated with a curious mortar-and-pestle motif in the same rose shade as the buttons. The skirt ends just above her ankles, revealing roller skates of dyed-pink leather. On her head sits an absurdly tall, stovepipe-shaped pink hat.

The skater weaves in and out among the pedestrians, careful not to bump into us. The effect she creates is comic, clownish, yet somehow enchanting. Her hands are thrust inside an enormous pink muff pressed against her stomach. One's gaze is drawn immediately to the muff, embroidered with the words "Dr. Williams' Pink Pills for Pale People."

As the skater passes, I take in, along with a whiff of her cheap perfume, the fact that she's been transformed into a mobile human advertisement. She must be the latest ploy in the worldwide sales campaign hatched by the audacious George E. Fulford. Once a druggist in sleepy Brockville, fifty miles from here, but now residing in New York, Fulford has been using every form of advertising imaginable to convert half the globe into believing his preposterous claims for his product—an innocuous pink tablet to which he bought the patent from some American inventor, I'm told, for fifty-three dollars. Just who Dr. Williams is or was we may never know; but Fulford is ensuring that every pasty-face from here to St. Petersburg knows about his miraculous cure-all. "These pills," his slogan goes, "make weak people strong." They're apparently concocted of iron, sugar and a bit of food colouring, and they've made him a millionaire many times over. It's only a matter of time before Sir John appoints him to the Senate.

I pop in at Ebenezer Browne's to buy a bottle of Monopole Sec for our approaching seventh wedding anniversary. Turning up O'Connor to the Hill, books under one arm and champagne under the other, I feel the sun flooding the back of my bowlerless head with glorious warmth. I cross Wellington, pass through the iron gates of Parliament, and am just admiring the noble spire of the Victoria Tower, its clock reading a quarter past two, when I become aware of a slight dark-suited gentleman converging from my left.

"We both bear our burdens," observes Joseph-Israël Tarte, addressing me in French.

I reply in his language: "Ah, but yours is heavier."

He switches to English, making me involuntarily wonder, as always, if something was wrong with my French. "As you can see, M. Pope," he says, "this is my day for bringing my *petits papiers* before the House."

This gives me permission to look directly at the black satchel resembling a doctor's bag gripped tightly under his arm. "So, M. Tarte. You'll have your innings today."

"Innings?"

"A sporting term. Your turn at bat."

"Ah, yes. But what a pity Sir John never saw fit to hear me out. This sad day might have been avoided."

That I doubt: Tarte has been desperately longing for his moment of truth for months. It's the reason he got himself elected to Parliament in the first place.

Although it takes me slightly out of my way, I fall into step beside him, curious to hear what else he might have to say. We proceed up the broad approach to the Centre Block, skirt the scalloped wall of the fountain, in full flow now that spring is here, and climb the steps between the two twenty-pound cannon. At the massive doors I step aside, telling Tarte I must deposit my parcels in my East Block office before entering the House. He too pauses. He sighs and regards me uneasily.

"This is a difficult day for me, M. Pope, more so than you may think. It is not the way I wish to introduce myself to Ottawa— bringing sad news of *malfaisance* from my home province. But I have no other choice. It is the only way we can bring such corruptions to an end."

"Of course. You want to get to the bottom of it."

"*C'est ça*, precisely. I am grateful you understand."

Tarte smiles, more to himself than to me, and passes alone through the open entrance. I wonder why he bothers justifying himself to me. Am I merely his conduit to Sir John? Or do I symbolize something more for him, the civil service perhaps? Even English Canada? I watch him mount the stairs, nod to the constable, proceed with his satchel up the wide corridor leading to the chamber. His seat is positioned on the Opposition side of the House; he insisted on running as an Independent, after all, despite his professed Conservative allegiance.

Finding Sir John in the Commons corridor fifteen minutes later, I make reference to the *petits papiers*. He already knows all about them. He tells me there's a rumour Tarte will bring to light new charges against McGreevy and Langevin, in addition to those he's already aired in *Le Canadien*. One story going the rounds is that McGreevy's office in Quebec City has a trap door leading down to a secret office where he transacts his shady dealings. Sir John greets some of his supporters, enters the chamber, and settles into his seat, while I retreat behind the curtain, both of us to await Tarte's revelations.

Mr. Speaker takes the chair, and nothing unusual happens for nearly two hours. There's a stir when the issue of Prohibition comes up. It isn't entirely clear whether McMullen, the Member who raises it, is more ardent to ban liquor, or more fearful the country will go bankrupt from the resulting loss of revenue. To the amusement of some, Sir John fields the question himself. When he tells McMullen the Government has several petitions supporting Prohibition under active consideration, it elicits jibes from the Liberal benches: "Not likely! Some chance!" Many

Parliamentarians, especially from Quebec, want nothing to do with Prohibition; but others of both parties have formed a temperance caucus to agitate for its imposition. They're a growing and increasingly self-righteous group, composed entirely of God-fearing, teetotalling, English-speaking Protestants. Somehow I doubt they'll carry the day.

At five minutes to five, just as eyelids are drooping and stomachs rumbling, Tarte rises in his place in the third row on a question of privilege. Members have been acting as if they didn't know this was coming. Even some in the Opposition are leery of seeing men of their tribe, veterans of this House since Confederation, dragged into the mud. Members interrupt their conversations, set aside their newspapers or letter writing, and attend to what Tarte has to say.

Speaking in French, Tarte declares he'd be more comfortable addressing the House in his own language, but he knows the great majority wouldn't be able to understand him. He therefore continues in English. He says they'll soon be able to decide for themselves whether, being in possession of a voluminous and incriminating correspondence, he would have done better to remain silent.

Tarte looks aggrieved and unhappy, as if he could use some of Dr. Williams' Pink Pills. He continually refers to a sheaf of closely handwritten notes gripped tightly in his left hand, leaving his right free to punctuate his address with short slicing motions. By reading his text, he ensures that the English phrases emerge from his lips clear and exact. The silence is total except for the scratching pens of *Hansard* reporters.

Tarte claims to regret beginning his Parliamentary career with "grave accusations against old and important Members of this House." Nevertheless, he insists, he's about to perform "a great public duty," a service for which the voters of Montmorency sent him to Ottawa. With his evidence, he declares, lifting the black

satchel from his seat and displaying it like some small slain pre-
dator for all to see, he will prove the accuracy of each and every
accusation.

Like the lawyer he was before becoming a journalist, Tarte
lays out the generality of his case before getting to the particulars.
"Something wrong and rotten" has been going on in the harbour
works at Quebec City. It has been going on since at least 1882, and
the rot leads directly back to the Department of Public Works in
Ottawa. The confidentiality of the department's dealings with
private contractors has been continually breached, secrets rou-
tinely divulged, influence improperly peddled, and large sums of
money illegally spent—all for the personal and political benefit
of Thomas McGreevy, MP for Quebec West, and the Quebec
wing of the Conservative Party.

This immorality, Tarte says, with its past and present harm
to the public interest, is widely known throughout Quebec. He
terms the scandal "the doings of our Canadian Tammany Hall."
He insists that the documents in his satchel were thrust upon
him—by whom he doesn't say. Last year, after seeking the advice
of senior members of the Conservative Party (by which he means
Chapleau), he turned his evidence over to Sir John: "At the Right
Honourable Prime Minister's request, I left some of those papers
with him. A few days afterwards he gave them back to me stating,
with his usual kindness, that he had seen the Honourable Member
for Quebec West and had received from him positive assurances
that there was no truth whatever in those documents; and that
he had also received from the Minister of Public Works the same
assurances."

That much I know to be true. And what else could Sir John
have said? He had to accept those reassurances, coming as they
did from his old friend and trusted ally, the long-time leader of his
party in Quebec, Sir Hector Langevin. The fly in the ointment, of

course, is the commonly known fact that Thomas McGreevy is
Sir Hector's brother-in-law and lives in his house while residing
in the capital.

Consequently, Tarte claims, he has had no other recourse but
to appeal to public opinion through the power of the press. Not
true: he could have remained silent for the good of his party and
Prime Minister. But that isn't Tarte's kind of loyalty. He sees himself as the scourge of corruption, of "malversation and fraud." His
loyalty is owed to some higher power—or ambition.

Tarte manoeuvres in closer for the kill. At the heart of the matter lies Larkin, Connolly & Co., a contracting firm with connec-
tions to both political parties. The head of that company, Patrick
Larkin, is a well-connected Liberal; one of his partners is Robert
McGreevy, Thomas's brother and a Conservative; the other three
partners are Americans. Tarte describes the wrongdoers as "men
of very desperate character" but powerful nonetheless. They control the Conservative Party in Quebec and will accuse anyone
who opposes them of betraying the party and the flag. Sir Hector,
says Tarte, imposed Thomas McGreevy on the party's provincial
wing as its treasurer: "Is it surprising then, Mr. Speaker, that our
old party has been for a long time losing ground in that old Conservative stronghold, the province of Quebec?"

It's obvious this scandal is really about the question of who will
control the Quebec Conservatives. What began as a parochial
squabble for provincial influence and power is about to be blown
into a national crisis.

Tarte makes no bones about implicating Sir John, even if indirectly. Before the election, Tarte says, he came up to Ottawa to
complain about these evils, but in vain: "The power behind the
throne was too strong for us. We did not know the real nature of
the influences against which we had to contend." This makes me
very nervous indeed. Tarte now has for a pulpit not merely the

French-language press but the floor of the House of Commons, and he can do Sir John a great deal of damage.

He proceeds to summarize his evidence. Previously I wasn't especially impressed by the inherent gravity of Tarte's charges, nor by his remorseless and implacable attitude in prosecuting them. Now, listening to him rhyme off his evidence, I realize it amounts, if true, to a devastating indictment: a long catalogue of influence peddling and profiteering and kickbacks, marked by the corrupt dismissal and replacement of public servants, falsifying tenders to obtain contracts, padding contracts to conceal payoffs, and re-directing public funds into election campaigns. As Tarte painstakingly reads every word of his sixty-three-paragraph motion into the record, the stomach-churning sense of awfulness mounts.

As usual I can't read Sir John's expression because I'm situated behind him. He appears to be sitting erect and unmoving, concentrating on Tarte's line of argument. The same is true of Langevin and McGreevy as their sins are enumerated. I notice Hugh John Macdonald slumping in his seat two rows from the back, his chin propped on one hand, looking aside in extreme distress.

It all starts with Parliament voting three hundred and seventy-five thousand dollars in 1882 for work on the harbour at Quebec City. Thomas McGreevy is a member of the Quebec Harbour Commission. To secure his influence in winning a dredging contract, Larkin Connolly takes McGreevy's brother Robert into the firm as a partner, giving him a thirty per cent stake. This is supposedly done with the agreement of Thomas McGreevy, who even tells Larkin Connolly he's consulted Sir Hector Langevin about it. *Voilà*, Larkin Connolly wins the contract, signed and sealed by Sir Hector himself.

This sounds fairly routine, if shady. The next development is more sinister. Three engineers from the Quebec Harbour Commission in charge of overseeing private contractors are dismissed at the instigation of Thomas McGreevy. They're replaced by Henry Perley, Sir Hector Langevin's chief engineer at the Department of Public Works. Meanwhile the Harbour Commission hires Sir Hector's own son as assistant engineer—"although he has never been an engineer in his life," according to Tarte. From this point on, Larkin Connolly's business with the department picks up considerably.

When the Quebec Harbour Commission calls for tenders to build a wall and lock, three contractors submit bids; and McGreevy discovers Larkin Connolly's bid is the highest. Before the contract is let, he communicates all the bid figures to Larkin Connolly and advises them how to manipulate their offer to bring it down below the others, while buying the collusion of the competing bidders. In the end Larkin Connolly receives the contract, pays McGreevy twenty-five thousand dollars, and contributes money to a "Langevin Testimonial Fund" being raised by Sir Hector's political friends.

The next year it's a new dock at Lévis across the river. This time Larkin Connolly guarantees to McGreevy any excess over fifty thousand dollars if it wins the contract from the Harbour Commission—which it does, at a price of seventy-two thousand.

Not satisfied with its successful manipulations at Quebec City, the firm tenders on building a new dock at Esquimalt, the naval shipyard on Vancouver Island. McGreevy divulges to Larkin Connolly confidential financial information from Public Works, helping them to win the competition. He later obtains richer contract terms involving changes to the construction, enabling Larkin Connolly to realize bigger profits. Out of these they pay "large sums" to McGreevy. The scheme entails the dismissal of Public Works officials working at Esquimalt, whose only error has been to incur the ill will of Larkin Connolly by insisting they work within the terms of the original contract.

And on it goes. In 1887 McGreevy makes a deal with Larkin Connolly to receive twenty-seven thousand dollars for helping win a contract at Quebec City, of which seven thousand goes into his re-election fund. On another tender, McGreevy obtains from Perley all the competing bids and shows them to his friends. In the end the contract goes to a bidder named Gallagher, who turns out to be a front man for Larkin Connolly instead of a legitimate contractor.

The barefaced arrogance of it all is astounding—almost risible in its cunning and perverted creativity. Tarte estimates that Mc-Greevy's own income from all these transactions has amounted to nearly two hundred thousand dollars over the years. That alone makes him a wealthy man. He's also received public benefits from the Gaspé–New Brunswick ferry service, since he owns the vessel in question, and from the Baie des Chaleurs Railway construction, from which he's pocketed forty thousand dollars. All told, public monies spent on the contracts named in Tarte's motion total over five million dollars.

Tarte pauses. No one in the chamber so much as coughs. They're waiting for the next blow.

So far Tarte has said nothing about trap doors leading to secret offices. His deposition contains nothing that he hasn't already divulged at various times in the French press, but the cumulative effect of it all, the deliberate, cynical pattern of deception and fraud, is staggering. And all of it on Sir Hector's watch.

Tarte's next step is to move that a select committee of the House be created to investigate his charges and get at the truth. He even suggests which MPs of both parties, including himself, ought to sit on the committee. To strengthen the case for an inquiry, he reads into the record a public statement by the Justice Minister, "in whom I have the fullest confidence." In February John Thompson said that, since it was insinuated that the Minister may have known something was wrong at Public Works, ministerial responsibility demands that Parliament conduct a thorough investigation, even if it proves that only departmental officials knew about the incidents. "In nothing with regard to those scandals," Tarte quotes Thompson as saying, "will the electorate of Canada be in any way deceived."

From the front row on the Government side, Thompson raises his stately, plump, handsome head in Tarte's direction, acknowledging that those were indeed his words and they still represent his position.

Swallowing hard, Tarte concludes: "I verily believe, Mr. Speaker, unless I am face to face with a long succession of forgeries, which to my mind is not possible, that I shall have the painful duty to prove every statement I have just made."

No applause, only silence, as Tarte sits down. With slow dignity, Sir Hector rises to Sir John's immediate left. Langevin's face is flushed beneath his white beard. There's an audible tremor in his voice, which could easily be a symptom of age, but is much more.

His own intention from the very start, Langevin states, was to move for a Parliamentary investigation; he's held back only to let Tarte have his say first. Sir Hector asserts his complete innocence. He never communicated or caused to be communicated any confidential information about tenders or contracts let by his department. He knows of no departmental officials guilty of breach of trust. Mr. Perley he has known for years as a faithful and honourable officer of the department; if Perley has done anything wrong, it was without Sir Hector's knowledge. He himself never asked for contributions to his testimonial fund and has no knowledge of contributions from the parties named. As for Thomas McGreevy: "He is in his place, and of course it is for him to say what he has to say."

Sir Hector insists he's ready to meet the inquiry at any time and answer any and all questions. He sits down, struggling to hold his head high. He receives sustained applause led by Sir John, who stands and pumps his hand. Some Liberals applaud too, but with greater restraint. Sir Hector is, after all, a Father of Confederation. Even if we've all known he's no saint, it's a shock to see him painted quite as black as this.

Now it's McGreevy's turn to protest his innocence. He doesn't equivocate: "The whole charge is false and untrue from beginning to end." Defiance colours McGreevy's cheeks and strains his unmusical voice. His air of wounded pride is dramatic, if nothing else: "It is a foul conspiracy concocted by a clique to damage me for their own benefit, because I would not be their tool and instrument to obtain for them what they wanted. They used my name, not only by writing letters but forging my signature. I am prepared to prove this. I am very glad this charge has been made, and I hope a speedy investigation will take place. I am prepared to defend myself. The result will be that the whole thing will be proved a false conspiracy."

When McGreevy sits down, Tarte concludes his case: "My wish, Mr. Speaker, my sincere wish, is that the words used by the Honourable Gentleman may be found to be quite true. He speaks of forgery. If the letters signed in the Honourable Gentleman's name are proved to be forgeries, Mr. Speaker, I will not only apologize to the House—I will have no other treatment to expect from this Parliament than to go out of it, and that very quickly."

James Edgar rises. He proposes that the inquiry be conducted by the Standing Committee on Privileges and Elections, consisting of all the lawyers sitting in the House. A picture flashes into my mind of Edgar, his wife in tow, head bent forward, conversing privately with Tarte at the reception after the opening of Parliament. Edgar's amendment is accepted, and Tarte's motion speedily passed.

Sir John immediately moves adjournment. It's five minutes to six: only one hour since Tarte rose to speak. But an hour can be an eternity in politics. Sir John doesn't linger on the floor as I expect him to, to confer with his Ministers or speak consolingly with Langevin. Instead he wheels about and proceeds promptly up the aisle to the corridor where I'm standing, his face pale, his expression clenched in utter fury. He strides straight past without seeing me.

Sir John

A little anger is a tonic for an old chap, but pent-up rage can kill a man. My fingers are trembling so much I can barely hold a sheet of paper between thumb and forefinger. Is this mere moral indignation? Or something more serious? And I haven't been on the burst for months.

Hearing Tarte self-righteously enumerate McGreevy's acts of self-enrichment, I can't tell which of the two makes me more furious. After all the betrayals and self-seeking deception I've witnessed in a life in politics, you'd think I'd take this in stride. I must calm myself: must take the long, considered view, calculate the balanced equation of events.

Yes, Tarte is a slippery weasel and hypocrite. True, McGreevy is an irredeemable scoundrel, steeped to the lips in corruption. Agreed, Langevin is an old fool who can't change his past or escape from his mistakes. These are facts, givens: easy enough to accept in themselves. One allows for them.

Taken individually, these men are minor figures, incidental players. It's their role in the greater scheme of things that gives them importance. The process of politics makes them larger than life; their words and acts, previously immaterial, suddenly swell with significance. Each of them has become a crucial gear in a machine now lurching into awful, destructive life, a monster that will do no one good save annexationists and separatists.

Patience. My beloved game. My trusted companion and ally in cooling the fevered brain. Lay the cards out on the table sacred to the purpose. Turn them face up, read their message with a clear and dispassionate mind. The game has the same soothing effect on me as a cigar upon a smoker. The cards always suggest a solution—almost always. And if they don't, the alternative remedy is time. They can call me Old Tomorrow as long as they want, but time and I are a match for any ten men.

Tarte is as addicted to intrigue as Coleridge to laudanum. I used to believe attaining government was Tarte's goal, but now I see him differently: governing would merely bore him. He seeks a different and more thrilling kind of power.

McGreevy. For all his attempts to cover his tracks, he's as transparent as glass, as only a man can be whose single governing principle is greed.

Langevin. I've gone through my political life with a simple creed: be to our faults a little blind, and to our virtues always kind. For all his weaknesses and limitations, Hector is a man after my own heart. He doesn't stay in politics for himself, much less for the money—both of us could have become far richer if we'd stuck to the law. When Hector sins, it's from the highest motives. For the public good. In the national interest.

But such a high-wire act, carried out in full public view, demands not only sound judgment but consummate skill. Unfortunately poor Hector has neither—only faith. His poor judgment has allowed McGreevy to lead him, and by extension me, into a foul blind alley, and all it takes is an incendiarist like Tarte to send the whole dreadful business up in flames.

Tarte is completely without conscience. In attacking Hector, he has no qualms about sacrificing his long-standing patron and protector, his journalistic Maecenas. Tarte wheedled Conservative capital out of Hector to buy his newspaper; then he begged government printing contracts to keep it afloat. Tarte looked to Hector as his shield against justice when he couldn't pay his debts. Tarte craved and got Hector's protection against the powerful enemies he made through his columns. It was only thanks to Hector that Tarte could insult and libel others with impunity while playing the high-minded idealist and moral absolutist. And yet once Hector told me Tarte is "a brave and important voice." What a dear foolish man.

Tarte even had the gall to portray himself as Hector's political conscience. In his columns he laid down the line for all Quebec Conservatives to follow, while he himself zigzagged all over the line—from clergy-worshipping ultramontanist to French-Canadian nationalist to Macdonald Conservative to Laurier Liberal. The cheek! And now, for all Hector's pains and Christian tolerance, we get Tarte's utter contempt.

Stare Tarte's evidence in the face, of course, and it's hard to disagree: McGreevy is a barefaced liar and thief. The press screams about patronage, but what McGreevy did isn't patronage at all. McGreevy stole public funds to benefit only himself and his friends. Patronage spends public money to benefit the public, ensuring that something gets done that the country needs doing while having it done by friends of the government. That's an important distinction. The government's friends don't rob it blind.

I'll be relieved to see McGreevy's end. The question is, who will go down with him?

Tarte is known in Quebec as Judas Iscariot. I feel his hot breath on my cheek already. Referring in his address to my "usual kindness"! Who will be next to receive his kiss?

Laurier, of course. It's only a short step from Tarte's seat as an "Independent" to the Liberal benches, fulfilling a pact made no doubt behind my back. But I also happen to know that some of the

McGreevy boodle ended up in Liberal coffers in Quebec. The vomit will land on Laurier's plate before long.

What do Laurier and Tarte hope to gain from all this, aside from power? Their roots in Quebec soil are as deeply intertwined as two parsnips. With the French, it goes down through the generations. Their forebears farmed and prayed together in the seventeenth century, studied and soldiered side by side in the eighteenth. Did I not once say that if we treat the French as a nation, they'll act as a free people always do—generously? And if we call them a mere faction, they'll become factious? But that was years ago. Ask me now and I'd say that no matter how fairly you deal with them, no matter how much you treat them as equals, they'll always find more natural and trusted allies in each other. Party and political philosophy run far shallower than blood and religion and language. And when a George Brown or a Dalton McCarthy attacks them and threatens their liberties, they instantly forget they're just as free as other Canadians, blessed with the selfsame rights and privileges—they fear a return to oppression and subjugation and subservience, and bind ever more tightly together.

Tarte prides himself on his claims to purity in both religion and politics: to him they're practically the same. He says his rosary every day, goes to confession every week, and openly believes the Church should interfere in the affairs of government. He even refuses to serve on boards of companies (the fool). But he's as biased against the English as any Orangeman against the French. He insists Langevin is an apostate captured by the English section of our party, a *vendu*—and, it goes without saying, far too close to me.

I well remember Tarte's stand on Riel. He published it, after all, in both languages. Tarte refused to believe Riel was sane. "Completely demented," were his words, "mad with the folly of religious reform." On those grounds he demanded I spare Riel from the noose, and when I didn't, he resorted to the old cry of *la race*. He bellowed about English prejudice and alleged that both judge and jury at Riel's trial should have been French. By that logic, we should have deformed justice—should have let treason and murder go unpunished, all because they'd been committed by a Frenchman.

Later Tarte paraded with Laurier and the rest of them on the Champ de Mars, protesting Riel's execution. By turning a traitor into a martyr, they raised the ghosts of French-Canadian humiliation and rage and embraced in full public view their precious belief that they'll never receive justice in this country, despite everything I've worked for all my political life—all my pleading and chivvying and negotiation and compromise to guarantee them equality under the law and a rightful place in government. But why should I expect gratitude from the French, or loyalty or love? Why should I expect anything? You have to take people as they are.

Tarte is a Riel in the making. I can see it in the burning coals of his eyes. But unlike Riel, Tarte has a strategy. By destroying Langevin, he hopes to install Chapleau at the head of our party in Quebec. Then he'll scheme to control Chapleau and thus wield the whip hand over me.

The strategy isn't going to work. Chapleau is a damned poor choice for a Messiah in any case: French interests are far safer with me. I know Chapleau of old, I've seen through his élan and charm and bonhomie. Chapleau's ambitions are utterly unscrupulous, his taste for plotting and intrigue worthy of Tarte's. Why else would I keep Railways and Canals out of Chapleau's hands all this time, even to the extent of running it myself? That ministry would give him enough scope for graft to debauch a committee of archangels. Then we'd see corruption! McGreevy's tawdry little acts would seem as nothing compared to what Chapleau is capable of.

Thanks to Tarte, the Conservative Party is now doomed in Quebec. We may as well hand the province over to the Liberals, let them take it straight out of Confederation.

What an intractable mess. The great imponderable, which even I don't know, is whether only our Quebec party will be destroyed or something far greater: the national party, even the country itself. In the end they're the same thing: the Conservative Party a simulacrum of the federation. I built them both. One can't stand without the other. And yet as Prime Minister I have less power to save them than Tarte to destroy them.

Let someone else turn back the tide. Damn it to hell, I no longer have the strength. Let Thompson or Laurier or, God knows, Cartwright and his squalling minions—let them all have a stab at it. They'll have less success than I. Then collapse. Chaos.

False Alarm

Having succeeded in getting an inquiry into Langevin's dark closet, the Liberals are seeking another vulnerable target. We hear they're now building their case against Sir Charles Tupper. Sir John shakes his head wearily at this incessant obsession with scandal and vilification. "The people elected us to govern," he tells me, "but the Liberals spend all their energies obstructing our efforts. That's the trouble with being in Opposition. The mind never climbs out of the gutter."

The festering problem of the Bering Sea has arisen, with all its old menace; it has the potential to make the McGreevy and Tupper affairs seem trivial. New arrests of our Pacific sealers demonstrate that the Americans aren't waiting for the conference to resolve the dispute. Despite agreeing to negotiate, they're bent on achieving a *fait accompli*. Their pressure tactics will destroy our West Coast seal fishery and leave us little choice but to accede to their claims, however dubious legally. Reaching a fair compromise on sharing the resource seems to hold no interest for them.

At a quarter to four I'm in the outer room of Sir John's Parliamentary office when he comes striding in from the floor of the House. He goes straight through to his inner office in silence, then, in an unusually abrupt tone, calls me in after him. The Colonial

Secretary is making nervous queries about the Bering Sea again. Lord Stanley requires Sir John's guidance in framing a response; rather than hosting us up at Rideau Hall, His Excellency prefers to come here for a briefing. He arrives in ten minutes.

Sir John seems distracted and irritable, but there's something else. An odd hesitation, an uncharacteristic hitch in the flow of his words, like a stutterer's painful pause, gives me a premonition of danger.

He tells me to go at once and fetch John Thompson to take part in the meeting. There's no time to lose, he insists. Hurrying down the corridor, I consider how Sir John turns to his Justice Minister in a crisis; it confirms my feeling that Thompson is his most trusted Minister.

I report back that Thompson will join us in a moment, and Sir John looks me in the eye, seeming seized by a wild desperation. "He must come at once. He must—speak to Lord Stanley for me. There's something the matter with my speech."

And now I see it: the left side of his face is twisted, the jaw pulled horribly downwards, as if by a lead weight.

Thompson arrives from the House, his face flushed and broad chest rising and falling. It's clear his bulk tells against him. I have reason to know Thompson is privately critical of "the old devil," as he refers to Sir John among friends, and even more caustic on the subject of Lady M. But now, sensing at once our chief's alarm, he clasps Sir John's hand and looks at him intently.

Sir John turns to me in mute appeal. I tell Thompson that the Prime Minister wishes him to act as his spokesman with Lord Stanley. I don't tell him the reason why, because I don't entirely understand it myself. I summarize the occasion for the visit. Thompson nods soberly; he's intimately familiar with the Bering Sea stalemate, having co-authored the Canadian position with Sir John after the first American hostilities.

Lord Stanley arrives precisely at four with a new aide-de-camp, Captain Walsh. Today His Excellency reminds me in appearance of a fastidious storekeeper with a good haberdasher, rather than a peer of the realm. I usher them into the inner office where the Prime Minister and Thompson are stiffly waiting. Sir John appears embarrassed, carefully keeping the left side of his face averted. This behaviour is so contrary to his usual ebullience that Lord Stanley picks it up at once, and he too begins acting embarrassed, smiling nervously and glancing about the office as if he's never seen the polished desk or drooping Union Jack.

Sir John is at least able to open the conversation. Speaking in a barely audible voice, he welcomes His Excellency and tells him that due to a sudden attack of exhaustion, he has asked Thompson to speak to the issue. Lord Stanley strokes his beard and murmurs words of understanding.

As incisively as only a former Nova Scotia Supreme Court justice can, Thompson lays out Canada's two main lines of argument: the legal principle of international access to the Bering Sea, and our legitimate claim to damages. These should not be excessive, he says, in fact might almost be considered symbolic of the larger issue, but ought to be sufficient to compensate our sealers for the loss of their equipment and livelihood. Finally, Thompson states that these principles are interdependent; they must be negotiated together, not separately, as the British Government seems to prefer, since that would only weaken Canada's case and would undoubtedly result in a less satisfactory settlement.

Lord Stanley nods reflectively while his ADC takes notes. Pondering the matter in silence a moment, His Excellency stares out the window toward the river. "It sometimes strikes me, gentlemen," he muses, "that Canada is much like a young man—at the stage of life where he mightily resents being led, and for good reason, no doubt, but not quite ready to stand alone."

To this there is no diplomatic reply. Thompson, a bit like the hypothetical young man, isn't ready to speak out; Sir John would like to but can't.

With Lord Stanley's assurance that he has no wish to dilute the Canadian position, we get on with drafting the wording of the telegram to London. In a few minutes I've taken down the complete text. I realize that nobody has yet sat down.

The purpose of the meeting fulfilled, the visitors still aren't willing to leave: the unasked question remains hovering over us. Finally Lord Stanley repeats how dreadfully sorry he is that Sir John feels unwell. "We must leave you in peace, Sir John, to conserve your strength. Perhaps it would be wise if you lay down for a good rest?"

"Thank you, Your Excellency. I'm afraid that would be no use. The machine is quite worn out."

Lord Stanley looks questioningly at Thompson and me but evidently can't think of a reply. He bids us all good afternoon and says he hopes to find Sir John in better health at their next meeting. As he turns to go, he glimpses Sir John's left side more clearly. He pauses for a second, sharing a revelation with himself, before moving toward the exit.

Lord Stanley, Captain Walsh and Thompson gather in my office, and I shut the inner door to give Sir John some privacy.

"Good Heavens above, gentlemen," His Excellency says under his breath, "I've seen those symptoms before. And I dread telling you this, but they belonged to a man who had suffered a terrible paralysis that later proved fatal. Of course Sir John's symptoms may simply go away. I certainly hope I'm sounding a false alarm. Still, you must get him to a physician at once."

His Excellency leaves, asking to be kept informed, but Thompson lingers. Pursing his full lips and frowning, he seems highly exercised. "The old man can't go on like this," he whispers resolutely. "He's doing for himself."

"Yes, but you know how he is. He's never learned to ease up."

"What's his dear wife got to say about it?"

"Sir John goes his own way."

Thompson sighs heavily. "He must keep his health, if only for the good of the country. If I were his doctor, I'd insist he get well away from here. Lie low and wait out the storm. We can handle the McGreevy business while he recovers his strength."

Thompson asks me earnestly to communicate this point of view to Sir John and leaves to return to the House. I think what solid judgment the man has, what integrity—a Justice Minister who actually cares about justice—and what a remarkable experience it would be to work under a chief barely a decade older than myself.

Sir John emerges from his office. He seems to be seeking my company, as if he can't bear to be alone. For the first time I see in his face the stigmata of fear. "I suppose they talked about me," he murmurs.

"They're of one mind, sir. You must see the doctor and rest up. A holiday was mentioned. Perhaps you'd consider leaving early this year for Rivière-du-Loup?"

"You know, Joe," he says, looking down at his lapel as he rubs it between thumb and forefinger, "I'm afraid of paralysis. Both my parents died of it. And," he adds slowly, "I seem to feel it creeping over me."

I telephone the front entrance for a cab to take him home. At least he'll have some peace and quiet there, and he'll receive a visit from Dr. Powell, and Lady M. can keep her eagle eye on him.

He says he feels chilled. He returns to his office to put on his coat but comes back a bit sheepishly, saying of course it's not there; since the day began sunny and warm, he told Lady M. he wouldn't be needing it.

Impatient with the delay, I ask Sir John if he feels up to walking down the Parliament Hill grounds to find a cab. He grunts, and we proceed along the main corridor and outside into the late afternoon brightness, all at a slow stately pace quite befitting a man of seventy-six. On the front steps I pause to let him catch his breath. The long green lawn shines brilliantly under a clear sky, several fat robins peck for worms. With no Buckley or any other cabman in sight, he agrees to walk all the way down to Wellington Street. Passersby tip their hats and smile in greeting, seeing nothing amiss in their Prime Minister enjoying a quiet afternoon stroll.

Buckley is just pulling Rosie up by the entrance gate. Apologetically he explains he'd taken another fare; he hadn't imagined Sir John would be leaving for home so early. Sir John steps up and climbs inside without difficulty. Planting my foot on the runner, I beg him to let me accompany him, but he won't hear of it: "No need for that, Joe, thank you." Settled in his seat, he drags the familiar rug of doubtful cleanliness across his lap, as though it were still winter. "You must be careful," he adds, before signalling Buckley to depart, "not to mention a word of this to Agnes."

A ball takes place at Rideau Hall tonight. The Macdonalds sent their regrets some time ago, and I'm attending as Sir John's representative and will report privately to Lord Stanley on his health.

On my walk down Sussex, I turn in at Earnscliffe. The twilit northern sky is full of innocent promise, the air hinting at some half-forgotten, revitalizing mystery. As I let myself in through the gate, the shadowy mass of Earnscliffe rears up ahead of me and seems suddenly tragic—a noble structure, helpless against the racing of time. A stark melancholy sweeps through me. I have to pause and wait for a moment beside the rose bed.

Rather than enter by my private door, I ring at the main entrance, since I'm not expected. Alice goes to fetch Lady M., who seems glad to see me. She doesn't find my visit especially odd—there's any number of reasons why I might need to see my chief of an evening—but steers me aside into the front parlour before I go upstairs.

"Remember, Joe, when I begged leave to share my worries with you?" Her expression turns anxious. "Tonight I don't know what to think. First he came home two hours earlier than normal. Then he asked for Dr. Powell to come and give him 'a good look up and down.' It's very unlike him, don't you think?" She peers at me with those great dark eyes.

"Did he say why he needed Dr. Powell?"

"He mentioned chest pains and shortness of breath—I think after climbing stairs at the House. Clearly that worried him. Apparently Dr. Powell found no *serious* cause for alarm, but he very much wants Sir John to take some time off. So I want to ask you—do *please* repeat Dr. Powell's advice to Sir John. If he hears it from all of us who truly care for him, I pray it will have some effect."

"Most certainly, Ma'am. I'll do what I can."

Climbing the stairs, I feel torn this way and that. Sir John's orders were unequivocal, and I must follow them; but what if his orders go against his own best interests for health, for life itself? Even then I must follow them. I know no other path.

I find him sitting upright in bed reading the London *Spectator*, with the *Saturday Review* discarded beside him. The New York *Nation* lies face down on his lap, holding open the article he'll read next. It's always been his custom to read for two hours or more before sleep, and tonight seems no exception.

The southern sky is luminous beyond his window, throwing into precise silhouette the dark branches of the maples. He inquires after my family, commiserating with me over having to leave them alone this evening, and it's clear from his first words that his speech is completely restored.

I ask about Dr. Powell's diagnosis.

"Powell is worried—but then he always is. I described my symptoms for him. I confided I've been feeling a lack of power in my left arm for some time now. Also an odd tingling in my left hand and fingers. More a nuisance than anything. When I hold a sheet of paper in my left hand, I can't grip it as tightly as in my right.

"Powell turned *très grave* and explained my condition in some detail. What happened today resulted from the heart being lazy, apparently—not able to pump enough oxygen to the brain. I was attacked by what he called 'partial brain anemia.' But now that I've had some rest, I feel quite normal."

He falls abruptly silent.

"And Dr. Powell's prognosis, sir?"

"Prognosis? That today's event is a warning. If I continue my duties in the usual course, the prognosis is—unpromising, I suppose. At any rate he didn't mince words."

"It sounds serious, sir."

"He advised rest."

"Ah. Then Dr. Powell and Lord Stanley and John Thompson and Lady Macdonald are all in complete accord. Unusual unanimity, sir."

He smiles and shrugs. "But in my case, unhelpful. As long as the House is sitting, rest is out of the question. And my absence from Ottawa isn't possible."

"Did Dr. Powell say—?"

"Now, that's enough of that. Off with you to drink my health with the Stanleys. Just tell them I'm sticking to my old habit of going on living. But before you go," he adds, his eyes darting to the dressing table, "pour both of us a small sherry from that decanter, if you please."

I pour. He sips abstemiously, sighs, closes his eyes. Before bidding him good night, I remark, with a stab of self-loathing for my cowardice, that Lord Stanley will be relieved he was right in thinking today's incident a false alarm.

Dinner Party

Now that both party leaders are absent with illness, the House is a changed place. It quickly becomes obvious how much the nation's business depends on these two men. The Members bicker and insult each other like bad-tempered schoolboys whose master has left the class; it's everything the Speaker can do to keep order. If Sir John were in his office down the hall, all it would take is Langevin sending a page to fetch him, and his steadying hand would be back on the helm. Laurier's presence too would have a calming effect—and not only on his own supporters.

Remarkably, it's the older of the two who returns from his sickbed first. For three days Lady M. succeeds in persuading Sir John to follow Dr. Powell's orders and avoid the stresses of Parliament. But on every one of those days, he calls me into his study to work with him on correspondence or draft legislation, in which he always takes a keen interest. At the end of the third day, he declares impatiently, "I feel like a fish out of water," rises from his desk, and stares out the bay window at the cedars blocking his view of Parliament Hill upriver. "I shall go back on Monday."

He insists on proceeding with his Saturday dinner party. To my eyes he still looks weary and pale during dinner: shaky on his feet, distinctly puffy about the eyes. Lady M. repeatedly begs him to sit back and let his guests entertain themselves, instead of feeling he must preside.

But by Monday afternoon the colour is back in his cheeks, and some of the customary vigour restored to his voice and step. His trim erect figure moves actively about the House once more, supplying encouragement here, telling a story there, giving the direction his supporters crave to shore up their confidence and sense of purpose. Everyone on the floor and in the gallery studies him closely, assessing his recovery. And all week he seems almost his old self again. He intervenes over and over in debate, serious or jocular as the moment demands, in command of the facts, the precedents, the flaws in his opponents' arguments.

John Thompson and I stand watching from behind the Government benches, and Thompson leans over and echoes my thoughts: "He seems perfectly well and bright again, doesn't he? Honest to God, I don't know how the old devil does it." Thompson isn't half so lively or cheerful himself. His beloved youngest daughter, Frankie, a vivacious and charming child, has become crippled with troubles in her hip joints. She's at the Royal Victoria in Montreal, where she faces a very difficult operation to be performed by Dr. Roddick, our best orthopaedic surgeon. There are doubts she'll see her tenth birthday.

By Friday the supply debate is in full swing. The steamy atmosphere inside the House is due only partly to the premature arrival of summer. Sir Richard Cartwright has enumerated a long list of Government budget items he considers offensive, if not downright immoral, and one of these is Sir Charles Tupper's salary. Having exhausted his store of excoriating adjectives, Cartwright gives William Paterson, MP for Brant South, the job of savaging Tupper. All concerns for Sir John's fragile health have now evaporated—but then he himself would expect nothing less.

"Might I ask the First Minister," bellows Paterson, "if the High

Commissioner told the truth to the people of Kingston?" Sir John is chatting pleasantly on the backbenches and ignores Paterson, who obligingly turns the volume higher. "My question to the First Minister is this: did Sir Charles Tupper speak truly when he said Sir John Macdonald had sent him to that electors' meeting in his constituency? And had given him a message to convey to the voters of Kingston? That is a question that can be very easily answered, if the First Minister will simply favour us with a reply."

Sir John returns to his seat. "Mr. Speaker, I cannot resist the seductive tones of my honourable friend. Sir Charles Tupper did indeed go to Kingston at my behest. I was laid up at the time, and he made his speech at my instance. And I fancy it had quite a considerable influence. In the previous election I'd been elected by a majority of only seventeen, but this time I was elected by a majority that only wanted seventeen of five hundred. And so to my Honourable Friend I say, yes, Sir Charles came out from England to give us all the benefits of his skill, his influence and his eloquence, and he did so at my special request."

Taken aback by Sir John's cheerful frankness, Paterson retorts, "Well, the constituencies east of Kingston went pretty solidly Liberal. The High Commissioner must have lost his eloquence as he travelled east."

"I'll tell you what he lost," the chief replies to delighted laughter from his supporters. "He lost his voice."

Before the dinner recess, Sir John decides he needs a shave and a haircut, and I accompany him down to the Parliamentary barbershop. He doesn't like to go anywhere alone anymore. We pass through the Senate lobby, where the walls are hung with oil portraits of past Speakers of the House. At Lady M.'s insistence he's taken to carrying a walking stick, a stout piece of black walnut, and he gestures abruptly with it toward the paintings: "Just look at them, Joe. Good men, mostly. Colleagues of mine. All gone now."

As we proceed downstairs, he says that whenever he comes this way he recalls one of his favourite stories. He doesn't ask if I've heard it before, so I've no idea if he remembers telling it to me at least twice.

Somewhere in the mountains of Europe there exists an isolated monastery, where a portrait is painted of each monk after he dies. In time an extensive portrait gallery has grown up, housed in a special room and cared for by one of the order. One day the caretaker monk, who's grown old himself by now, is showing the gallery to visitors. He tells them, "When I consider how all these years I've been gazing on these unchanging faces, and when I reflect on all my departed companions, I feel sometimes as if *they* are the realities, and we the shadows."

We reach the barbershop just as Sir John finishes the story. Napoléon Audette jumps up at our arrival and signals his staff to do the same. Audette is inordinately fond of Sir John, whom he's been shaving for years. They always enjoy a bantering conversation about politics, Audette being a staunch Conservative—or so he claims, perhaps claiming the opposite when he shaves Laurier.

After the hot towel is removed from his face, Sir John orders one of the attendants to bring over a framed photograph hanging forgotten behind a hat rack in the corner. He beckons me to his side. "Have you ever seen this, Joe?" I admit I haven't. Surveying a phalanx of forbidding-looking men in old-fashioned whiskers and black robes, I read the caption aloud: "Judges of the Special Court assembled by the Provincial Parliament on its opening, 4th day of September, 1855."

"That's right, ten years before *this* place opened for business. The Legislature sat in Toronto that fall. These august gentlemen were the leading judges back when I was Attorney General of Upper Canada—lions of the bench, the *crème de la crème* of our legal system. Look at them: Bowen, Loranger, Mackay, Beaudry,

Dunkin, Short, Meredith, Lafontaine, Drummond, Cherrier . . . All gone. All gone."

He settles back to let the barber do his work. Afterwards he reaches deep into his pocket and pulls out all his silver. "Now, Audette, I not only owe you for this visit but for the last time you came out to Earnscliffe." Settling their account, he distributes all his remaining coins to the attendants. As we depart, I notice them carefully sweeping the wispy grey remnants onto the front page of the Ottawa *Citizen*. I wonder if they're going to save them.

The House debates the supply motion all evening. With the week-end imminent, the Members' mood progressively improves. Many drift in late from the Parliamentary saloon with a few drinks under their belts, slouching carelessly and listening to their colleagues with vast amusement, shouting unparliamentary remarks like spec-tators at a boxing match.

Sir John leaves the speaking chores to his supporters but fol-lows the debate closely. I notice the eldest of the pages, a tall slim lad of fourteen in trim knickerbockers and a smart black jacket, rise from the steps in front of the Speaker's chair and shyly approach the Prime Minister. Sir John cocks his head to listen, and in a moment they're conversing earnestly, mostly Sir John speaking, the boy listening with rapt attention. Tomorrow when the chamber is empty, the "Pages' Parliament" takes place. The boys will divide into Government and Opposition, sit across from each other, and conduct a mock debate on some topic of the day. This lad will be playing the Prime Minister, and Sir John has agreed to coach him.

Adjournment finally comes at eleven. The mean-spirited taunts give way to cheers and laughter, joking and backslapping. I join Sir John on the floor to await final instructions before going home. Mackenzie Bowell, the Minister of Customs, comes over, pulls his watch from his vest, and says, "Sir John, don't you think it's time boys like you were home in bed?" They walk out of the House together arm in arm, and I follow.

Outside on the front terrace we pause to draw breath. It feels wonderful to escape the stifling chamber, to inhale the fresh quickening of a May night and stare at a black sky teeming with stars. A breeze blows the rich scent of lilac toward us from the heavily laden bushes rimming the terrace. The city sleeping beyond Parliament Hill lies at peace. Home to the legislators' sweaty quarrels and cigar smoke and feverish plotting, Ottawa always seems to remain blissfully indifferent to it all, going about its business of being a city where ordinary people work and spend and raise their families and struggle to live out their lives, long or short.

"Yes, it's late, Bowell," Sir John remarks after a moment. "Let's get ourselves home. Good night!"

Cabinet drags on all day Saturday. By half past four they still have several agenda items to get through, and I can see there won't be time to go home and dress before dinner. I slip out of the meeting to telephone Minette and tell her to meet me at seven at Earnscliffe, where I keep an extra suit of formal attire in my office against such emergencies.

After the meeting, the Ministers chat in small groups while Sir John huddles with Langevin, Thompson and Haggart at the far end of the Council table. I approach with some papers for him to sign, but Langevin gestures to me to stay away until they're finished. Sir John signals me to remain, saying simply, "Joe is one of us." After nine years at his side, you'd think they'd know by now.

Haggart is in the middle of pressing his suit for Railways and Canals. He isn't pleading this time, but attempting to make a case on practical grounds: Sir John is heavily taxed by the duties of the premiership, should consider lightening his burdens by off-loading the department to another, etc. Watching Haggart elaborate his argument with some skill and care, I wonder if I've misjudged the man. I must admit he's achieved considerable success, given his limitations. I notice his soft, liquid, almost effeminate eyes, a curious mismatch with his greying moustache. Do those eyes bespeak a sensitive heart beating away in that portly chest? Is that why Haggart holds such appeal for certain women? But there's no getting away from his blatant self-seeking—and now I hear that "Haggart's Ditch" was so poorly planned and engineered that it isn't even deep enough to handle the intended traffic from the Rideau Canal. This hardly inspires confidence in his ministerial abilities.

Seeing Sir John has no wish to discuss the matter further, Haggart claims an appointment and excuses himself.

Thompson interposes, "He makes a valid argument, Sir John, as far as your workload is concerned. Railways and Canals is an onerous portfolio. One might ask whether it's possible for a Prime Minister to take on *any* department and administer it effectively."

Thompson certainly isn't afraid of offending his chief. No other Minister would challenge Sir John's judgment to his face.

Far from taking offence, Sir John wrinkles his brow in thought: "A fair point, Thompson. But we know much can go wrong in these departments where contracts and patronage abound." Langevin reddens, as so he should. "The only reason I've held on to Railways and Canals so long is that no one I trust implicitly is available. If Chapleau can't have it, much as he's slavered over the prospect for years, how can I justify giving it to Haggart?"

"There must be *someone*, Sir John," Langevin suggests.

"Perhaps," Thompson states with judicious neutrality, "you could find a man already within Cabinet. Young Charlie Tupper might be moved into Railways and Canals—he has more probity than his father."

"Now, Thompson!" Sir John chides. "Anyway, we need Charlie for Marine and Fisheries."

Langevin moves off, commenting that he looks forward to seeing us all this evening. Sir John has invited him to dinner—a show of continuing support for his old comrade, a boost to Langevin's collapsing prestige.

Glancing quickly at me, Thompson leans in close to Sir John and lowers his voice: "These McGreevy hearings will be taking a lot of my time. They'll certainly delay getting the Criminal Code through the House. But I assure you, Sir John, it will be far better in the long run if everything in the case is allowed to come out. I do hope you agree. We must stick by that approach come what may."

"Come what may to Hector, you mean? Of course. The public must see that their Government has nothing to hide."

"And it has the added merit of being the right thing to do. That's why I've offered to equip both Tarte and Langevin with counsel at public expense. The people will thank us for it eventually. They'll understand that once we saw wrongdoing, we rooted it out. Tarte has no monopoly on virtue."

"As we have none on vice. But I'm afraid *you'll* have to carry that business through, Thompson, because I won't be there to help you."

Thompson looks startled, but Sir John just carries on: "Which brings us back to the party leadership. With Hector gone, who?" He looks hard at Thompson, who glances involuntarily away—the difficulty, with which I'm so familiar, of returning that unblinking, illusionless stare. "Now, I've no wish to embarrass you, Thompson. I know how you feel about the disability, if I may call it that, of your religion. It matters not to me, only to others. And I'm fully aware that Sir Charles Tupper has many detractors in the party, and you're among them. But either one of you would make a capital leader, in my opinion. If you're both out of the running, there's no obvious successor. I've been worrying this question for ages. In the end, I must confess, I'm settling on the idea of a stop-gap—a provisional leader with no serious enemies in the party. Someone without personal ambition, who can hold this Government together until a solution is found. And Thompson," he adds softly, having perhaps arrived at this decision so recently he can scarcely speak it aloud, "I've come to the conclusion that when I'm gone, all of you will have to rally around Abbott. Yes, I'm persuaded of that now. Abbott is your only man."

Thompson's broad face remains impassive, unembarrassed. This possibility will have occurred to him, too. John Abbott, the venerable Senator from Montreal, distinguished railway lawyer, former law dean at McGill, is a dull decent sort who enjoys people's respect. But sitting in the Senate, he's unable to enter the Commons; this would mean Thompson could operate as Government leader in the House, where it counts—the *de facto* Prime Minister. And Conservative Orangemen could find comfort for their delicate sensibilities in having a Protestant as titular head of their party.

Only a few months ago, Sir John assured me that Abbott, who holds a well-known abhorrence of politics, possesses not a single qualification for the office of Prime Minister.

"Good heavens, John, it's already past six. What's kept you all so late?"

Lady M.'s peevishness and cross words are a mask for her anxiety. I wonder how long she's been hovering inside the Earnscliffe gate, pretending to inspect the flower beds while watching for our arrival.

With painful slowness, Sir John steps down from the cab. She takes his bulging briefcase, the inevitable companion of his returns home, and scowls at me: a reminder that I should have been carrying it along with my own.

He does look awful. It's the end of a week of long days, and they all flew by so fast, and the pace is too much for him. He stands there in the drive silently submitting to Lady M.'s inspection. She makes a flapping gesture of exasperation: "Well, we'll simply have to postpone the dinner party. We can't entertain with you feeling as you do."

"My dear—how do you know my feelings?"

"Just look at you!"

"Our guests will be arriving in less than an hour. We can hardly send them packing."

"We can let them know by telephone."

"Too late. They may be nowhere near a phone. And besides, think who's coming."

"Then let me play hostess while you stay in bed."

He shrugs offhandedly, signifying there's no way on earth he'd allow such a thing to happen, and no point in bothering to say so.

Just before seven Sir John descends the Earnscliffe staircase at a measured pace, Lady M. on his arm. The transformation in both of them is astonishing. In forty-five minutes he has somehow re-created himself. His old resilience, his instinctive pleasure at entertaining in his own home, has risen to the occasion, bringing the light back to his eyes. Could this improvement reflect anything more than the simple benefits of rest? Yet I've often noticed how his wife, when not busy disapproving of things, can act on him like a rejuvenating tonic. She too is beaming.

Radiant in her ebony gown, Lady M. wears dangling silver earrings, and a silver pendant against her throat. As expected, her annoyance at me has evaporated, replaced by delight that Minette has arrived. The two of us are stationed at the foot of the stairs to greet them. For Minette's sake Lady M. will forgive me almost anything. Her sense of propriety even forgives the décolletage of my darling's pearl-grey satin gown, all on the grounds of her being French.

Tonight's is no routine dinner. Sir John has decreed that we make this a special occasion. Instead of the usual miscellany of MPs needing their ambitions encouraged and loyalties firmed, he's invited Laurier and the Sir Sanford Flemings, as well as the Thompsons, the Langevins, the Dewdneys, Martin Griffin, who has left the editorship of the *Mail* to become Parliamentary Librarian—and, to make Laurier feel a little less outnumbered by Tories, the new editor of the *Globe*, John Willison, a likeable and open-minded Liberal about my age. Such interesting company fills me with far more enthusiasm than usual; it's the reason Minette has been invited.

Once the guests have all arrived and assembled in the drawing room, Sir John leads us down the hall escorting Lady Fleming. Sir Sanford is next with Lady M. on his arm, and Minette and I bring up the rear. As we approach the dining room, I remember to look up to the second-floor landing, where Sir John has had a little balcony built to accommodate Mary's wheelchair. There she perches, as always, behind the railing, silently fulfilling her yearning for society. She peers down at the unsuspecting guests as we file past beneath her. Mary and I exchange our little ritual wave, and a small sad smile of pleasure spreads across her features.

Lady M. has placed John Willison between Dewdney and Thompson, where the Conservative Ministers can have good access to the *Globe* editor, well away from the embattled Langevin. Sir John believes in making the press as welcome and as useful as possible, rather than avoiding them. Educating Liberal newspapermen, he once told me, is a life's work, but also a means of seeking a constructive if not necessarily friendly response to his policies. No doubt Thompson will give Willison the benefit of his well-informed and balanced views. And yet a few weeks ago I overheard Lady M. trying to dissuade Sir John from even inviting Thompson, whom she considers arrogant and overly influential in Cabinet. For no discernible reason she also detests Thompson's spirited wife, Annie, now making charming small talk across the table with Laurier. "See here," Sir John told his wife at the time, "it was I who begged Thompson to come to Ottawa in the first place." I surreptitiously observe Annie Thompson, her fine eyes intent on Laurier's words, and think how heartsick she must feel, facing the possible loss of a child.

Minette and I are placed either side of Laurier, who is temporarily a bachelor again, Madame Zoë having returned to Arthabaskaville. He makes a point of declaring himself fully recovered from his bronchial attack and receives congratulations from the entire table. Laurier will have Minette to converse with about doings in their home province; sitting between the Popes insulates him delicately from his adversaries.

We're no sooner seated than Sir John rises, and we all rise with him: "To the Queen!" We observe the toast in flutes of excellent chilled champagne, quickly followed by more toasts, to the Dominion of Canada and the health of all present. Everyone is immediately enveloped in a mutual sense of warmth and fellow feeling. Ben Chilton fills the crystal wineglasses with a fine Margaux. The silver candelabra up and down the table glow brilliantly; the electric lights have been turned off. Flourishing his carving tools with elk-horn handles, a gift from the CPR on his transcontinental journey, Sir John addresses the enormous side of roast beef set before him. The rest of us follow Lady M.'s example and start in on the Nova Scotia lobster bisque. The dinner is off to an excellent start.

Conversation at first revolves around railways. Talking as he carves, Sir John can't help noting that the deadline to complete the CPR line all the way to British Columbia was the first of this very month—yet the last spike was already driven more than five years ago. Laurier smiles indulgently at the cries of "Hear, hear!" He's willing to share in Sir John's pride in such a crowning national achievement, despite having once termed the CPR "a monstrous monopoly" and perhaps still thinking so. Railways, however, have conquered the world, and Canada has grown into one vast, unlikely continental nation because of them.

None know this better than the Flemings, just back from Paris and a journey on the Orient Express. Sir Sanford's stupendous engineering career, from surveying the trans-Canada line ocean to ocean down to his invention of standard time, has been built on railways. The Orient Express he pronounces a superlative line, in a class by itself. His snowy-white beard positively blazes in the candlelight as he describes speeding across the lawless Balkans to Constantinople, replete with oysters, caviar and a five-star Parisian chef who would put the CPR to shame.

This leads Annie Thompson to ask if it's now possible to travel by rail from Constantinople to India. Although Lady M.'s own appetite for adventure is well known, she interjects, "But why would anyone wish to make such a journey?" She suspects the Indian subcontinent of medieval darkness, dirt, disease and superstition. Madame Langevin quickly agrees, adding that even the thought of Indian food makes her ill. But Annie Thompson persists. Smiling vivaciously at the older women, she declares, "Why, those are the very things I'd find fascinating about the place. I'd *love* to go there someday and visit the Marabar caves." Mrs. Thompson is a Halifax sea captain's daughter and apparently not averse to a little adventure herself.

Heading off the imminent charge of his wife's reply, Sir John reminds us that Lord Lansdowne, his favourite Governor General, went directly from Ottawa to India to become Viceroy with dear Lady Lansdowne at his side, and she has found it quite bearable. Willison takes up the theme, observing that Sara Jeannette Duncan, formerly one of the *Globe*'s writers, now lives in Calcutta as wife of an English museum official. A Canadian in India! This strikes me as thrillingly exotic; it reminds me of the CPR advertisement "Around the World for $600." Nowadays Canadians feel themselves nearly equal participants in Imperial affairs, I remind myself, and it's high time I saw more of the world.

"Miss Duncan," remarks Lady M., refusing to be sidelined, "once attended one of my Saturday teas. Marvellously clever young woman, but she insisted on publishing an article about it afterwards."

"Dear Lady Macdonald," Laurier says in his most gravely seductive manner, "as a gifted writer yourself, how could you possibly object?"

"M. Laurier, you are very kind. But if all my guests did that, I'd never entertain."

Annie Thompson speaks up again, mischief playing about her lips: "Your teas, Lady Macdonald, are the stuff of legend. As are your kindness and compassion. My husband and I were recently at dinner with Senator Boyd, who told a most interesting story. Evidently he was present years ago when you and Sir John visited the model asylum for the insane in New Brunswick." Several guests lean forward in fascination, wondering where this story could possibly lead. "The Senator recalled that you were approached by an inmate, a lovely young girl suffering from religious melancholy. She stared at you and said, 'Ah, Lady, I love you, may I kiss you?' And you made her very happy, the Senator said, by planting a kiss on her pale forehead."

Lady M. lowers her eyes, but as far as I can tell is not displeased.

"Capital!" Sir John cries. "That is exactly how it happened."

Between mouthfuls of beef, roast potato and fresh asparagus from the Macdonalds' garden, Sir Sanford Fleming takes the floor to remind us, apropos of nothing in particular, of the need for a Pacific telegraph cable from Canada to Australia. Sir Sanford considers undersea communication an immediate necessity to strengthen our political links—not only with Great Britain but the entire Empire. Imperial Federation is the coming thing, Sir Sanford believes. His old associate, Principal Grant of Queen's, keeps pushing it as the best way for Canada to outgrow colonial status without cutting ties to the Mother Country. As long as Britain conducts our foreign relations, Sir Sanford argues in his light Scottish brogue, we're little more than a dependency of

England. But Federation, with Canadians sitting in an Imperial Parliament in London, would give us a voice in the conduct of the Empire and a genuine role in world affairs.

Willison weighs in enthusiastically, and Sir John listens to their proselytizing with an indulgent smile. But the drift of the conversation makes Laurier uneasy; I notice him wringing his napkin under the table. If Canada were to throw in its lot with these grand Imperial designs, it would make the French an even smaller minority in an immense Anglo-Saxon sea. If I could, I'd assure Laurier he has nothing to worry about—Sir John has told me he considers Imperial Federation completely unworkable. But there's a tacit understanding that domestic politics are off limits this evening, so instead of joining the discussion, Laurier strikes up a conversation with Minette in French. Lady M. leans toward them, signalling a desire to be included. She prides herself on her command of the language.

Martin Griffin pleasantly redirects the conversation, recalling that Sir John visited him in the Parliamentary Library recently to inquire about some precedent set by Disraeli. Martin asks if Sir John would be willing to recount the story he told then, and Sir John obliges:

"It's simply that Dizzy had rather a way of putting forward his Jewish lineage. This was especially true when speaking in a heart-felt way. On the night I was his guest at Hughenden, he described some remarkable characters from days gone by, the Count D'Orsay among them. 'D'Orsay,' he told me, 'was a strikingly handsome man—as handsome as Saul.' An ordinary Englishman would have likened him to Apollo.

"Then he asked me how long I'd been in public life, and I told him thirty-five years, most of that time in government. 'Ah,' he murmured, 'I beat you. I have been forty years—as long as David reigned.'"

Ireland receives an airing over the salad course: Home Rule, the machinations of Lord Randolph Churchill to ally the Conservatives with Parnell, the stern policies of Arthur Balfour as Secretary for Ireland. Even this topic has a Canadian dimension. With our large Irish population, Home Rule emerged as an issue two elections ago, and Dewdney is especially exercised against it. Laurier is more sympathetic, of course, although diplomatically so. Others find the politics of Ireland and its sectarian squabbling thoroughly tiresome. I confess I'm one of these and feel relieved when Sir John displaces the subject with a wave of his hand.

Since Churchill's name has come up, he says, he has a choice bit of gossip for us. An English confidant reports that Lord Randolph's rich and attractive American wife, Jennie, has recently been besieged by none other than Sir Charles Dilke. The outraged Lord Randolph, who had been neglecting his wife for politics, has tried to knock Sir Charles's block off. "But as Sir Matthew Hale said long ago, 'There is no wisdom below the belt.'" This brings barely suppressed guffaws from the gentlemen, tutting from Lady M. and Madame Langevin, and an amused snort from Annie Thompson.

Thompson mildly disparages the morals of the aristocracy today, in particular their effect on our own youth. Shaking his white head, Sir Sanford replies that his youngest son, Hugh, is engaged to the Gormullys' daughter Ethel, who smokes cigarettes and drinks Tom Collinses and thinks nothing of riding a bicycle all over Rockcliffe Park in the masculine style. She defends these habits by saying, "They do the same at Rideau Hall." Sir Sanford would call her fast if she didn't charm him utterly.

With a faint smile, Laurier asks, "Is there any truth to the rumour, Sir John, that you've been offered a peerage? I hope so, because it may be the only way I'll ever defeat you."

"Ah, Laurier, you must know something I don't. But if it were offered, I'd have to respectfully decline. I can do more mischief in Ottawa than in the House of Lords."

"If it *were* to happen, what title would you take?" Laurier asks. Sir John replies without hesitation: "Lord Tomorrow."

Red-cheeked in the candlelight, sipping more dessert port than Lady M. would like, he leans back to take in the spectacle of his guests. He openly relishes their enjoyment of his hospitality, their willingness to get along together so freely and generously. From time to time he leans thoughtfully forward to make private conversation with Langevin, careful to ensure his old friend doesn't feel eclipsed by the political shadows looming over him.

Dessert is plump fresh Ottawa Valley strawberries mixed with blackberries imported from British Columbia by Lady M.'s special supplier and slathered with Devon cream. When everyone has finished, Sir John rises. He offers more port and invites us to take our glasses into the drawing room, where coffee and chocolates, brandy and cigars, await. Not for him the custom of separating the women from the men after dinner.

At last the guests depart, drifting off gradually in couples and groups, disappearing into the rapidly cooling night. They feel privileged, I'm sure, to have experienced such a rare and insouciant occasion.

Only Minette and I remain. The air in the Earnscliffe drawing room has grown close with the presence of such a large company and acrid with cigar smoke. Sir John asks me to throw open some windows before we go. He collapses into a chair in front of an open window looking toward the rounded charcoal shapes of the Gatineau Hills.

Lady M. appears gratified and relieved after all her pre-dinner anxiety. Offering a last chocolate truffle to Minette and selecting one for herself, she smiles. "Sir John," she says coyly, "do you think it quite the thing for your private secretary and his wife to be seen so frequently in the company of the Leader of the Opposition?"

Sir John calls from across the room, "In my own home? Certainly."

We leave him sitting there, black tie askew, spent but happy, cooling his flushed brow in the breeze off the river. It fills and billows the filmy lace curtains.

The River

The next day is the Queen's birthday but also the Sabbath, so the fireworks celebrations must wait until Monday. After a beautiful Mass at the Basilica I feel at peace with my soul. Minette and I spend a sunny afternoon outside in the garden *en famille*, playing croquet with the children, munching egg-salad and ham sandwiches, sipping iced tea. She has a kind and uncomplicated gift for making me forget the world.

On Monday morning I arrive at the East Block feeling rested and ready to work, only to find my assistant in a peculiar state: fidgety, not sure what to do with himself. With scarcely a word of greeting, he thrusts at me an unsealed note marked "Urgent." It's written in an ungainly scrawl on Earnscliffe stationery:

Monday, May 25, 7:30 a.m.
    Dear Mr. Pope,
Yesterday afternoon was summoned to see Sir John. Found him prostrated with a bad cold, voice very weak. Has once more a feeling of constriction across his chest on breathing, pain when coughing—quite severe, he says. It causes him to hold back his cough, which further oppresses his breathing. I applied a hot poultice and returned last evening to find him

somewhat relieved. Applied another poultice and gave him five grams of Dover's Powder. This morning I find him awake and alert and claiming to feel more comfortable. Slept well through the night, his usual six hours. I am keeping him in bed today and henceforth until further improvement.

Yours Faithfully, R. W. Powell, M.D.

The symptoms match those of three months ago in Kingston: the old bronchial cold, contracted this time, I presume, from sitting too long in the chill breeze on Saturday night.

I reply to Dr. Powell by messenger, promising to keep Sir John free of disturbances. Of course this won't prevent me from visiting Earnscliffe later in the day to make inquiries of Lady M. and the staff and get a better idea of what's going on.

I make the round of Ministers' offices, starting with Langevin's, informing them Sir John will be away from Parliament today. I'm careful to avoid raising the alarm. It's only a cold.

This time he remains in bed for two full days. The newspapers run brief items noting the Prime Minister is "slightly indisposed" and confined to home. I try to keep my visits to Sir John brief, limited to questions of substance on which I must have his guidance; but he wants a briefing on everything. He's restless and talkative and won't let me go, climbing out of bed to pace about the room in his dressing gown with his spindly shanks exposed. Despite continuing chest pains, he can't tolerate the inactivity.

He's put out that he'll miss the Press Gallery dinner at the Russell House tonight—always a raucous and potentially scandalous occasion. He reacts dismissively to Senator Howlan's newspaper interview advocating construction of a tunnel under Northumberland Strait to connect Prince Edward Island to the mainland: "Preposterous. Engineers think they can do anything nowadays." He fumes at the news that U.S. Customs has quarantined some

Canadian swine on suspicion of hog cholera, even though we have our own stringent inspection measures.

The Supreme Court has begun hearing *Barrett vs. the City of Winnipeg*, a case that will test the constitutionality of the Manitoba Schools Act. It's my opinion, which I venture cautiously to Sir John, that Manitoba's establishment of non-sectarian state schools is meant to prejudice the rights of the province's Catholics. He doesn't divulge his own views on the matter. No matter which way the decision goes, it will create problems for the Government.

He's most exercised by the Liberals' filibuster over the estimates for Sir Charles Tupper's office. Laurier and Cartwright have become quite obsessed with Sir Charles's expenses on his visit home during the election campaign. Yesterday's debate dragged on for eight hours. "The devils," Sir John says under his breath, "they're just wasting Parliament's time. Mark my words, they'll turn around and accuse *us* of delaying the business of the House."

The McGreevy inquiry has also begun in earnest. Tarte himself is playing the role of Grand Inquisitor, having declined Thompson's offer of counsel. He's been challenging Thomas McGreevy, who has taken the witness stand, to explain the incriminating contents of certain letters he wrote to his brother Robert at Larkin Connolly. Sir John listens to this without a word. Finally he takes a deep gulp of air; it's as if he's been holding his breath.

On Wednesday morning his impatience gets the better of him. After tea and toast he insists on dressing, coming downstairs, and joining me in his study to attack the correspondence. In just a few hours we get through a staggering volume of work. His capacity for answering letters with solicitousness and humour never flags, no matter what the state of his health. Over lunch, which he scarcely touches, he continues dictating, and I'm unable to do justice to my chop.

Lady M. hovers nearby, ordering the servants about in peremptory tones that she'd like to use on her husband. Over coffee she inserts family matters into the conversation, and I wonder if this is a signal I should leave; but Sir John gives no such indication.

Back in his study, he seems tired and slips into a reflective mood. He asks after the progress of my research on his memoirs, laughing gently at his own question: "Not that you've had any time to spare, poor fellow. When are you supposed to work on it, in your sleep?"

On the pretence of serving more coffee, Lady M. enters and suggests, for the second time in an hour, that he take an afternoon nap. He smiles patiently, reminding her he never naps during the day.

By mid-afternoon we've come to the last remaining letter: a reply to an anxious inquiry from the Ontario lumber baron Edward Wilkes Rathbun. How often I've seen the advertisements on page one of the Montreal *Gazette* for sashes, doors and telegraph poles from the Rathbun Company of Deseronto. Long a Conservative supporter, Rathbun wants to know what Sir John proposes to do about the planned American import duties on Canadian lumber products.

"My dear Rathbun," he dictates, going on to commiserate with the millionaire over threatened access to the U.S. market for his lath and railway ties. Sir John's reply looks ahead to the autumn conference and the negotiation of new trade tariffs with the Americans. "I don't think we should take any action until we see what the twelfth of October will bring forth," he concludes. "Believe me, Yours faithfully, etc."

With that, only housekeeping matters remain. We tot up three months' worth of Buckley's cab fares for reimbursement by Parliament. Sir John recalls the occasion when the estimates contained an item of a hundred and thirty-four dollars for his cabs, and some dimwitted backbencher objected. Between us we manage to reproduce, almost to the letter, the reply he gave then on the floor of the House: "I am sorry that the Honourable Gentleman objects to that small item. I do myself. But there it is, and here I am, in the last days of my life, unable to afford to keep my own footman, horse and carriage. Sad to say, my limbs are getting weak and weary and I cannot walk as I used to. That is the common lot of mortals—but it does seem hard if the Prime Minister can't be permitted to ride occasionally to and from his residence on public business."

He laughs and shakes his head. "I'm guilty of manifold sins of omission and commission, Joe, but enriching myself at public expense isn't one. I'll die a relatively poor man, considering the opportunities."

He carries on in this philosophical vein. "Procrastination, now that's another matter. I'll never live down Old Tomorrow. Guilty as charged. I suppose you know how I came by that?"

To other men it would be annoying or embarrassing to discuss the epithet their opponents use—not to Sir John. "I've heard it had something to do with Chief Crowfoot," I answer.

"It was actually Colonel Irvine who coined it when head of the Mounted Police. There was a chap who desperately wanted a commission in the Force and tried to get it through me. I didn't consider him qualified, so every time he came to see me, he was told, 'Come back tomorrow.' When Irvine heard about this, he told some friends, 'That's just the name for Sir John—Old Tomorrow.' He then gave the Blackfoot name for it, 'Apenakwis,' and it got attributed to Crowfoot. There now. Something to put in your wee book."

He suggests we move onto the terrace. I hesitate, wondering if being outside is quite the right thing for a sick old man, but find myself following him through the drawing room and the French doors and onto the rear terrace suspended above the cliff.

It's a splendid afternoon: dizzyingly bright, temperature approaching high summer, the spacious wooden terrace pulsating with heat. The Ottawa glistens as it surges toward the St. Lawrence. The far green shore shimmers in the haze. We've had no rain for nearly two weeks, and forest fires are burning over on the Quebec side, far up the Ottawa Valley. Dark smoke smudges the undulating horizon as far as the eye can see. A breeze from the west carries the unpleasant smell to our nostrils, like burnt toast, overlaid with the sour stench of sulphur from Eddy's mill. Sir John stares fixedly at two small tugs working patiently around the edges of a log boom anchored to the shore.

The majesty of the river, and his long silence, embolden me: "When you consider the past, Sir John, do you ever wish you'd done anything differently?"

"I certainly can't conceive," he replies after some deliberation, "why anyone would consent to live his life over again."

I realize he's taken my question in a more sweeping sense than I'd intended. "But what if you had all your accumulated experience to guide you?"

"Ah," he says. "That's an entirely different matter. We were speaking a moment ago of procrastination. Now, in most things I'd probably still delay. One of my favourite books, as you know, is Stanhope's *Life of Pitt*, and Pitt was fond of saying, 'The first, second and third requisites of a prime minister are patience.' But in other things I'd be more resolute."

"For instance?"

"Oh—the North-west Rebellion, I suppose. Some in our party think I failed to read the warning signs. They're right—even if they themselves did no better. But as we know now, if we'd acted more promptly on the Metis grievances we might never have had our little uncivil war. All those deaths, Joe. Executions." He pauses and looks away toward the curtained drawing room, as if down a long tunnel. "Perhaps Laurier was right. If we'd taken as much pains to do justice to the Metis as to punish wrong, they'd never have broken the law in the first place. Laurier's a good chap, you know. If I were twenty years younger, he'd be my colleague."

"Perhaps he may be yet," I venture.

He shakes his head sadly. "Oh no. Too old, Joe, too old."

I bring him back to the subject. "Without the rebellion, sir, we might not have got the railway finished." It's growing unbearably hot. I'd dearly love to remove my suit jacket but know that would give me an unfair advantage. Sir John would never permit it for himself.

"Oh, the railway would have got finished one way or another." He turns back to face me. "It would have been stupid to invest so much and leave it incomplete. Even the Liberals would have seen that."

"They'd have reversed their position?"

He looks mildly amused. "Yes, but I'd have been long gone by then. So you're right: the rebellion gave us the lever and the hammer. It saved my political life. And finally put the finish to Riel."

"Do you actually believe you could have stopped them from rising?" It excites me to be on the scent of my research again.

He strolls to the far end of the terrace and leans his elbows on the railing, whether to seek support for his weary limbs, or to better glimpse the Saskatchewan River valley in his mind's eye, or just to get away from mc. I move near his right shoulder to encourage him.

Finally he says, "I never thought I'd have to deal with Riel again. Surely we'd seen the end of him once he exiled himself to Montana. He'd even become an American citizen! When he turned up in Saskatchewan I was astonished. He was so unpredictable. He'd spent time in that asylum, remember."

"For good cause, do you think?"

Sir John shrugs noncommittally. "At first he acted quite sane. He did everything a good politician should—everything *I'd* have done. Meeting with his constituents, building bridges to the white settlers, and so on. I was worried he'd raise the Indians—it would have been like committing arson in the vicinity of a powder magazine. But he gave no sign of doing so."

"His intentions seemed peaceful."

"The man's a born leader, I told myself. All he wants is justice for his people. Some renegade whites were agitating for secession, but the Metis only wanted title to their land. As far as I was concerned, they could have it. They could live in security under the law like any other citizen. Settlement of the West would flow on around them like a tide around an island. But instead of being a little prairie Ireland with Home Rule, they'd be surrounded and swallowed up eventually by an English-speaking sea, indistinguishable from their neighbours."

"That would have been the best outcome."

"Oh Lord, yes." Sir John sniffs the thickening smoke and turns to face me. His nose twitches, irritated. "I started expecting Riel to behave in certain ways. Reasonable ways. That was my first mistake. I told Lord Lansdowne he'd likely draw up a list of grievances and bring a delegation to Ottawa. We'd parley. If we treat the Metis generously and liberally, I said, we can make them into good subjects."

"You'd dealt with Riel before, after all."

"We'd had an understanding over Red River. Why not again? Instead he crossed me. He started making outrageous demands."

"He thought the Government owed him something." That I remember well. By '85 I'd been in Sir John's service for three years, and most of the contradictory and baffling reports about Riel's strange behaviour were passing through my hands.

"Well, we did owe him something. He had his own land claim— his family property at Red River, forfeited when he was banished. I was prepared to make good on that. But when he sent a personal demand for a hundred thousand dollars in damages . . ."

". . . he became just another blackmailer."

Sir John begins striding in a small circle about the terrace, suddenly agitated. "But how could we be sure the demand was genuine? It came through Father André to Commissioner Dewdney, and through Dewdney to me. Riel had already broken with his Church. He'd declared himself a prophet. He was all set to appoint a new Pope and rename the days of the week and months of the year and all the continents and oceans, and God knows what other lunacy. Father André reviled him. But neither Dewdney in Regina nor I in Ottawa knew if André was truthfully representing Riel's position or just painting him as black as possible, so we'd crush him like a bug."

"You were confused."

"I was furious. I thought I was dealing with a cynical adventurer instead of a spokesman for his people. It didn't help that the Metis' petition for land didn't even come through Riel. So what did he *really* want? How could I negotiate with a will-o'-the-wisp? If only he'd communicated directly with me. . . ."

"But by then the CPR was threatening to fall apart."

"Exactly. We had all we could handle just to keep the railway alive."

And at the time I was too distracted myself, too busy mastering my own responsibilities, to appreciate the depth of Sir John's dilemma and frustration.

"Perhaps," I suggest, "the distance between the Ottawa and the Saskatchewan was simply too great." He gestures offhandedly to say that's self-evident. "You and Riel were relying on rumours and go-betweens. How could you possibly have understood his intentions?"

"And how could he understand ours? We set up that commission to settle their land claims. But the Metis either didn't understand it or didn't believe in it. According to Dewdney, most of them were illiterate anyway, it was impossible to explain things to them. But Riel was far from illiterate. He and I could have parleyed. Neither of us took the first step, and once violence broke out, it was too late. I must confess, I was almost grateful. I knew we'd at least salvage the railway."

"And what could have mattered more?"

Still, Sir John doesn't look content. His agitation has subsided into gloom.

"Sir John, have you ever seen the country as united as when it put down the rebellion? Remember the troop trains packed with volunteers. The crowds were delirious to see them off. And even bigger crowds welcomed them home."

"Oh yes. Nothing like a foreign devil to rally the clans. Even Montreal sent the Sixty-fifth Battalion, and it marches in French." He sighs mirthlessly. "The Metis, poor devils, had no idea how much the world had changed. They thought Riel would rescue them again as he had at Red River. But they didn't have a chance. The railway finished them."

"Yet they started by killing our soldiers," I protest, surprised by the heat in my voice. "Some settlers too. They sealed their own fate!" I feel foolish for saying this. Who am I to remind *him*?

"Listen to me, Joe. You'll never hear this again—not from me anyway. I understand Riel's position completely, if only in hindsight. He didn't plot the rebellion. He didn't plan the skirmishes, the killings. We don't *plan* such events, they just happen, and we're dragged along after them as helpless as everyone else. Our best hope is to hold on and live to fight another day. I lived. Riel didn't. That doesn't mean I wanted him dead."

I'm bewildered. "You'd have saved him?"

"Oh absolutely." The Scots accent is suddenly vivid, radiating through his words.

"But you had—"

"—my chance to do so? Not really. I had no free will in the matter. My final mistake was imagining the French would get over his execution. 'We're in for lively times in Quebec,' I told Lord Lansdowne, 'but the excitement will soon die out.' How wrong I was! Lansdowne never held it against me, for which I'm eternally grateful. But the fact is, neither he nor I believed the French would make a martyr out of Riel—a man who'd abjured the Church and been willing to abandon his own people for money. We couldn't believe the death of a single Halfbreed would undo my alliance with the French."

I work up my courage. "I should be the last to say this, Sir John, but I suggest you were misled by the clerics. The Roman Catholic Church let you down. It was a failure of intelligence."

"Perhaps. Even so, what could I have done differently? Told Cabinet to commute Riel's sentence after his appeals failed? And on what grounds? Placating the French? Then the English would have revolted. They'd have had grounds to string *me* up for asking their sons to make the ultimate sacrifice." He gazes across the river. "I was stuck, Joe. Pinioned like a butterfly—just as Riel was. However much the Metis deserved our sympathy, he'd committed high treason. He'd attacked the state and killed its representatives. I wouldn't have been much of a Prime Minister if I'd pardoned him. His only hope was a finding of insanity."

"Did you believe he could tell right from wrong?"

"That's why I created the medical commission. It was Langevin's idea, to give him credit. He thought it would show Quebec that every reasonable effort had been made."

I'll never forget my own role in that penultimate scene in the drama: the rainy overnight train journey through the autumn woods along the less-travelled line to Kingston, via Sharbot Lake, to brief Dr. Lavell, who had been appointed to the medical commission. My job was to dispatch Lavell on the first train west to examine Riel's mental state. As warden of Kingston Penitentiary, Lavell was assumed to know something about madness. In the end he'd deliver the fatal verdict of sanity.

Sir John permits himself a wan smile. "I have one last untold tale for you. No doubt you remember the French member of the commission, Dr. Valade. His opinion was far more ambiguous than Lavell's. Valade considered Riel an accountable being in some degree, but not when it came to politics or religion. On political matters, Valade believed, Riel was completely deluded—effectively insane. But when Dewdney telegraphed the commissioners' findings to me, he omitted that point. He led me to believe Valade too considered Riel sane and accountable."

"Dewdney lied?"

"He interpreted, distorted, obfuscated, whatever you want to call it. Valade himself drew it to my attention, but only after it was too late."

We look at each other. I don't know what to say, except to ask my question one last time: "But you yourself, sir: do you believe he was sane?"

"Lord, no. He was mad beyond a doubt. Not that it makes the slightest difference now." Sir John turns to re-enter the house. "Come, it's sweltering out here. As you can see, hindsight in politics is quite useless."

Sir John

Why I shouted out loud I don't know.

I was sound asleep. When I awakened, an ancient memory immediately sprang to mind, unbidden: waking in the Westminster Palace Hotel in London years ago to find my curtains and bedclothes on fire. On that long-ago morning I immediately pulled down the curtains and emptied the water jug over them and smothered the rest of the flames with pillow feathers. It was only when Cartier ran in from his room next door that we discovered my back and forehead were as scorched as beefsteak. Three days later I proposed to Agnes.

What was the alarm this time? By now I've learned to be more careful with candles. Another dream? Agnes rushed in as soon as she heard my cry. Was it she I was calling to?

I haven't even budged from my bed. She leans anxiously over me, her face hovering like a frightened moon in the long shadows.

She rocks me gently by the shoulders. "John, are you awake? Are you awake now, for pity's sake?"

"Yes, of course I am. It's all right," I reply. "Only . . ."

"What?"

"I can't seem . . ."

"What, John?"

". . . to move my arm. Never mind, it will get better in a minute."

"Whatever do you mean?"

"The feeling will come back. It takes time. It's happened before."

She draws back stiffly, frowning, bewildered. "When?"

"You remember. That day I came home early. But it's different this time—I can speak perfectly well. It's the arm that's gone."

I begin to feel alarmed. My left arm appears to be inert, useless—no longer mine. I try to move my left leg and my worst fear is realized. There's nothing down there but a faint, distant tingling, like the sound of a telephone ringing somewhere down the street.

By degrees I come to realize that my entire left side is paralyzed. Somehow Agnes knows it too. She's patting me helplessly, aimlessly, here and there, her hair and nightgown gleaming against the darkness, her flesh warm and sweet in my nostrils, and she's weeping.

"Your face," she says, barely able to get the words out. "This side of your face, John. It's twisted."

Standing up, she wipes both cheeks with the backs of her hands and turns practical. "Have you any sensation at all?"

Experimentally I waggle my right arm and leg, raising them one after the other, demonstrating their aliveness. "My right side seems to be fine." I sink back onto the pillow. "I'm half alive, at least."

I don't feel any particular pain: only a vast eerie numbness all the way down one side of my body, from shoulder to toes. But the numbness is powerful and seems to be spreading—leaching into my spirit, seeping ever so quickly into my thoughts. I sense myself metamorphosing into something else, something I don't recognize. I'd prefer to go more cleanly and decisively than this, not disintegrate by stealthy stages. Waking decay. Death procrastinating cruelly with Old Tomorrow.

Agnes preoccupies herself pouring me a glass of water, turning on the lights, hurrying downstairs to telephone Dr. Powell.

Left alone, I see myself anew, as if from a vantage point some-where near the ceiling. Looking down, I see a charcoal sketch, perhaps one of Bengough's caricatures in *Grip*: a jaunty-looking ancient in a nightdress tucked helplessly into his four-poster. But the artist's rubber has erased my entire left side, leaving me incomplete: literally a shadow of my former self.

"It's gone half past two," Agnes announces when she returns. She stands stock-still and stares at me, almost accusingly. It's difficult for her to accept I can't move.

Powell arrives at three, clumping upstairs in the semi-darkness. I'm relieved not only by his presence but the discovery that my own alarm has ebbed somewhat. But perhaps that's not good; perhaps I'm adjusting too quickly to my altered state. Ah, you can get used to anything, as my infinitely wise old mother used to say.

"See here, Powell," I tell him, "I'm dreadfully sorry for disturbing your sleep. I was just thinking what a good thing it's such a mild night, he won't mind a walk in the dark."

"Now Sir John, best not to talk. Try to conserve your vital powers."

"My vital powers are fine, it's my left side that's the problem. The point is, I *can* talk—not like last time. The worse for you."

Powell listens to my heart and investigates my symptoms, putting a series of questions to me, asking me to attempt a series of movements of my limbs, and it strikes me I'm the only calm one in the room. Powell's face is screwed into a grimace; he asks if I can stick my tongue out. Of course I can. He peers at it and mutters darkly to himself, "Tongue skewed visibly to the left."

Looking on, poor Agnes appears lost. In some sense she's already bereaved. I wonder what I can say to brighten her spirits. Having washed my face and hands and taken away the chamber pot, she needs something else to do. As Powell goes about his examination, I tell her lightly that all will be well and ask her if I've wakened Mary. Without a word she goes down the hall to look in on the child.

This presents me with a chance to interview Powell. "So, Doctor. Are we finally preparing for the last supper?"

"Oh, come now, Sir John. I certainly wouldn't say that. Not in the least. But I presume you'd prefer I were honest with you."

"Of course."

He pauses: how to put this to the old chap? "It's really too early to tell how serious your condition is. We'll have to see how it progresses. I should think by this evening we'll have a better idea."

"Ah, the dreary prospect of another day in bed."

"More than a day, I'm afraid, Sir John. I shall have to insist this time—really, your body is insisting for you. Not only must you curtail your official duties but suspend them entirely. You have no other choice. This is very serious indeed."

"A warning shot across my bows."

"*Another* one, Sir John."

Powell insists on remaining in the house until first light. I'm sure we could manage all right without him, but he's conscientious. He withdraws to take a cup of tea with Agnes, and I fall asleep.

By the time I'm conscious again, the pre-dawn sky is brightening, promising yet another lovely day. These short nights and long days appeal to me. More time to do nothing. Agnes and Powell are standing side by side at the foot of my bed, waiting for me to open my eyes. It feels odd to be observed like this, like some rare, unpredictable species of wildlife, possibly dangerous.

Powell puts me through my paces with the same succession of arm and leg movements and this time seems slightly more optimistic. "Partial recovery of power in left leg," he remarks softly when I manage to draw it a little way toward my body. "No apparent change in left arm."

Agnes is calmer now. She smiles beautifully at me, which gladdens my heart. "Your recovery has begun," she says.

By nine o'clock the sun is pouring in on my face. The warmth feels marvellous, and I quote my favourite Italian epitaph: "I was well, I would be better, and here I am." I'm now able to draw my left leg all the way up to my chest, although it requires a gradual and determined effort; Powell is rather impressed. My arm is no better than before, but I see no reason why it shouldn't imitate the leg. Patience is all.

Powell decides it's safe for him to take his leave. Poor devil, what a profession. He tells me he'll return after lunch, and in the meantime would I have any objection to his calling in two colleagues for a consultation? They're specialists from Montreal, McGill graduates like himself, George Ross and James Stewart. They can be here in three or four hours.

Agnes nods encouragingly at me; they have obviously discussed this already.

"The more the merrier, Powell," I reply. "We'll convene a little salon."

Shortly after the doctor leaves, Pope enters carrying his briefcase, as if it's just another day. No doubt he's been downstairs in his office, waiting. All these comings and goings create a reassuring sense of normalcy: the universe unfolding as it should. After night terrors, it's always a relief when daylight restores the banality of reason.

I wave my right hand in greeting. "I'm sure you've been briefed about my latest theatrics," I tell Pope. "I'm improving by the minute."

He appears less in command of himself than usual. "I'm delighted to hear it, Sir John. I must say you look very . . . settled. Composed, if I may say so."

"Now, about the two resolutions we discussed yesterday, before getting distracted by Riel—"

I impress on him that the matters dealing with the North Shore bonds and the Intercolonial Railway are quite urgent, and I must get them both before Parliament without delay. I instruct him to draw up the resolutions this morning, so I can give notice in the House on Monday. I want to know they'll be presentable.

As Pope starts down to his office, I call him back. "Oh, another thing. Is that estate document ready?"

He assures me it is, and Ben Chilton conveniently nearby to act as witness. "Do you wish to sign it now or later, sir?"

"Now," I tell him. "While there is time."

Pope, the good chap, has left behind the morning papers, and my eyes are instantly drawn to a headline in the *Gazette*: "Lord Salisbury Yields." The Prime Minister has made an announcement I knew was coming but still find dreadfully disheartening. He'll introduce a bill at Westminster prohibiting British subjects from catching seals in the Bering Sea, pending arbitration of our dispute with the Americans. Naturally enough, President Harrison and Secretary Blaine have received the news with great satisfaction. They'd been debating whether to dispatch three warships from San Francisco to reinforce their revenue cutters. Why do I have to hear this from a newspaper? It's the sort of thing that happens when you get sick and out of touch.

On the other hand, newspapers are a wonderful cure for a preoccupation with eternity. They create the illusion that whatever is happening at this very moment is the most urgent thing in the universe. Nothing else compares in importance with the latest news, so there's no need to look backwards or forwards or inward, just stay anchored in the present. I plow through today's *Gazette* and Ottawa *Free Press* and *Citizen*, as well as yesterday's *Empire*, *Mail* and *Globe*, which is enjoying itself spreading rumours of my imminent demise, political and personal.

Pope returns bearing a sheaf of documents. I sign the estate paper and some letters from yesterday, all done up in his copper-plate hand. He explains he's been able to prepare only one of the resolutions for the House, the other requiring him to go in search of documents in the Parliamentary Library. I find this disappointing and urge him to make haste.

As we're discussing the legal and political aspects of the second resolution, Agnes arrives with a tray of boiled eggs, toast and tea. Pope retires downstairs. I try to eat a little for Agnes's sake, although I haven't the slightest appetite, and she asks if I feel able to receive a visit from Mary. But of course I do! Far better my dear sweet Mary than anyone. "I just don't want you to become overexcited," Agnes says.

Powell reappears, black toolkit at the ready: time for more tests. He agrees to let Agnes remain. It's better for her if she's involved as he works away on me, having me move my arms and legs from one position to another. To my great relief, both left limbs get higher marks this time. Sensation and power have been steadily returning: I can now raise my hand to touch my nose and draw my leg toward my chest farther and more easily than before. What astonishing feats. How odd to be praised for doing what any infant can! Agnes gives me a kiss on the forehead, Powell a brotherly pat on the shoulder. I feel oddly moved.

I'm ready to get up and try walking, but Powell won't hear of it: he wants me strictly recumbent when Doctors Ross and Stewart arrive. Luckily there isn't long to wait. They come striding into the room like a pair of well-dressed plumbers on a house call, one short and moustachioed, the other stern and beardless. I've met them before on party occasions. As they're quick to mention, they were both present for my seventieth-birthday festivities at the Windsor Hotel in Montreal. I imagine they never expected to see me alive again.

After summarizing the latest developments, Powell stands aside to let Ross and Stewart observe my arm-and-leg tricks.

They seem pleased to see I'm able to extend my left arm behind my head, then outwards at a right angle to my body. They examine my face intently, as if they've never seen it before. "Left side still shows a slight deformity," Stewart tells Ross, who grunts in agreement.

"Tongue?" Ross asks me.

I extrude my tongue.

"Hmm," he says.

The three doctors excuse themselves to hold a consultation. Agnes and I make small talk about the household help and her plans for dinner, both of us desperately conscious the whole time of the deep, semi-audible voices from the hallway, half-fearing what those sombre rumblings might mean. The doctors sound as if they're debating some obscure, ultimately unknowable mystery.

At last they come back in, Powell acting as spokesman: "We're in full agreement, Sir John. A lesion, in all likelihood a small extravasation of blood, has occurred in the right hemisphere of your brain. The rapidity of your recovery leads us to believe the lesion is rather slight. This naturally gives us hope. With great care and perfect rest on your back, we may be able to avert a return of the symptoms—perhaps for a considerable period of time."

The extreme tentativeness of all this dampens my spirits. "Thank you, gentlemen. I'm sure you have to be cautious in predicting the course of these events. I don't know whether to feel blessed or cursed."

"Sir John," Ross breaks in, "the cardinal point is rest. If you accept the absolute necessity of rest in the recumbent posture, you may be able to ward off a second attack for weeks, even months. If not, it could come at any time."

"We apologize for not bringing better news," Stewart adds in funeral tones. "We felt it better to leave you and Lady Macdonald in no doubt about the situation."

I exchange glances with Agnes. Struggling to keep her courage up, she betrays no alarm.

"I think we both understand the reality, gentlemen," I reply. "We're much obliged to you for your frankness. Although to be equally frank, I don't know how I can just lie here with my eyes shut for weeks on end. It will drive me mad."

I ask Agnes to fetch Pope. In his presence, I explain to them all the necessity of informing Cabinet about my condition and issuing some sort of bulletin to reassure the public. We must be careful to keep the language sufficiently general and vague. I understand alarmist rumours have been put about, portraying me at death's door, which will do nothing for public morale, not to mention the stock exchange.

The doctors step away to confer once more, quickly returning to say the wording for the press can be quite guarded, given how quickly I've rallied since my attack. "After all," says roly-poly Ross, "there's no reason why, with great care, you might not recover completely."

"An optimist after my own heart," I tell him.

Pope has pen and paper, and we agree on the wording of a brief statement for release to the press. The medical posse departs. Powell, accompanied by Pope, is going directly to Parliament to meet the Cabinet at six.

After showing them all out, Agnes comes upstairs and strides to my bedside. Settling, she clasps my right hand in both of hers, giving me a long, moist, unwavering regard of heartbreaking tenderness, which seems to look right inside me. "Well, John," she says. "We have our work cut out for us, you and I."

What an exceedingly lucky old devil I am. How can I ever make adequate admission of gratitude for my great good fortune? The Deity, in His boundless wisdom, has blessed my life with second chances—in marriage and family and fatherhood, no less than in politics. Once declared politically dead, I rose to fight another day. Once a dissolute widower, I found the gift of Agnes. Once mourning the death of my first child, I received the joy of Hugh John's and Mary's births and the balm of their love. It's like being given two entire lives to live within a single span. It would be too much—too unreasonable and greedy and proud and sinful—to ask for a third, even though I do. God willing, I'll be up and about again in a few days or weeks. I'd just like a little more time, please, Sir—just enough to correct a few errors of judgment and neglect, some sins of omission or, more likely, commission. And a little more time to spend with Agnes. I move my previously truant left hand to enclose both of hers and squeeze as hard as I possibly can.

Attacks

In front of the entire Cabinet assembled in the Council chamber, staring into those drawn faces expecting the worst, Dr. Powell reads aloud the brief, cryptic bulletin:

> Earnscliffe, May 28, 1891, 5 p.m.:
> Sir John Macdonald has had a return of his attack of physical and nervous prostration, and we have enjoined positively complete rest for the present and entire freedom from public business.
>
> (Signed) R. W. Powell, M.D.,
> George Ross, M.D., James Stewart, M.D.

This is bad news but far from their worst fears. Seeing his listeners' uncertainty and discomfort, Powell offers to answer questions. He performs exceptionally well considering he's never met any of Sir John's Ministers before. He shows great tact in responding to all questions, no matter how foolish.

Knowing he's in a more intimate, privileged relation to Sir John than any of them, the Ministers assume he possesses complete knowledge of the situation. When will the chief be well again? How long before he returns to us? And the unspoken question:

how long must we wait before abandoning a lifelong habit of depending on his mastery of our fortunes?

Over and over, in words that barely vary, Powell makes it clear he has no idea. There's no answer to such questions. There are limits to what medical science can predict.

The next morning I confess to Minette that the state of complete uncertainty troubles me also. After nine years of givens and sureties in working for Sir John, I no longer know what to expect, even in the next hour. The world has begun to change.

I visit the East Block just long enough to leave instructions for the day and continue by streetcar to Earnscliffe. The last order Sir John gave me—in a whispered aside, while Lady M. was preoccupied with the doctors—was to summon John Graham Haggart and Collingwood Schreiber, MP, for ten o'clock this morning. I must get there before they do and prepare Lady M. for their arrival before she unceremoniously throws them out.

I find her in the kitchen with Alice. Lady M. says that Dr. Powell insists Sir John is to have only light nourishment to begin with. This is to consist mainly of beef tea and a little milk, to which whisky can be added to calm the nerves. Later he'll graduate to more substantial meals.

Lady M. listens gravely as I explain the imminent arrival of the two MPs. To my surprise, she accepts it with equanimity. "My guiding principle from now on, Joseph, is simply to do what's best for him. If Sir John asked you to invite Mr. Schreiber and Mr. Haggart this morning, he must have had a good reason. It would upset him more to prevent their visit than to allow it."

This strikes me as eminently sensible: the workings of a well-ordered mind. Lady M. is so unpredictable. I'm forever worried she'll see me as part of the cabal of forces that threaten her, constantly spiriting her husband away, burdening him with cares and demands beyond endurance, menacing his life. And yet she's fully aware that her own position in life is directly attributable to those same forces. Somehow she makes her private peace with this contradiction.

"Joe," she continues as we walk down the hallway, "let us agree, shall we, that the gentlemen will keep their visit as brief as possible. They must confine themselves to hearing what Sir John has to tell them, then leave at once. There's no need to prolong their stay beyond that. If you share my view, there will be no need for me to be present at the meeting."

I assure her I'm in full agreement. I ask how Sir John spent the night.

"I'm so pleased—he slept without disturbances and got his six hours. The moment he awoke, he began reading. His arms are strong enough to hold a book again. It's a marvellous sign, don't you think?"

"I'll pop upstairs now to give him my regards. When his visitors leave, I'll leave too."

She considers this. "Joe, it does him so much good to see you, just as and when he normally would. You are a vital part of his day. Without your presence . . ."

". . . his world would seem *too* changed?"

"Exactly. A very happy way of putting it. I trust you to keep him calm and untroubled, Joe. We're of the same mind—and, if I may say so, of the same loving nature. His life is in our hands now. We are his gatekeepers."

I find this a disturbing thought but say nothing. I only bow, retreating backwards into my office.

Sir John's reason for summoning Haggart and Schreiber is purely practical. Several matters within his portfolio of Railways and Canals require urgent attention, and knowing he won't be able to attend to them for an indefinite period, he's placing them in other hands. He's chosen Haggart because he wants to observe how competently he'll perform in the role he craves; and Schreiber because he doesn't trust Haggart. As the former federal Engineer-in-Chief, Schreiber understands railroads and can ride herd on his colleague to ensure he doesn't do anything too venal or stupid.

As soon as the pair arrive in my office, I lead them upstairs. Both are sombre and nervous. Neither has been in the *sanctum sanctorum* before.

We find Sir John placidly reading his newspapers, looking as if nothing untoward has happened and nothing in the papers per-turbs him. A silver tea service sits on the little parquet table by his elbow. For once he shows no interest in political chitchat. He thanks the two men for coming, clearly explains the matters to be addressed, and instructs them to deal with them jointly, reporting on their progress through me. As for why he's assigning these duties to both of them, he matter-of-factly points out that only Haggart has been sworn in as a Minister, but he has enough to do already as Postmaster General and can use help from a knowl-edgeable associate.

When Sir John asks if they have any questions, both are too intimidated by the situation to speak. "Well, if any difficulties arise," he tells them, "be sure to inform Pope." He gives them a smile and a little wave, sending them on their way. I've never seen Haggart so meek and submissive, yet he must be thrilled to be getting his hands, however briefly, on the coveted portfolio.

When they're gone, Sir John asks me what letters have come.

"Not many," I reply. "At least none of any importance." I hes-itate before adding, unable to repress the habit of years, "Should I bring them up?"

"Of course," he says impatiently, as if I should already have the correspondence to hand.

I don't fetch all the letters, only a few minor ones, to which he dictates brief replies. A more appealing task is responding to the cable just arrived from Princess Louise, Queen Victoria's youngest daughter and the wife of our former Governor General, Lord Lorne, expressing grave concern about his health.

These efforts seem to tire him quickly. I feel all the more justified in holding back the other letters, one of them a malodorous rant from a powerful Toronto businessman and party supporter demanding commercial favours. Some of these men have no shame.

I'm about to leave him in peace when Lady M. strides in, frowning. "Mr. Thompson is here, John. He knows he hasn't an appointment and will gladly come back another day."

"Oh no, my dear, send him up at once. I have something to say to him."

Thompson enters, twisting the brim of his bowler. His impassive face—he occasionally puts me in mind of the Buddha—is damp, and he pats his forehead with a huge hankie. Apparently the weather outside has grown hot while we've remained in the coolness of the old stone house.

Thompson apologizes to Sir John for disturbing his convalescence. He merely wishes to offer best wishes for a speedy recovery. But surely Thompson wouldn't come out of his way to visit Earnscliffe if there weren't something weightier on his mind.

"I'm glad you've come, Thompson," Sir John says. "Tell me about Frankie. Did the operation go well? I understand Roddick is excellent, up on all the latest procedures. We had him examine Mary, you know—her legs."

For a moment Thompson seems almost overcome. "You're very kind to ask, Sir John. Frankie's condition is still highly indefinite. Her operation should be under way at this very moment. I'm afraid we won't know for some time. . . ." He continues fidgeting with his hat.

"That's so often the way," Sir John replies gently. "You must have faith, you and dear Mrs. Thompson. Lady Macdonald and I had faith that Mary would get better—which she did, insofar as possible."

He asks about the House, and Thompson doesn't spare him: "I'm afraid it has deteriorated badly in the past forty-eight hours. I know the medical bulletins are meant to reassure, Sir John, but they've given rise to all sorts of rumours. They get wilder by the day—not one of them worth repeating. On our side confidence and morale are sagging. The other side is buoyed up. The Grits are quite without principle—like a lot of pirates preparing a mad attack. We have a plurality of twenty-seven, yet they boast they only have to win over fourteen of our men to be in the majority. Edgar and Cartwright egg their men on to be reckless in debate. Laurier only sits back and watches and waits."

"Hell's teeth," Sir John says. "What good's a leader who can't lead?"

"Sir Hector does his best. At the moment, of course, his authority is dimmed. . . . He's called a caucus meeting for Tuesday to rally our men."

"But behind whom?" Sir John is becoming agitated. Thompson glances at me nervously.

"I wish there were a clear answer. If we were to—"

"There's nothing for it," Sir John says abruptly. "The party needs an heir apparent. A man waiting in the wings. A man in whom everyone has faith, who can act as interim leader and then step into my shoes."

Thompson appears uncomfortable. We all know such a man doesn't exist. He asks, "Have you given any further thought to Abbott?"

"I have. I know what I told you last time—that he was your only man—but I've changed my mind. Abbott is too selfish. He hates politics, you know. He told me so himself. Any man who hates politics can't lead the country."

Thompson appears dismayed. "I must admit, I'd come to think of Abbott as an inspired choice."

"I've sometimes maintained, Thompson, out of your hearing of course, that the best thing I ever invented was *you*," Sir John exclaims. "Now you'd prefer Abbott, and he'd prefer Thompson. What's to be done with such people?"

"What about Sir Charles Tupper, sir?" This is my voice speaking. I can scarcely believe I'm offering an opinion on a grave political matter—yet Sir Charles seems the obvious alternative.

Thompson immediately scotches the notion. "If you'd been in the House this week," he tells me sharply, "you'd know that's impossible. Sir Charles is everyone's *bête noire*."

I retreat into my silence. There's no love lost between Thompson and Tupper.

"Leave it with me," Sir John says. "I now have leisure in which to contemplate the succession. I will let Cabinet know my preference in due course."

Thompson is disappointed. I suspect this is what he's always found so exasperating about our chief—his insistence on keeping power close to his vest, not showing his hand until the last possible moment. Thompson is a man of principle but also a man of action. He believes in collective ministerial responsibility rather than presidential authority. He'll make a superb First Minister one day, if he ever gets the chance.

Thompson asserts himself: "At the same time, Sir John, I do hope you'll consider giving up Railways and Canals. The workload is heavier than ever. It's easily enough for a full-time Minister."

"Assuredly. I will give you my answer tomorrow."

Thompson can see Sir John is exhausted and observes that it's lunchtime. Gently bringing the visit to an end, he exits as gracefully as he can. I accompany him as far as the entrance for a glimpse of the weather.

The Earnscliffe grounds are parklike and somnolent in the sun. The city's faint rumble reaches us over the arching treetops. "I'll say this for him," Thompson remarks as we linger on the step, a hot breeze stirring the shiny new leaves, "his mind is as acute as the day I met him. He never changes. Old Tomorrow forever."

I say something about Sir John's formidable constitution.

"Even so, I can't imagine he'll be in the House again this session, if ever." Thompson slowly and solemnly shakes my hand, with something like affection. "Good day to you, then, Pope. I hope to see you on the Hill before long."

Lady M. and I share a cold luncheon in the kitchen. Picking at her potato salad and bread and butter, she seems distracted and morose. It's pointless trying to converse; she doesn't even make her usual inquiries after Minette and the children.

Sir John has been having a visit from Dr. Sullivan, his Kingston physician, who has dropped by to pay his respects, and Ben Chilton informs us Dr. Sullivan is ready to take his leave; also Sir John has asked to see the latest *North American Review*. Lady M. rouses herself to see the doctor out, while I fetch the magazine from the mail tray in my office. It contains a piece from Washington speculating about who will run for President next year.

I'm conversing with Sir John about the Langevin inquiry when Dr. Powell arrives for his afternoon visit. He pulls up a chair by the bedside, as if they're two old friends about to have a comfortable chat.

I hover in the background while they talk. Sir John patiently answers the doctor's questions. I'm conscious of a deep drowsy stillness in the big house. At the heart of it lies this battered old man, whose illness now seems the epitome of his career, his entire existence. As long as he draws breath he refuses either to complain or to submit.

Knowing Dr. Powell will want to conduct a physical examination, I turn to go.

"Oh, don't leave us yet, Pope," Sir John commands lightly. "Stay with me and the good doctor a while. We happy few, eh? We happy, happy few."

He yawns uncontrollably, opening his mouth wide, not bothering to cover it with his hand. He lies back onto the stack of pillows and closes his eyes.

Suddenly Powell leans forward tensely in his chair. He rises. Pushing open Sir John's eyelids, examining each pupil in turn, he lifts the left wrist and counts the pulse. For a long moment he stands frozen, head on one side, shoulders hunched, the two of them making a disquieting *tableau vivant* against the white sheets and pillows and curtains undulating in the breeze.

Powell raises his head slowly and turns to meet my eyes.

"Stroke," is all he says.

He still breathes. Slender as it is, that is our one hope.

My capacity to think and act is paralyzed. Fortunately Powell knows exactly what to do: we must find Lady Macdonald, tell her what's happened. He'll look for her on the upper floor, I'm to see if she's still downstairs.

I descend the staircase in double time.

She's not in the kitchen with Ben and Alice. She was there a few moments ago, they say, and may have gone outside. I want to conceal from them what's happened but it's impossible, they can see it in my face.

Without a word I rush down the hall to the front parlour, into Sir John's study, through the drawing room and out onto the terrace. Empty. I even look into my office, exiting into the front garden, and make a complete circuit of the grounds past the henhouse and the tethered cow before returning inside and encountering Powell in the front hall. He hasn't found her either.

Conscious of the awfulness of leaving Sir John alone, we race upstairs intending to search the upper floors more thoroughly. We look into Sir John's room first. There she is, standing by his bed, staring down at his immobile face, one hand extended to his brow, shoulders quaking.

Five

JUNE 1891

Vigil

Rereading the advertisement, I still can't seem to take it in:

Campbell's Quinine Wine. Invaluable in case of loss of appetite.
Also recommended for indigestion, malaria and lowness of spirits.

Invaluable in case of loss.

I throw the *Ottawa Free Press* aside. Habits deeply ingrained have become useless. The habit of being the instrument of my chief's will. The habit of being by his side at all times. The habit of making my every breath an extension of his intimate mind. I feel rudderless, lost. My instinctive knowledge of his thoughts, opinions, desires, suspicions, values, hopes, fears, limits, my anticipation of his needs, my sense of what he considers right, wrong or possible, are all suddenly superfluous. Thank God, Dr. Powell's grasp of what the situation requires is sound. His deep unhurried voice transmits endless reassurance. I think he's been preparing all his life for this moment.

I assure Dr. Powell I'm available at any hour to do whatever is needed. I'll accept any task, any responsibility, any role he wants to assign me. I accept. I accept. I cannot be anywhere but here.

Sir John is paralyzed down the entire right side of his body. That half of him is, in a sense, dead—from his face to his toes. (Yet he lives.)

He has also lost all power of speech—a disaster, when one considers that his voice has always commanded the nation. (Yet he lives.)

And then a miracle. After Dr. Powell administers some croton oil to improve his circulation, Sir John awakens. He opens his eyes, slowly and as if from a great distance, onto the scene before him. He stares at us all. He blinks occasionally, fixing us with a mute, wondering, deceptively familiar, utterly foreign and strangely rigid regard. He's undeniably conscious—but to what extent is unknowable.

For Lady M. these signals of renewed life are enough. To her they mean he'll soon be speaking again, if not moving, walking and living as her husband of old. This isn't just a pipe dream, she tells me with triumphant authority. She clearly suspects me of callow unbelief. She reminds me that Sir John's splendid constitution has surprised everyone over and over, and it will do so once more. And from the back of my mind, from the back of the hall, I hear that inebriated supporter at the rally in Toronto bawling, "You'll never die, John A.!"

Dr. Powell's next orders are directed to me. I'm to dispatch messengers to two leading Ottawa physicians, asking them to attend immediately at Earnscliffe. One is Dr. Wright, a medical man of considerable reputation, and the other Sir James Grant, who treated Sir John twenty years ago for his gallstone attack. By the same messengers I convey brief notes written by Powell on Earnscliffe stationery to Lord Stanley and Sir Hector Langevin, informing them of Sir John's stroke in simple, unambiguous terms. Finally, a carefully worded note goes out in my own hand to Hugh John Macdonald, who like Sir Hector is at this moment attending the sitting in the House. My pen quivers as I write.

The messengers leave Earnscliffe at five forty-five. By half past six Hugh John arrives at the main entrance in Buckley's carriage. The poor old cabman is beside himself, on the verge of tears; he too wants to stay and help. He assures me he'll light candles for Sir John tonight.

Hugh is grim-faced but rock-steady as he embraces his step-mother in the front hall. Before going upstairs to his father, he hands me a sealed note from Sir Hector Langevin addressed to Dr. Powell. With my long habit of opening Sir John's correspondence, I unthinkingly tear open the envelope and read the note inside:

My dear Doctor:
I have just received your letter and I am so grieved that I can hardly write. Please let me know at the House of Commons by letter how he is after eight o'clock.
Yours truly, Hector L. Langevin

I go upstairs. Sir John is conscious and struggling to say something to his son. He plucks at Hugh's sleeve with his good hand, but no words emerge, not even a grunt. He is mute yet imploring. Hugh looks stricken and pats his father's hand.

By the time Doctors Wright and Grant arrive, the deep golden light of early evening is flooding the downstairs rooms with beauty, mocking our sorrow and fear. The physicians join Dr. Powell in the bedroom. For the next half hour, Lady M. comes in and out of my office, squeezing her palms together, pressing down the folds of her skirt, abruptly taking the tray with Mary's supper away from Alice and carrying it upstairs herself. When the doctors emerge from their examination, leaving Ben Chilton and Alice in charge of Sir John, they ask Lady M., Hugh and me to join them in the drawing room.

Sir James Grant's beard is silver, his accent Scottish-patrician. As the senior of the three physicians, he pronounces the diagnosis: "We are unanimous, Lady Macdonald. Sir John has suffered a brain hemorrhage into the left hemisphere, chiefly confined to the motor area. Considering his poor health prior to this attack, and his advanced age, we do not expect him to recover his speech."

I watch Lady M.'s face as she absorbs this blow. She blinks. Otherwise her steadfast expression suggests she'll hold on to her private hopes, whatever expert opinion might say to the contrary.

"We believe it very fortunate," Sir James continues, "that Sir John was resting in a recumbent position when the stroke came. That is the most favourable circumstance for such an event, as the heart wasn't overly disturbed. Under other conditions, there would have been greater extravasation—and greater damage to the nerve centres of the brain."

This portentous information is followed by silence. Exchanging a pained glance with Hugh, Lady M. waits for further details, but the doctors seem reluctant, or unable, to provide them. Hugh, his expression sadder than I've ever seen it, faces forward like a good soldier, ready to accept the cheerless finality of the verdict. I want him to scream, to cry out in protest and outrage and disbelief.

"In that case, gentlemen," says Lady M., taking in all three doctors with a sweeping imperious glance, "what can we do to make my husband more comfortable? Happier?"

A system of four-hour watches by the bedside is agreed on. The order of precedence in the new hierarchy is clear: at its apex is Dr. Powell, advised by his two physician colleagues; then Lady M., who will assume general charge of Sir John's nursing care under the doctors' supervision; then a male nurse—yet another James Stewart, shortly to arrive from the Dominion Police—followed by the rest of us. Performing watch duty with Lady M. and Hugh

John and Ben and me will be Sir John's old colleague and friend from the North-west, Edgar Dewdney, now Minister of the Interior, whom I'd begun to think of as Riel's real executioner. Sir John's diet will continue as prescribed earlier by Dr. Powell, provided he can still swallow nourishment. My first shift is tomorrow morning.

The doctors have jointly prepared a medical bulletin; I take it into my office to type, with several carbon copies for official purposes. While Powell remains in the room with Sir John—he fears another emergency could occur at any moment—Sir James Grant and I will drive to Parliament to deliver the bulletin to the press gallery and the requested note to Sir Hector.

Signed by all three physicians, the bulletin describes Sir John's condition as precarious:

He experiences great nervous prostration, although quite conscious. No diversity of opinion as to the present state, which is the result of hemorrhage into the brain.

Sir James Grant's note to Sir Hector is blunter:

I have seen Sir John. Brain hemorrhage. Entire loss of speech. Condition hopeless.

Word comes from Rideau Hall that Lord Stanley is on his way to Earnscliffe on foot. He wishes a briefing by the doctors, and an hourly report afterwards by telephone.

Buckley drives Sir James Grant and me to Parliament Hill at speed. We proceed directly to the Commons where the evening session is in progress. The MPs are hotly debating Laurier's motion to censure Sir Charles Tupper for breaching his diplomatic duties. Cartwright is just completing his attack on the

Government's perfidy, his voice etched with sarcasm, and Mackintosh, the Conservative Member for Ottawa City, is rising to defend Sir Charles, as I step from behind the curtain and slip down through the Government benches to hand the medical bulletin and Sir James's note to Sir Hector.

Head bent forward, Sir Hector stares at the note without moving. After an interval he transfers it to his left hand and takes an equally long time to read the medical bulletin. Finally passing them to Thompson, he crosses the floor to whisper in Laurier's ear. Laurier looks stunned. He and Sir Hector look wordlessly at one another.

Mackintosh breaks off his remarks, bows to the Speaker, and sits down. Sir Hector is recognized. The Members are uncommonly quiet, knowing what this must be about. Sir Hector speaks in halting phrases: "I have the painful duty to announce to the House . . . that the news from Earnscliffe just received . . ." He reads out the text of the medical bulletin, stumbling over the words, and makes a motion to adjourn at once, which Laurier seconds.

At first the House is strangely immobilized. Members lean toward each other muttering and gradually rise in twos and threes and fours on both sides to stream down among the benches and converge in the aisle. Conservatives and Liberals mingle in random confusion, addressing one another in low tones, forgetting their rancour in a rare instant of shared feeling. Some of them delicately approach Langevin, who appears about to collapse. He hands the note around from one to another, then sits frozen in his place staring straight ahead, tears streaming down his cheeks.

The spirit filling the chamber comes as a revelation: we at Earnscliffe are far from alone in our grief. These battle-scarred men of action, some of them rough characters hardened by years of no-holds-barred politicking, are asking themselves how the nation can possibly go on without him. We've never known an hour when he wasn't at or very near the helm. All of us knew this day had to come, but now that it's here we don't know what to do.

Toward midnight the Cabinet assembles at Earnscliffe. The Ministers arrive in a succession of cabs, solemnly doffing their hats and entering the house, faces set. They know they can't see Sir John but want to pay their respects to Lady M., and she seems gratified by their presence. Erect and unbroken, she nods graciously at their fumbling attempts at consolation, their clumsy but sincere assurances of loyalty and friendship. The Ministers mill about the drawing room sipping tea and sherry and trying, not always successfully, to avoid slipping into their customary conviviality.

Shortly after one o'clock, much to the relief of the household staff, they depart. I decide to leave with them. A part of me wants to stay, if only to keep Lady M. and Mary company, but they won't lack for support. Hugh John and his family have moved back from their hotel to be here, and Dr. Powell is taking up residence in the servants' quarters; a small leather trunk containing his instruments, medicines and clothes has already arrived. Even so, it feels wrong to abandon my chief to the fate of staring at the walls. I have to force myself to break away from Earnscliffe's iron grip and go home.

The next morning's papers carry a front-page story from London. Lord Salisbury, "wishing to please the Canadians," is hesitating before agreeing to Secretary Blaine's demands for exclusive American rights in the Bering Sea. Evidently the uproar of protest across Canada has taken the British Prime Minister by surprise; perhaps public opinion has some effect after all. Meanwhile the warship USS *Bear* has already left the port of San Francisco for Alaska, where it will enforce a closed season on seals—closed, that is, to

Canadian boats—and police the sealing grounds until a settlement is reached. It seems preposterous that Sir John doesn't know
any of this.

Just as she once used sign language to communicate with him
in the House, Lady M. has devised a novel method of communi-
cating with her husband. He still has the use of his left arm and
leg; even better, we've determined he can understand what is said
to him. And so she has him responding to questions by a squeeze
of his left hand in hers—an answering pressure means yes, the
absence of pressure means no. By this means he's already telling
us whether he wishes to take nourishment or be turned in bed or
sip a little milk doctored with whisky.

"It does no good," Lady M. instructs, "to ask him a question
that can't be answered yes or no. Best of all is to say, 'If you wish
such-and-such, squeeze my hand.' You'll soon see—he knows
exactly what he wants."

And it's true: when I feel Sir John's dry old hand in mine as I
ask him some elementary question, his gnarled fingers press my
palm in response. Behind the impenetrable wall of silence, his
powers of observation and thought are still functioning, however
improbably. Through that hand, his will speaks to me as clearly as
ever, and more intimately.

His eyes speak too. At one point during my second shift, they
begin darting agitatedly downwards, accompanied by odd wag-
ging motions of his left hand. I'm at a loss to understand what
he wants. I'm alone at the time, Lady M. busy elsewhere in the
house and Nurse Stewart taking one of his brief naps. Finally, as
I sit down at the end of the bed, Sir John startles me by giving
me a sharp kick in the backside with his left foot. Wriggling his
leg, he points his toe toward the bedpan on the vacant chair
alongside.

And so, with much awkwardness and embarrassment on my
part, I position the thing in place and witness my chief's privates

for the first time. This little ceremony performed, he closes his eyes and drifts off into apparently contented sleep.

The torrid heat continues, the skies remain cloudless. The sun looks unnaturally red both at rising and setting. A sultry smoke-scented wind blows down the Ottawa Valley and across the river, bringing the taste of ash.

As the hard glare beats down on Earnscliffe's roof and walls, we work to keep Sir John as comfortable as possible. The blinds and curtains in his room remain closed, filtering a mysterious light on Lady M. as she moistens his face, chest and arms with a cloth soaked in scented water. Visits are restricted to family and very close friends and colleagues. Even they are instructed to tread quietly on the gravel paths below Sir John's window. Disturbances of any kind must be kept to a minimum. Orders have been given to remove the bells on the Sussex streetcars that warn passengers the tram is about to start. Tugboats towing the log booms on the river must muffle their engines and no longer sound their whistles as they pass beneath the cliff. The doctors believe the first forty-eight hours after a stroke are the most dangerous, the most likely to bring on a second, possibly fatal attack.

Even as the world beyond the hushed bedchamber keeps a respectful distance, it remains highly aware of the battle being waged within. From Balmoral, the Queen cables Lord Stanley expressing her sorrow; she asks His Excellency to give her sympathies and fondest hopes to Lady Macdonald. Lord Stanley himself visits several times a day accompanied by Captain Walsh. Perhaps because there's little Vice-Regal authority he can exercise in the matter, the Governor General has forbidden cricket matches and other entertainments at Rideau Hall until the Prime Minister is out of danger. From India, the Viceroy also sends a cable; sadly, the contents make clear that Lord Lansdowne has been misinformed and assumes Sir John has passed away.

Such tales keep circulating, we know not from where or whom. In an attempt to keep rumour at bay, Dr. Powell and his colleagues issue four medical bulletins a day: at 6 a.m., 11 a.m., 2 p.m. and 6 p.m. The latest reads:

> The Premier passed a quiet day, and we find no alteration in his general symptoms. He retains consciousness and is much as in the past two days. He is free from suffering.

People of all ages and classes stop to read the bulletins as I post them on the Earnscliffe gate. Among them are reporters from every daily in the nation. On the lawn outside the wrought-iron fence, the Canadian Pacific Railway has pitched a bell tent to house a telegraph operator and key, and the newsmen cluster there around the clock, within steps of Lady M.'s zinnia bed, supplied with the means to keep their papers informed of the latest developments. They frequently glance up to the curtained second-storey windows, as if expecting something or someone to materialize, or willing events to speed up so they'll have something new to write about.

Sir John drowses through the heat of the day. He is liveliest in the early morning and evening, when his eyes stay open an hour or two at a time, taking in everything with seeming interest.

The most dangerous forty-eight hours have now passed. Although Dr. Powell refuses to speculate publicly, he confides to Lady M., who confides it to me, that the sheer passage of time may have permitted the brain tissue to absorb some of the blood, easing the pressure of the hemorrhage—but to what extent, and with what result, is unclear. To judge from the radiant smile on her face, Lady M. takes Powell's observation as grounds for encouragement. Overhearing her optimistic explanation to me, he glowers behind her back and emphatically shakes his head.

Lady M. remains in the room morning, noon and night. At first I thought this was because she didn't trust us to perform our duties properly, but now I realize she simply can't be away from him.

"Mother," Hugh John tells his stepmother, "it's after midnight. You simply must get some sleep. Don't be afraid—rest as long as you wish, Joseph and Dewdney and I will manage until you wake up."

Reluctantly she acquiesces and leaves the bedroom, but returns barely an hour later just as Hugh John and I are finishing a round of cards by lamplight. She couldn't sleep any longer; she'd rather not lie in the dark with her eyes open, she explains matter-of-factly, and needs to be up and doing things.

This sounds like a recipe for exhaustion and collapse. Yet I know exactly what she means: I too must be here, close to him. Even when Sir John worked me off my feet, I've never felt as bone-weary as I do now, but still want nothing else than to keep my place in the rotation of strictly scheduled four-hour watches. The rotation can put me at his bedside at dawn or in the mid-afternoon or late at night. After a few days of this, I lose all sense of time. Between shifts I attend to his correspondence as he would wish me to, acknowledging the countless sympathy letters that pour in daily and, in those rare instances where the writer is unaware of Sir John's illness, providing a holding letter "until such time as he can reply himself"—this on Lady M.'s instructions.

One such letter comes from South Africa, postmarked nearly a month ago. It's written by the Prime Minister of the Cape Colony:

Cape Town, 8th May, 1891
    Dear Sir John,
    I wish to write and congratulate you on winning the elections in Canada. I read your manifesto and I could understand the issues. If I might express a wish, it would be that we could

meet before our stern fate claims us. I might write pages, but I feel I know you and your politics as if we had been friends for years. The whole thing lies in the question Can we invent some tie with our mother country that will prevent separation? It must be a practical one, for future generations will not be born in England. The curse is that English politicians cannot see the future. They think they will always be the manufacturing mart of the world, but do not understand what protection coupled with reciprocal relations means. I have taken the liberty of writing to you; if you honour me with an answer, I will write again.

Yours, Cecil J. RHODES.

At other times I stand greeting the few visitors to Earnscliffe who have special dispensation to enter the grounds, while others are turned away by the policeman on duty. Or I find messengers to carry prescriptions to pharmacies for Dr. Powell, or type up the latest medical bulletin and walk down the gravel pathway to post it on the gate. It gets to the point where I feel drained and order myself home. Minette never knows when to expect me; she's given up asking. I fall into a dead sleep for a few hours, then jerk awake, dress, eat, and return to Earnscliffe to resume my place in the vigil.

We vigil-keepers rely on visitors for news of the outside world. Some of the stories reaching our ears are consoling, others appalling. On Sunday morning, the latest medical bulletin was read from the pulpits of churches across the Dominion; sermons were delivered about Sir John's great services to the country, and prayers uttered by all faiths that his life be spared. In the House of Commons, some relic-hunter has stolen Sir John's nameplate from his seat, where it has been ever since the Parliament Buildings opened. In Toronto, the newspapers keep floods of inquirers at bay by posting hourly reports from their Ottawa correspondents.

Even so, two of the less responsible Toronto papers have prematurely reported Sir John's death; the "news" spread across the city in no time and was contradicted only with difficulty.

The political gossip is becoming more virulent. The initial outpouring of communal grief for Sir John has passed, and the Liberals have begun plotting to bring down the Government as soon as possible, or force creation of a new one. One Liberal paper has published an editorial urging the Opposition to take full advantage of Sir John's illness and push the Government into submission. The *Globe* too is up to its usual mischief. First it speculated on Conservative plans to form a new Cabinet in the event of Sir John's death; now *Globe* editorialists are musing on the possibility of a coalition government. Even though the Conservatives have no need to entertain such a desperate notion, the *Globe* airily dismisses a coalition as unacceptable to the Liberals! Such a thing is "out of the question," the paper sniffs: "The Liberals would not coalesce with Tupper or Langevin upon any terms, nor join Abbott or Thompson except upon a clear understanding that the National Policy should be abandoned in favour of free trade with the United States. Whoever Sir John's successor may be, the task before him is one of extraordinary difficulty. With Sir John, it has always been, 'After me, the deluge.'"

The organs of the Opposition are acting as if he were already in his grave. To compound this crude and tasteless presumption, the Montreal *Gazette* repeats the *Globe* editorial even while condemning it. The *Gazette* goes on to demolish a Liberal-sponsored proposal to dissolve Parliament on the grounds of national emergency and hold an election immediately after Sir John's death.

To ensure that Lady M. doesn't run across such upsetting articles, Hugh John and I ban all newspapers from Earnscliffe.

Liberal machinations are increasing the pressure on the Governor General to name a new Prime Minister. Although some Conservatives would welcome such a move, Lord Stanley adamantly refuses to make any such appointment as long as Sir John lives. He already has a Prime Minister, he insists; he will do nothing to compromise that article of faith.

The Governor General's stand upsets John Thompson, who shares his indignation with me during a visit to Earnscliffe. Knowing Thompson has declined the highest office himself, I'm surprised he opposes His Excellency's position and in all innocence I ask him why. His reply is testy—or perhaps, in my exhausted state, I'm simply more thin-skinned than usual: "My dear Pope, if you were a constitutional lawyer, you'd know that the Governor General of Canada has no right—*no right*—to be without a government and a First Minister one hour longer than he can help. Anything less is a betrayal of democracy."

I see his point immediately. But as irrational as it may be, imagining any other man occupying Sir John's place seems a gross imposture. Gagged and bound, he still rules Canada. He'll rule it until he enters its earth.

The press views Dr. Powell as aloof and secretive and overly inclined to withhold information. He takes me aside in the stifling shadows of the sickroom, Sir John sleeping behind us, covered by a single sheet and lying in a state of utter repose I've become used to, as if he's only now getting the rest he so richly deserves. Powell confides he's under tremendous pressure to publish details of Sir John's symptoms and vital signs: temperature, pulse rate, digestion, etc. He understands why the papers are so hungry for information, but it troubles him that colleagues in the medical profession are bombarding him with letters urging him to divulge these facts to the press. Why? he asks. Nosiness? Professional rivalry? Sheer morbid curiosity?

"In any case, I won't do it," Powell insists with some heat. "It's bad enough trying to maintain scientific objectivity amid a sea of emotion coming from all quarters, starting with the Premier's wife. But if I tell the whole country his pulse has gone up or down in the past six hours, they'll never understand the significance of it. They'll misinterpret the information, and it will just lead to more pointless speculation and second-guessing. I'm damned if I'll give in."

The strain is clearly telling on him. I advise Powell to silence his critics by confronting them: issue a public statement giving his reasons for keeping information confidential, particularly when it can change by the hour. State clearly that such details are meaningless without a wider knowledge of Sir John's medical history and best left in the sickroom, which is the only place where a sound diagnosis can be made.

Powell gratefully agrees to adopt this strategy. He also plans, he tells me, lowering his voice still further, to write his own detailed account of Sir John's "case" for publication after the Prime Minister's death.

I look across to the pale draped figure lying in bed: the so-familiar wisps of silver encircling his forehead, the sheet drawn up to his chin. Sometimes it takes an effort to remind myself he's still living.

Rising to the challenge of too little real news, the newspapers have begun inventing ever more imaginative stories about Sir John's epic battle with what the *Gazette* is pleased to call "the Angel of Death." Reporters have taken to impersonating a camera lens: picturing for their readers the scene inside the bedchamber in which I now spend so much of my existence. The astonishing thing is how many details they get right. They must be suborning the servants. I wonder if any money changes hands.

The papers accurately report that fanning brings Sir John some relief from the heat. That Hugh John and I sat by the bedside last night. That Lady M. is there at all hours and going almost entirely without sleep. They duly observe the comings and goings of the sorrowing Professor Williamson, and the visit by the Reverend Bogart, Rector of St. Alban the Martyr, who celebrates Holy Communion in the sickroom.

The newsmen keep the gardens under observation, peering through the iron bars to report the moment when little Jack emerges from the house in his Jack Tar suit carrying his toy sailboat to sit on the grass under the maples. As he watches the breeze flutter the sails, the reporters call out to get the boy's attention. He looks up: "Grandpa is very ill," he tells them solemnly. They record Lady M.'s brief solitary stroll among the rose beds to take some air. They stay up all night, afraid of missing anything. From Sir John's window after midnight, I see several of them patrolling the well-worn path between the bell tent and the gate. They stand smoking in the checkered shadows cast by the lantern hung on the lintel, under canopies of dark foliage swaying in the wind. I'd be surprised if any reporters are left in the press gallery. Yesterday Hugh John took his seat to inform the House of his father's condition.

When I scan the newspapers during brief visits home, I see the other long-running story is the baccarat scandal unfolding in London. The Prince of Wales has been testifying about gambling cheats at a country house. As if that weren't embarrassing enough for a prince of the realm, he's also been named by Lord Brooke as co-respondent in His Lordship's divorce suit; and it was Lady Brooke who broke the gambling scandal in the first place. What tame lives we lead here!

Today the heat has broken. Fluffy clouds fill the sky, the temperature has fallen, and fresh northern breezes coming through the window seem to revive Sir John. He stays awake longer than usual, right through his lunch of beef tea, milk and champagne mixed with Appollinaris water. And then occurs a scene that any newsman would pay a ransom to witness.

At half past two I hear Lady M. in the hallway outside the bedchamber chatting with little Jack. "I want to see Grandpa!" he pipes. His grandma tells him he can't—indeed, he hasn't been allowed in the sickroom at all. But Jack, who's rather spoiled, insists. Perhaps since Sir John is still wide awake, Lady M. relents and leads him inside by the hand.

At first Jack hesitates, hanging back to study the strange sight of his grandpa swathed in white and surrounded by men standing around his bed: Dr. Powell, Ben Chilton and me. Overcoming his shyness, he cries, "Grandpa!" and runs to the bedside. He grasps Sir John's hand—the good one, fortunately—and begins telling him about an encounter outside with the cow.

As Sir John listens to Jack prattle on, his eyes widen with interest. Smile lines unseen since before the stroke crease his cheeks. His gaze moves from Jack's face to the little hand placed in his own. Sir John is rediscovering something—some revelation of innocence and delight whose existence he'd forgotten.

Lady M. is transfixed. Realizing the positive results the boy is producing, far greater than anything we adults have achieved in the past five days, she rushes out and returns pushing Mary in her chair. Mary has been visiting her father daily, but only briefly. She appears startled but happy to have another chance to see him, her thin face illuminated by a lopsided grin. In a moment she's sitting alongside Sir John, exchanging wordless adoring smiles, while Jack, sensing that limits are being removed, climbs onto the counterpane.

The old man listens intently to his grandson's chatter. His watery eyes are full of sympathy and pleasure, but he can say nothing in reply. Not understanding why Sir John doesn't answer, Jack repeats himself pleadingly: "Grandpa, Grandpa, what's the matter? Can't you *hear* me?"

Sir John's smile wanes. He begins to look alarmed. Mary leans forward, grasping Jack's hand and stroking it. "Dear Jack," she croons tenderly, in her peculiarly drawn-out, measured way, "you know Grandpa is ill, don't you? We mustn't get him tired out, now, must we? It will just make him sick, you know. Come, dear, kiss Grandpa on his forehead and say bye-bye. . . ."

Jack likes the idea of kissing Grandpa. He plants a kiss on his wrinkled forehead, then one on each cheek. Sir John receives the kisses with a look of wonderment. Mary coaxes Jack down off the bed, and Lady M., blinking back tears, ushers them both outside as Sir John watches hungrily after them.

It's soon apparent that this emotional excitement has drained his meagre store of energy. He slips into unconsciousness.

The breeze grows chillier. The windows are closed.

Thursday blends into Friday, separated by a brief night, and Sir John sleeps on, in infinite exhaustion but apparent comfort. The papers Minette saves for me mirror the changed tone of the medical bulletins. The reassuring tone of earlier headlines has given way to MUCH WEAKER—SIR JOHN'S CONDITION BAD AS EVER and ACTION OF HEART MAY STOP AT ANY MOMENT.

Dr. Powell is finding it onerous to shoulder the chief responsibility for treating Sir John around the clock. He telegraphs George Ross in Montreal, asking him to return for another consultation. Dr. Ross arrives on the next train, and all four physicians jointly sign the following, which I type for the newsmen at the gate:

June 5th, 1891, 2 p.m.
At our consultation today we find Sir John Macdonald altogether in a somewhat alarming state. His strength, which has gradually failed him during the past week, shows a marked decline since yesterday. He shows still a slight flickering of consciousness. His respirations number 38, his pulse 120, more feeble and more irregular than hitherto. In our opinion his powers of life are steadily waning.

As I'm typing the doctors' names at the bottom, I become conscious of Lady M. standing behind me, reading over my shoulder. She leaves my office as wordlessly as she entered.

Even though he's surrendered to pressure to publish Sir John's pulse and respiratory rates, Dr. Powell goes ahead with making his concerns public. His statement to the press begins, "I desire to state in the strongest terms that the public are demanding of me more than I can give. While I have no desire to delude, I must respectfully decline to manufacture information."

The press isn't content to let him make his point with dignity; this too must be turned into melodrama. Playing it up with their usual nose for conflict, the papers term his statement "Dr. Powell's protest" and interview other medical men to obtain their opinions about the "peculiarly worded bulletin." Fortunately for Powell, his colleagues support him.

Sir John has a brief stirring of consciousness early on Friday evening. It's enough to permit him to swallow a bit of nourishment before he falls into another deep sleep. Robins sing their tuneless songs on the boughs outside his window; everything appears outwardly normal, or as normal as it's been all week. But the scene is shifting. By 10 p.m. he can't be roused for another feeding. He remains comatose throughout the night.

Shortly after dawn on Saturday, the doctors murmur to each other about his altered breathing; it has become laboured and shallow. They seem alarmed. Evidently his pulse is now so irregular, varying from one hour to the next, that it can't be easily counted.

Powell describes Sir John's breathing as "almost entirely abdominal." Lady M. and I are both present as he gently prods and squeezes Sir John here and there. The doctor remarks, addressing no one in particular, "The reflexes have become abolished." Lady M. receives this as she receives everything now, stoically, without comment. She looks only at her husband.

The hours move slowly. I forget to make my daily visit home. I can't remember when I last slept. Several of us take an early supper in the dining room. Someone says something about "the last flicker in the socket," which strikes a sour note with me, and I have to go outside for air.

Standing on the terrace where I conversed with Sir John only a week ago, I see, as if for the first time, what a sylvan setting this is. The sky is clear, the lush meadows on the Quebec side splashed with late afternoon sunshine. The rumble of the city is distant and unthreatening. I can distinguish the faint roars of both the Chaudière Falls upriver and the Rideau Falls downriver, their tumbling white waters mingling in my eardrums and merging in nature, preparing to enter a third and final river to the sea.

I return to Sir John's room. Hugh John and Lady M. are there, sitting unspeaking side by side. They watch while Dr. Powell cradles Sir John's wrist and tries to count.

Shortly after sunset, as shadows lengthen across the walls, Dr. Powell asks Hugh John to summon the rest of the family. Hugh returns escorting his wife, who pushes Mary and positions her wheelchair beside her mother, close by her father's head. The three women hold hands.

"Doesn't he look at peace," Lady M. says, speaking for all of us. Her voice is crystalline as water.

Sir John is still breathing, with such extraordinary delicacy and infrequency that it's almost imperceptible.

I enter the darkness of the garden. I force my legs to move against their will, against the black air's solidity, and hurry along the gravelled pathway carrying the bulletin typed on Earnscliffe stationery.

As I reach the gate, two reporters approach from the direction of the telegraph tent, a corporals' guard keeping watch overnight on behalf of the others. We regard each other warily through the bars, in the light flickering from the lantern overhead. I recognize their faces.

"Gentlemen," I tell them, my own voice terrifying to me, "Sir John Macdonald is dead. He died at a quarter past ten."

This is the news they've been waiting for. They can only stand in silence, disbelieving. Slowly they remove their hats.

Vale

The doctors are unanimous: there will be no autopsy. Shortly after 11 p.m. Mr. Rogers and his staff respond to Dr. Powell's long-expected call, the casket secured to the rear of their carriage by heavy ropes. Even before their arrival, the bells begin.

The City Hall tower starts first, deep and resonant despite the distance from Elgin Street, tolling once for each year of Sir John's life. Long before it reaches seventy-six, it's joined by church bells to the east and west, their peals rising and falling until it's impossible to distinguish one from another. The long rolling mournful sound rides to us on the dark wind.

When I consider how long it took Sir John to die, it seems that life didn't want to give him up. Now, after all the waiting, his death has become the cue for action. Edgar Dewdney leaves in Buckley's cab to fetch Major Sherwood, Chief of the Dominion Police. I notify the messengers to report for duty. While they're en route, I compose and type the necessary communiqués to inform the Governor General, Sir Hector Langevin and Wilfrid Laurier. Then I telephone Minette.

Officially, Lady M. is personally in charge of the mourning arrangements. In fact she's nowhere to be seen. She attended to most of the planning earlier, while still calm and practical and able to tell herself it probably wouldn't be necessary.

The body will rest at Earnscliffe for two days. The casket is a replica of the one in which President Garfield was buried—an odd choice to my mind, since Garfield was assassinated, but evidently the Macdonalds attended his funeral a decade ago and admired the design of brushed steel with a rosewood finish and silver lifting plates in the shape of a wheel attached to seraph's wings. Sir John will be dressed in his Imperial Privy Councillor's uniform and sword. His Grand Cross of a Knight of the Order of the Bath will adorn his left breast.

At half past midnight Ben Chilton carries Dr. Powell's small leather trunk downstairs to the front hall. Ben looks utterly miserable, as does everyone. The doctor and I have agreed to leave Earnscliffe together.

One of the police officers securing the gate sticks his head inside the front door, apologizes, and tells Powell the reporters are demanding an interview. At first Powell refuses, but he changes his mind when informed they've already interviewed Doctors Wright and Grant. He asks me to accompany him to the gate.

The little club of newsmen has grown alarmingly large in the past two hours, augmented by ordinary mourners and the just plain curious. Since the streetcars have stopped running for the night, everyone must have driven out or walked here from the city. I notice the final medical bulletin is already missing from the lintel where I attached it.

"I am reluctant to answer questions at present," Powell tells the crowd. A little self-consciously, he explains that he's writing his own account of Sir John's last days, which they may read in due course. After the reporters persist in pelting him with questions, he agrees to entertain a few brief ones.

The first is about the stroke that preceded the fatal attack. The second is about the official cause of death: "Hemiplegia," Powell asserts, drawing confidence from medical terminology, "induced by hemorrhage of the brain. Sir John passed away very peacefully. He was surrounded by members of his family and others close to him associated in the watching."

One young reporter blurts out, "Had you ever any hopes of his recovery?"

"None," Powell replies without hesitation. "I gave up his recovery as hopeless from the very first. You cannot find a single bulletin in which I expressed any hope."

Abruptly he turns on his heel and strides to the house, ignoring the anxious questions hurled at his back. I hurry to keep up with him. Reporters call out my name like a reproach.

Ben intercepts me in the front hall and says Lady M. is waiting for me in the drawing room.

I find her already veiled and shrouded in black. She seems translated into another state of being. Her voice too is transformed, lowered to a deeper pitch, oddly thrilling.

"I have something for you to deliver to the Governor General." She thrusts into my palm a small envelope closed with wax and stamped with the Earnscliffe seal. "Do not give it to an ADC or Lady Stanley or anyone else at all. You must put it directly into Lord Stanley's own hands."

Her manner alarms me: outwardly controlled, inwardly hysterical. "Tonight, Lady Macdonald?" I mumble stupidly.

"Yes, Joseph, at once. Tomorrow it will be too late."

"Of course. Dr. Powell and I were just about—"

"I have ordered another carriage to take the doctor home. Buckley will deliver you and my letter to Rideau Hall. Thank you, Joseph. Good night."

Explaining matters to Powell, who gives me a peculiar look but says nothing, I set off with Buckley. He talks all the way to Rideau Hall about Sir John's many kindnesses to him over the years, so that I scarcely have to speak.

"I drove Sir John for thirty-eight years, winter and summer, and can scarce believe he's gone," Buckley laments above the sound of hooves. "I never knew him to be out of temper. Never heard him say a cross word, not once, no matter how rough the road or how careless I might drive. Do you remember that grey suit of his, Mr. Pope? One time I called for him when he was on his way to meet some toffs and he was wearing a different suit. 'Sir John,' I said to him, 'why don't you put on your grey suit? You look ever so much better in it.' And God strike me if I lie, but he went back in and changed his clothes. I could take those liberties with him, Mr. Pope."

Seen through the elms, Rideau Hall is ablaze with light at every window. Expected even at this hour, I'm shown into the smoking room, where Lord Stanley greets me with solemnity. He offers a sad and kindly smile. "You look exhausted, Pope. Such devastating news. I'm so sorry."

"Thank you, Your Excellency. My deepest condolences to you also. You've lost your First Minister."

We stand a moment in shared sorrow.

"Lady Macdonald said you bring a letter." I hand it to him, glad to be free of the burden of it, and he immediately tears it open. "Excuse me, but I may need to send you back with a reply."

Once he's scanned it, he looks aside. "Extraordinary. Did she actually really write this tonight? After Sir John . . . ?"

"I believe so, Your Excellency."

"I'll set it aside for now. Would you care for a drink? You must be parched after your labours."

Decanters and glasses are arrayed on a sideboard. I accept scotch whisky and decline soda.

"Sir John would approve, I'm sure," His Excellency says. "Why ruin good whisky? Here's to him, then: one of the Empire's greatest statesmen!"

"To Sir John."

Everyone assumes he was a scotch drinker. Oddly enough, he seldom touched it.

"Now Pope," Lord Stanley murmurs, closing his eyes to savour the first burning peat-flavoured sip, "I'm going to bind you to secrecy. At least until you're a pensioner writing your memoirs, and I'm long gone."

"Certainly, sir."

"I don't imagine you've seen the contents of Lady Macdonald's missive. It's written in her own hand. You see, she's taken it on herself to advise me—on the appointment of her husband's successor."

"Good heavens."

"Yes. Constance—Lady Stanley—sometimes says Lady Macdonald believes in her heart of hearts that *she* should be living here. I've always considered that a charming exaggeration. Now I wonder if there's something to it. At any rate, the letter has been written. I will probably decline to answer it, at least officially. If it was written tonight, it's a product of her heart's anguish, and therefore a communication of the most impulsive and private sort. She may even regret writing it tomorrow. Does that seem likely to you?"

"Certainly, Your Excellency."

"I want your honest opinion. You're more closely acquainted with the lady than I."

"Sir, I don't doubt that Lady Macdonald is feeling overwrought. Grief may have made her reckless."

He thinks for a moment, almost smiles. He samples more of the whisky. He's poured us large ones. "I've often wondered about the hold of Sir Charles Tupper's charm on the ladies."

"Sir?"

"Sir Charles is Lady Macdonald's nominee as the next Prime Minister of Canada."

"Ah."

"You don't think . . . ?"

"No, sir. I don't."

"Nor I. Such a principled woman. Loyal wife."

"Lady Macdonald is nothing if not loyal to Sir John in every respect—if I may say so, sir."

"Of course you may. We're entirely alone here. Nothing will go beyond this room, will it? But I'd also like your frank opinion on the reasons for her recommendation."

It's not only the whisky that loosens my tongue. Lord Stanley's open invitation to speak arrives on a tide of unspoken emotion that demands some outlet, however unsought and unlikely. And so I begin to talk. I tell His Excellency, who has only known Sir Charles Tupper as our High Commissioner to London, how a powerful bond between Tupper and Sir John was created and sealed those many years ago when the country was born. How Tupper believed implicitly in Sir John's conception of Canada and fought tirelessly for it. How deeply grateful Sir John felt to him for delivering Nova Scotia to Confederation over the hell-bent opposition of his opponents. How Tupper believed this nation has a future far greater than the sum of its parts, and at critical moments was the only political leader to display a generous optimism on that point equal to Sir John's—their alliance becoming a counterpart to the old, intimate comradeship-in-arms Sir John once enjoyed with George-Étienne Cartier. How, even after Tupper left active politics and moved to London, Sir John always knew he could rely on his old friend in his time of need. And since loyalty to Sir John has always come first with Lady M., it's natural she should now think of Sir Charles.

"Well argued," Lord Stanley replies. "Perfectly logical. Perhaps, then, Lady Macdonald believes she's speaking for her husband. It's not that she fancies herself in the role of kingmaker. But isn't Sir Charles a bit of a rogue?"

"The Liberals think so, sir. But then they always said the same about Sir John. Sir Charles also has enemies in his own party."

"And among the ranks of certain husbands, I hear. But clearly you admire him."

"I am a public servant, Your Excellency."

"Yes, yes, but put yourself in my position, Pope. I can scarcely ask a man to head my Government if he's held in low esteem by half the country. No, I think John Thompson ought to get the call. What do you say? Entirely between us?"

It's astonishing to me to be put in this position by the Governor General of Canada. But this is an astonishing moment in our lives and our history. I try to answer as Sir John would have wanted me to: "Your Excellency, John Thompson possesses exceptional qualities of mind and heart. He has great knowledge and judgment, both legal and political—in my opinion."

"I fancy I hear a 'but' in your voice. Never mind his religion, I like him. He's solid. I'm considering pressing him to take the office. But as you've suggested, many enmities exist among the Conservatives. Before I call on anyone, it's of the utmost importance that I know Sir John's own choice of successor. Surely he left behind some indication of his preference."

I remain silent.

"A codicil to his will, perhaps? As his private secretary, you are my most reliable source."

I find I'm perspiring despite the lateness of the hour. The whisky on a long-empty stomach is making me ill. "I'm terribly sorry, Your Excellency, Sir John didn't leave any such indication, none whatsoever. Certainly not in writing. Nor orally, to my knowledge."

"Damn it!"

The next day is Sunday, so thankfully there are no newspapers. Directly after eight o'clock Mass I resume my post at Earnscliffe, which has begun to feel like my true home: a perception I know I must surrender.

Sir John remains in the room where he died. Mr. Hamilton McCarthy of the Royal Canadian Academy is coming to take a plaster cast of his face. I feel very peculiar and queasy, knowing he's still upstairs while I'm in my office, answering his correspondence in his absence, as it were. I already miss with an aching heart the moment when he summons me to his side.

At Langevin's request, I attend an emergency Cabinet meeting in the evening. It takes place in Sir Hector's home; no sign of his boarder, Thomas McGreevy. An anxious, unsettled, fractious mood rules the group, turning Minister against Minister. Without an acknowledged successor to Sir John, they pull against each other in all directions, everyone bent on leading and no one on following. Chapleau arrives late from Montreal and acts high-handed with his colleagues. Thompson, who also had to return from Montreal, where he was visiting his daughter in the hospital, had no trouble getting here on time.

It's impossible to take minutes. There is little order or purpose to the discussion, and practically the only thing the Cabinet can agree on is the need to hold a state funeral. The body will lie in the Senate until the interment. I remind them that the Macdonalds plan a private family service at Earnscliffe tomorrow, so it's agreed the public viewing will last from Tuesday until Wednesday morning, followed by a state ceremony at St. Alban's.

I'm dispatched to Earnscliffe with a draft of the arrangements for Lady M.'s approval. It makes for another late night. She seats me across from her in the drawing room, lifts her veil with both hands, and scans my two-page draft where it sits on the side table. Her face is alarmingly pale. She clasps her hands in her lap. "It all looks perfectly fine, Joseph. A very majestic ceremony and a fitting way for the nation to honour him. I'm only glad I won't be there."

I assume I haven't heard correctly. "Not at St. Alban's, Ma'am?"

"I will not be in attendance. I'll say goodbye to my man right here at home where we were happy. Not in full public view so everyone can judge whether my widowhood is sufficiently noble and tragic."

She's not prepared to discuss the will either. There are one or two loose ends that need tying up, but they'll have to wait. Sir John has named me, along with Hugh John and Edgar Dewdney, as trustees of his estate—a task that includes responsibility for Mary's welfare, in the unlikely event she outlives her mother.

When I inquire how Mary is managing, Lady M. describes her as full of grief over her papa's death. "She said, 'I must try and be a comfort to you now, instead of a burden.' I told her we both have to be brave. It will not do to be weak. Papa wouldn't have liked it. He liked us to be cheerful."

I stand to leave, fully expecting to have more dealings with both women well into the future. The other executors have agreed that the responsibility for dealing with Lady M. on estate matters falls to me.

Next morning Lord and Lady Stanley are the first mourners to visit Earnscliffe. Mr. Rogers and his men have deployed their dismal arts to turn the dining room into a funeral parlour; they've transformed the hallway into an anteroom draped in black and hung with photographs of the Prince of Wales (taken long before the baccarat scandal) and successive Governors General. Once inside the dining room, the Vice-Regal couple, accompanied by all four aides-de-camp, behold the casket. It's swathed in white and purple silk and surrounded by lavish bouquets of summer flowers. Their perfume is cloying, almost overpowering. At the head of the casket, a gracefully folded Red Ensign supports a floral St. Andrew's Cross sent by Princess Louise and Lord Lorne. At its foot sits a handsome royal-purple pillow embroidered in gold, an offering from the officers and men of the North-west Mounted Police. The Queen's portrait sternly surveys the scene.

Sir John looks improbably small in his Privy Councillor's uniform. He's dwarfed by the grandeur of his tributes. For several minutes the Stanleys remain gazing down on his powdered features, as apparently unmarred by pain as any marionette's— features so intimately known, now rendered pale and alien.

Lady M. is nowhere in evidence. The official word is that she'll be present to welcome the evening visitors, while her niece, May Fitzgibbon, greets visitors during the day. From what Ben tells me, Lady M. still hasn't stirred from her bedchamber.

The Stanleys are followed by the entire Cabinet in mourning dress. They encircle their leader like ravens, peering downwards steadily or unsteadily, then looking away, as if seeking something else to look at. Afterwards hundreds of friends, dignitaries and senior civil servants pass through the house all day, by invitation only. The uninvited are kept at bay beyond the gate.

In the afternoon I return to Parliament Hill. It's the first time I've been back in ten days. My office looks much as I left it, except that the desk is heaped high with file folders prepared by my assistant, some containing memoranda from colleagues, others legislative drafts for Sir John's perusal, still others correspondence requiring his attention. His inner office is sadly immaculate. I can't bring myself to contemplate the appalling task of sorting his lifetime's worth of papers, or even to set foot inside his personal domain.

With an hour before the House opens, I immerse myself in the newspapers. The headline in the *Globe* reads SIR JOHN IS DEAD. In the *Gazette*, whose prose for the past week has been passionate to the point of delirium, the headline consists of the single word: DEAD.

Both papers' editorialists express sorrow, but move beyond it to envisage the future. In the ever-loyal *Gazette*'s opinion, the Conservative Party contains plenty of competent candidates ready to carry on Sir John's National Policy. Yet the editors betray anxiety over Lord Stanley's delay in appointing a new Prime Minister. The decision must not be postponed much longer: "Precedent enjoins speedy action." I've heard the same thing out of the mouths of certain Cabinet ministers. Thompson even speaks of the danger of a constitutional crisis developing; he's already christened it "Lord Stanley's Folly."

Naturally the *Globe* takes a different tack. Following a grudging and sanctimonious lead editorial, in which they postpone their assessment of Sir John's career until a decent interval has passed, the editors run a piece headed "The Next Premier." By some process of divination they claim to know that Thompson will get the call, with Dalton McCarthy inserted into Cabinet to placate the Orangemen. Not only that, but the new Government will have no choice but to abandon the National Policy since it has allegedly impoverished Canadian farmers and working men, who desperately need the revenue from their "natural market," the United States. Tupper can't be Prime Minister because of his record of corruption, "making Canadian politics stink in the nostrils of respectable men." And Abbott is out of the question, since government by him would mean government by Mr. Van Horne and the CPR.

Having determined the composition of the new regime, the *Globe* airily demolishes its prospects. Thompson "may succeed in patching together a new administration, but its days will be brief and troubled. Nothing but his own magical name enabled Sir John Macdonald to rule the curious omnium gatherum that calls itself the Conservative Party, and the task is impossible for his successor."

I dare say the oracle of Liberal Toronto stands to be wrong on all counts.

In the House of Commons every available surface is hung with hideous black crepe and cashmere. The public galleries are packed; everyone dressed in black; the women fanning themselves furiously. A stranger occupies Lady M.'s place. Sir John's seat on the floor is empty, save for a wreath of white roses placed there by the Conservative caucus, encircled with a purple ribbon emblazoned "Our Chief." He has become a gigantic corsage. Every other seat is filled, with the glaring and inexcusable exception of Sir Richard Cartwright's.

It falls to Sir Hector Langevin, as the Minister of longest service, to inform the House officially. The old man rises, trembling slightly. Since before Confederation he's served Sir John faithfully, if not always wisely, and now his career and reputation are ruined. Unconfident of his memory, he's written out his speech and apologizes to the House for reading it.

After bearing witness to the greatness of Sir John's statesmanship and the power of his patriotism, Sir Hector dwells on his "chivalry" toward Quebec and French Canadians. Sir John could have received far bigger majorities in his own province of Ontario, Langevin says, if he'd been willing to appeal to prejudice, and if he hadn't insisted on treating his French compatriots as equals. Because they understood this, Quebeckers had the confidence to enter Confederation a generation ago. Suddenly Sir Hector's papers drop to his desk. He's unable to read further. "Mr. Speaker, I should have wished to continue to speak of our dear departed friend, and spoken to you about his goodness of heart, the witness of which I have been so often. But I feel that I must stop. My heart is full of tears."

Laurier rises next. His friends tell me he was sick over the weekend, and today his chiselled beautiful face looks more pallid than ever. But his voice is strong and unwavering all the same, his tone limpid. First Laurier refers kindly to Langevin's grief. He fully appreciates the intensity of the emotion that has choked off the old man's words: "His silence is far more eloquent than any human language."

Grief over Sir John isn't confined to one party, Laurier says: his is a great national loss. "In fact, the place of Sir John Macdonald in

Canada was so large and so absorbing that it is almost impossible to conceive that the political life of this country, the fate of this country, can continue without him. His loss overwhelms us. For my part, I can say with all truth his loss overwhelms me, and it also overwhelms this Parliament, as if indeed one of the institutions of the land had given way."

These are more than polite sentiments to suit the occasion. Members of both parties, officials of the House, spectators in the galleries, even the cynical press gallery, all are moved by the personal quality of Laurier's sadness: "Sir John was endowed with those inner, subtle, undefinable graces of soul which win and keep the hearts of men. As to his statesmanship, it is written in the history of Canada. It may be said, without any exaggeration whatever, that the life of Sir John Macdonald from the date he entered Parliament is the history of Canada, for he was connected and associated with all the events, all the facts which brought Canada from the position it then occupied—the position of two small provinces having nothing in common but their common allegiance, united by a bond of paper and nothing else—to the present state of development which Canada has reached.

"Although my political views compel me to say that, in my judgment, his actions were not always the best that could have been taken in the interests of Canada, although my conscience compels me to say that of late he has imputed to his opponents motives which I must say in my heart are misconceived, yet I am only too glad here to sink these differences, and to remember only the great services he has performed for our country—to remember that his actions always displayed great originality of view, unbounded fertility of resource, a high level of intellectual conception, and, above all, a far-reaching vision beyond the events of the day, and still higher, permeating the whole, a broad patriotism—a devotion to Canada's welfare, Canada's advancement, and Canada's glory."

It's apt and, I think, rather wise that Laurier concludes his eulogy with a plea for the nation. He banishes all doubt about where he himself stands on the question of patriotism:

"Before the grave of him who, above all, was the Father of Confederation, let not grief be barren. But let grief be coupled with the resolution that the work in which Liberals and Conservatives, in which Brown and Macdonald united, shall not perish, and that though a united Canada may be deprived of the services of her greatest men, still Canada shall and will live."

For years to come, Canadians will tell each other about the words spoken today by Sir John's French opponent. Generosity on this scale is seldom witnessed in politics. These two men fought bitter battles over the years, exposing deep differences between them—differences in their origins and cultures and temperaments as well as their parties, and hence in their ways of seeing the world—yet now Laurier eulogizes Sir John with a fervent heart. When a man's epitaph is written by an enemy who holds him in such high regard, what more does history need to know?

Lady M. doesn't invite me to the family funeral. My status as an honorary Macdonald has expired.

I do attend at five next morning when Sir John departs Earnscliffe for the last time. The sun is already up and burning in a cloudless sky, and Hugh John, Patrick Buckley, Ben Chilton and I carry the casket outside to Mr. Rogers's waiting hearse. I'm staggered by the weight of it. I notice that the only words engraved in the brass plaque on the lid are "John Alexander Macdonald."

Reporters are present to record the scene for their readers. They try to maintain a respectful silence, but one of them can't resist inquiring if Lady Macdonald is coming too. We ignore him, piling into the hearse, to be followed by another carriage containing the flowers.

Our early departure is timed to avoid crowds of gawkers and

sensation-seekers. The Earnscliffe grounds were invaded last night by souvenir-hunters making off with roses and bits of turf and strips of bark torn from the maples. Hugh John had to summon a squad of Dominion Police to protect his stepmother's property and privacy.

It's not yet six when we pull up on the Hill. Several Parliamentary staff carry Sir John inside the Centre Block and down to the Senate. Rogers and his crew have completely transformed the Red Chamber, removing all the seats and desks, hanging black draperies, spreading a spotless white cloth over the floor. The public will be allowed in by the main entrance and will leave by an exit behind the throne.

The men tenderly place the casket on the dais prepared for it. The bouquets of flowers, still fresh and fragrant, are set all around.

For the next two hours, with no other duties left, I watch the crowds of mourners throng onto the Hill from all directions. They obediently form up into a long line snaking from the main entrance of the Centre Block around past the East Block and all the way down to Wellington Street, ending somewhere on Dufferin Bridge. Uniformed sentries are posted along the line, drawn from all four regiments stationed in Ottawa—the Governor General's Foot Guards, the Princess Louise Dragoon Guards, foot soldiers of the Forty-third Battalion, and artillerymen of the Ottawa Field Battery. While they wait, the crowds admire the soldiers, knowing the doors won't open until ten.

The Governor General and Lady Stanley arrive with their ADCs, slipping into the building by another door. They're followed shortly by the Cabinet. The casket remains open. Dragoons in plumed silver helmets stand stiffly at attention on either side. One by one the Ministers say their final farewells to their chief. Lord only knows what's passing through their minds or hearts.

Sharp at ten, the first mourners step timidly into a place where most of them have never set foot. They pass out of the tropical sun into the dim, hushed, scented cavern of the Senate chamber, moving steadily in single file toward Sir John's bier set behind a waist-high barrier. I see them wanting to stretch out the moment as long as they can, but they've been instructed not to stop even for a second; the line must keep moving at all times. Quickly they lean over the barrier, careful not to mar the casket's gleaming rosewood finish with their fingerprints, and peer boldly or meekly inside before moving on to the exit. Having had their moment with the dead chieftain, all are solemn, some openly tearful.

The expectant masses grow as the day wears on. This city has never seen anything like it. There's no break in the sweating streams of humanity surging onto the Hill, including hundreds upon hundreds of working men and their wives and children— beneficiaries of Sir John's National Policy, I hear the *Gazette* saying tomorrow—no, victims of it, the *Globe* will say. Many have come in from the countryside, to judge from the rough-hewn faces of farmers in their Sunday best. As I walk past the lineup on my way home for lunch, I note perhaps a third of them are speaking French.

On Wellington I encounter the Toronto journalist E. B. Biggar. He looks elated to be covering such a dramatic public spectacle: "This morning I stood beside an old white-haired boy," he tells me, "leaning on his cane. Did he know Sir John? I asked him. '*Know* him?' he repeated with a kind of astonishment. 'For thirty years I've known no other name.'"

Biggar is perfectly frank that his mission here is to collect stories about Sir John for a book he's planning. The old boy's story will be one of these, and he'd clearly like me to linger awhile and give him mine. I tell him I have an appointment.

The afternoon brings no respite from the sun or the crowds. Several ladies in the lineup faint, one falling down the flight of steps above the fountain. Everyone is sympathetic and helpful, buying from the water vendors to soothe the afflicted. No one acts badly.

Long into the evening, well past the late, blood-red sunset, they keep coming, until finally the doors of Parliament are closed for the night and the sentries tell the disappointed to come back in the morning. I linger on in the Senate, longing to be alone with Sir John for even a minute. The scent of lilies and roses hangs heavy in the shadowy chamber. Only a few attendants remain, tidying and straightening up in anticipation of the onslaught tomorrow. I can almost share his marvellous company again, can almost commune with him. I feel he knows where he is—unlike the rest of us, cut adrift and bewildered, lost without the certainty he gave.

The doors reopen early. The *Citizen* estimates one thousand mourners file past the casket every hour. By the time the visitations end at noon, nearly twenty thousand will have wished him Godspeed.

Today's visitors include many who have travelled long distances. Contingents have arrived by train from Montreal and Toronto. The dust on some people's clothing attests to their having driven all day or night by horse and wagon. An army of old men who have followed Sir John all their lives, turning out in all weathers for his speeches and rallies and political picnics, are here to make their final rendezvous. They haven't stopped following.

Kingston awaits his arrival tonight on a special train. The interment will take place in Cataraqui Cemetery tomorrow afternoon. His will instructs, "I desire that I shall be buried in the Kingston cemetery near the grave of my mother, as I promised her that I should be."

Soldier, engineer and patriot Sir Casimir Gzowski arrives, representing the Queen, and walks straight past the lineup. With self-conscious pomp and ceremony, Sir Casimir strides up to the casket, holding before him in both hands a spectacular wreath of enormous white and yellow roses. He leans forward and delicately places it on Sir John's breast. "From Her Majesty Queen Victoria," runs the inscription, "in memory of Her faithful and devoted servant." Tomorrow, we're told, a memorial service is planned for Westminster Abbey.

The noon gun at Nepean Point is supposed to end the visitation period, but too many people are lined up outside to close the doors. Finally it's necessary to shut the public entrance, regardless of how many still wait. The last mourner to witness Sir John in the flesh is a Mr. Prévost of Montreal. The casket lid is dropped and screwed into place.

Dr. Powell and I take our places in the procession behind the casket, immediately after Hugh John and little Jack dressed in a black sailor suit. The pallbearers are the thirteen Cabinet Ministers. At a quarter past one, we emerge through the looming Gothic archway of the main entrance into the light and heat, facing the massed crowds. They stand all along the processional route as far as the eye can see. At once the bells in the tower above our heads chime out mournfully, joined in a deafening chorus by every church bell in the city. Wee Jack covers his ears and looks terrified. I wonder if he's really strong enough for all this. His father must think he is, or has to be.

The straining Ministers—what about *their* old hearts?—lift the casket into the hearse to be drawn by six black-plumed horses. Hugh John picks Jack up, and they disappear into one of a long succession of carriages, joining Professor Williamson and other relatives. Powell and I are assigned to a carriage closer to the rear. Ahead of us are the Lieutenant-Governors of all the provinces, Justices of the Supreme Court, Senators, Members of Parliament, commanders of the militia, and mayors of many of the largest cities in the Dominion. The Vice-Regal carriage leads the procession toward the church. It occurs to me that all this elaborate ceremonial has been planned and executed without my lifting a finger.

As the procession takes us down Elgin Street, mismatched snatches of Handel's "Dead March" from *Saul* reach us from two regimental bands, one ahead of us, the other behind. We pass between lines of spectators jamming both sidewalks, past enterprising folk leaning off lampposts, craning out of upper-storey windows, perched on rooftops. The shopfronts are decorated in black and purple. Most contain images of Sir John—photographs, magazine clippings, even the painted plaster statuettes of him that were popular a few years ago. The spectators' garb is sombre, all part of this dark festival of death. The only colour is provided by the Foot Guards' scarlet tunics and the blue and green uniforms of the artillery and riflemen, marching with weapons reversed.

The procession turns left onto Maria Street and crosses the bridge over the Rideau Canal to Theodore. Students and seminarians from Ottawa College stand in the sun to sweat and stare. We round the corner onto King Street and proceed north toward Daly. Finally no more forward progress is possible; our carriage stops to let us out some distance from the church.

With its grey stone walls and long sloping roof, St. Alban the Martyr is modelled after a church in some English market town. To me it's always looked curiously lopsided, being built into a steep hill, which requires one side to be twice as tall as the other and reinforced with massive buttresses. St. Alban's is too small to hold any but the invited guests, but spectators thronging the sidewalks spill into the intersection; from the quantity of formal mourning dress I suspect many had hoped to get inside. A good Samaritan comes along with a picnic basket full of lemon wedges and hands them out to the grateful soldiers standing at attention with tunics buttoned to their chins. Dark clouds, I notice, are piling up in the west.

As we find our places inside the church, the organist plays Chopin's "Grand Funeral March." The casket rests under a canopy of imperial purple silk, edged with gold-lace imitations of oak and maple leaves. Surrounded by the flowers from the Senate chamber, the canopy is bathed in filtered, multicoloured light.

One of the stained-glass windows was presented to the church by Lady M. herself, whose absence is constantly being remarked upon by the mourners around me with barely disguised disapproval. They can scarcely credit or countenance the fact that she's missing her husband's funeral. I try to make it as widely known as possible that she's already been through a full Anglican service with Reverend Bogart—the same Reverend Bogart who now emerges from the vestry to stand before us and spread his arms benevolently wide. In a moment he's reading from the fifteenth chapter of 1 Corinthians, "Behold, I show you a mystery: We shall not all sleep, but we shall all be changed."

Aside from noting the differences between the Church of England service and our own, I can't enter deeply into the liturgy. I'm simply afraid of breaking down. I don't wholly give myself up to the prayers either, or allow myself to sing the hymns with feeling. But the man described in the sonorous prayers for the dead isn't the man I knew; I must bid him farewell in my own way, my own time.

When at last we follow the casket and Reverend Bogart and Venerable Archdeacons Lauder and Bedford-Jones outside the church, we discover the sky has turned gloomy. The air is still hot but has taken on a curiously yellowish cast. The clouds directly overhead are discoloured a shade of dark plum, creating a premature sense of evening.

The procession has been routed so that the carriages are still in their proper order for travelling on to the CPR station. We set off westward along Daly, accompanied by hundreds of spectators who no longer stand and watch but join in the lengthening march. The cortège turns right onto Cumberland, and we're just approaching Rideau Street when the wind rises, rattling the elm trees and exposing the pale undersides of leaves. Spirals of dust veer into the air. A fierce gust scatters a few fat raindrops, and for a moment there's nothing more—then a tremendous thunderclap crashes in the direction of Parliament Hill, and the deluge is ready to begin.

Some of us who have been stretching our legs scramble back into our carriages. Anyone without a carriage races for the shelter of doorways and overhangs. The wind intensifies, the heavens break, and slanting sheets of rain drench everything and everyone. Thunder drowns out the muffled drum rolls of the bands, and lightning plays across the sky in counterpoint. It's the capital's first thunderstorm of the season.

By the time we reach Parliament Hill once more, we present a sorry spectacle—a mere remnant of the original procession, with bedraggled horses and drivers, cowering passengers, soggy black bunting. The only marchers still on foot are the regimental soldiers and band members. Soaked to the skin but cooler than before, they've bravely continued marching in unison as if nothing has changed.

The rain stops as abruptly as it began. In a moment the sun reappears, and at the CPR station on Queen Street we discover another crowd waiting. All they've had to look at until now is the funeral train sitting on the main track, consisting of six cars, the engine decked in black and purple, and each car named for a different region of Canada—"Matapedia," "Assiniboia" and so on. The troops and cavalrymen form up along both sides of the track, their lines extending beyond the end of the platform. One of the bands takes up position at the far end of the platform and plays "Nearer My God to Thee."

I watch as the masses of flowers from the church are transferred into a car set aside for that sole purpose. I feel numb, utterly drained. I'm still standing at Dr. Powell's side, where it seems I've been for weeks, and he suggests we pay a visit to the funeral car.

Down the platform we approach the large express coach refitted to bear Sir John home to Kingston. Two sentries, Dragoons from the Senate, recognize us and allow us to enter the carriage. The dimly lit interior strikes me as sinister and ghastly. The ceiling and walls are smothered with great swags of gleaming black satin. They loop from the centre of the ceiling to the four corners, glimmering in the light of a single shaded lamp. Beneath this dreary canopy the casket lies on a silk-draped slab, adorned only with the Queen's oversized wreath. Therein Sir John lies and forever will remain. I turn away in haste, rushing back to the platform and the light.

I slip into a seat in the car reserved for the Cabinet. The Ministers have begun to chat and banter as of old, humorously chiding each other, firing up cigars. A porter hovers ready to take orders for drinks and dinner. William Van Horne himself bustles through the car, shaking hands and asking after the Ministers' comfort, his bulk filling the aisle. Van Horne has commandeered another special train for tomorrow to take the rest of the Parliamentarians to Kingston for the burial. A wave of nausea passes over me. I rush to lock myself in the WC, but instead of being sick I break down into helpless, uncontrollable sobs.

Afterwards I sleep a little, and when I awake I feel tranquil, serene. I lean back in my seat and keep my eyes closed while the Ministers carry on in their usual boisterous fashion, ignoring my presence. I'm grateful for the anonymity and illusion of solitude. Surrounded by these luminaries, I'm invisible.

Sir John and I are retracing our last train journey together. I stare out the window at the green dark forest, occasionally interrupted by a field of spring wheat or young corn or barley. A covey of ducks flies over a marsh. We pull in to the Smiths Falls station, where an overflow crowd is waiting along with the town band. Nobody gets on or off the train, and we sit on the track, bursts of steam escaping from the engine, to listen to yet another, less tuneful, rendition of "Nearer My God." Then the Member for South Lanark, John Graham Haggart, who is to be named Minister of Railways and Canals, steps onto the platform to shake the hands of the Mayor and the bandleader and thank them for their expressions of loyalty and patriotism.

As we travel southward toward Brockville and the St. Lawrence, the sun drops close to the horizon. The atmosphere outside has completely cleared, ushering in a lovely, cool, translucent evening. It feels strange to share a railway car with these men who will be directing the life of the nation under a leader yet to be named, and soon to be chosen from among them. With a couple of exceptions, they're a truly undistinguished, unprepossessing lot. Could any one of them truly lead the country?

For the moment, and possibly for a few more days to come, Canada has no leader. Or rather it does, but he lies mute in his coffin two cars ahead of us, never to be seen or heard from again. For now Canada's entire meaning, its only purpose, has resolved itself into seeing Sir John Macdonald buried in the soil of his creation.

The train passes through a dark stretch of dense bush. I feel glad when we emerge into the light again, into a scrubby landscape of blackish-green cedar and jutting rock and white pine, the southern extension of the Laurentian Shield. The last slanting rays of the sun are amber as honey. A well-kept snake-rail fence begins, the land flattens out—part pasture, part cultivated, rising gently toward a weathered barn. A low stone farmhouse sits next to it on the ridge, looking as if it's always been there, a modest storey and a half, with a peaked gable and a single window above the entrance. The farmer and his wife have walked down to stand by the track behind their fence at the bottom of the field. They're a young couple, slight and wiry, with perhaps a child or two sleeping back in the house. Her dress is pale blue, with a white apron. Tenderly he removes his hat and encircles her waist with his arm, and their raw sunburnt faces turn with the swift passing of the train.

Six

MARCH 1921

Epilogue

Of all the unlikely visitations to brighten a dark winter's day in Ottawa: a letter from Miss Mary Macdonald. It comes in the Saturday morning post at home. After returning from my half-day at the office, I share it with Minette over lunch.

Since her mother's death last autumn, Miss Mary and I have been carrying on a highly agreeable and entirely unforeseen correspondence. It offers the pleasure of two old friends catching up on each other's doings after the passage of thirty years. It also helps distract me occasionally from the burdens of running the Department of External Affairs, a job that's become far more onerous since the Great War and, quite frankly, too demanding for a man my age. Corresponding with Mary connects me to my younger, more impressionable, far more hopeful self.

Perhaps it does something similar for her. After telling me how much she likes her nice new flat in Hove near Brighton on the English south coast, she writes, "Your last letter seemed a link with the dear old times at Earnscliffe." She inquires after the health and whereabouts of Ben Chilton, of Ben's sister, who was once her nurse, of Alice the cook, and others who frequented the house in the days when Sir John was alive.

It touches me to realize that her father's long-vanished era lives on in Mary's memory as vividly as in mine; and that her mind, once considered little more developed than a four-year-old's, has become capable of writing such a thoughtful adult letter on the typewriter she calls her "pride and joy"—a device, come to think of it, I first showed her how to use.

The remarkable and unexpected changes in Mary began while she was still in her twenties, after moving with her mother to England. Lady M. had found it impossible to remain at Earnscliffe, or at their country home in Rivière-du-Loup, or indeed anywhere in Canada. Every place in this country reminded her of Sir John— how they'd been happy here or been royally entertained there— and only served to bring back her loss more painfully. "There is hardly a sadder woman tonight," she once wrote to me, "as I sit alone and dream of the dear old days."

At that point she'd been named a peeress and had just signed the deed of sale to Earnscliffe. She hadn't set foot in Canada for ages and never would again.

Lady M. (I could never get used to calling her Baroness) often wrote to me from England or the Continent of her worries about Mary, her anxiety about how best to provide for her daughter's care, should her own passing leave Mary alone in the world. Both parents had always assumed Mary would predecease them; yet she was reasonably sound physically and mentally, her doctors agreed, apart from her inability to walk and look after herself, and now that she'd lived this long, there was a good chance she'd live to become an old woman. Still, "the horror of leaving my poor helpless dependent darling in any but the best possible circumstances is dreadful to me," Lady M. wrote.

Even then I found her dread, though natural, misplaced. It was Hugh John who'd pointed out to me, during one of our vigils at Sir John's bedside, that both Lady M. and Sir John had kept his stepsister childish by treating her as a child. I saw how right Hugh had been when I visited mother and daughter in England in 1893 and again in '99. In just a few years Mary had already changed a good deal: she was reading magazines and entire books—silly popular romances, but books all the same—and beginning to delight in the London theatre. Her mother arranged for tickets, transportation, a lady companion and porters to carry the wheelchair in and out of the theatre, and Mary was able to attend *The Great Millionaire* or *Iolanthe* or *Véronique*. She displayed a broader mind and more youthful sensibility than her mother, enjoying entertainments that Lady M. deplored as immoral. Mary has ever been an attentive observer of human behaviour, not a judge.

Mary's belated growing up was greatly assisted by Lady M.'s chronic need to keep moving, to avoid the hated English glooms and alight continually, like some aging butterfly, in sun-drenched Mediterranean gardens. Mary vastly preferred London and the south coast to her mother's retreats on the French and Italian Rivieras. After a few jaunts to the Continent, Mary began asserting her independence; instead of being dragged halfway across Europe, she asked to be allowed to stay near friends and relatives who took her on outings to the South Kensington Museum or Hyde Park. Seeing the advantage to herself in travelling unencumbered, Lady M. slowly surrendered her guilty doubts and agreed to leave her daughter behind on occasion—especially since she'd found for Mary an English maid-companion whom she liked and trusted implicitly. The companion's name was Sarah Coward. Mary loves her dearly to this day, calling her "my Coward." The pair now reside comfortably together in Hove.

Lady M.'s other great anxiety over the years, aired and elaborated with me in countless ways, in person and by letter, was money.

Sir John's will had provided handsomely for both women. Yet Lady M. remained in the grip of an obsession: her means were surely going to fall disastrously short of her needs, and someday she and Mary would be stranded in debtors' prison. In fact, her inheritance was perfectly adequate, provided she curbed her longstanding tendency toward extravagance. But since I was Lady M.'s only real confidant among Sir John's executors, she spilled out her fears to me, and her finances became almost as absorbing a concern as my responsibilities in setting up Canada's foreign service.

I half expected Lady M. to take up her writing again during her quiet Italian winters. I'm sure *Murray's Magazine* in London would have been pleased to publish her lyrical impressions of Italian gardens; she also told me she was considering writing the story of her married life, and all the great events she'd shared with Sir John, but I don't believe she even started it. She never wrote for publication again. If she had, it would at least have brought in a little money to alleviate her financial worries.

These finally vexed her so much that they led to the terrible rift between us which I regret to this day.

It began with our difference of opinion over the best way to invest and manage the capital on which she depended. Then came the awful revelation that the man I'd appointed to be her solicitor was far less prudent, competent or honest than I'd thought. To my horror, I discovered he'd been pocketing some of Lady M.'s interest income; in addition, he'd kept her financial records in a chaotic state. Naturally I fired him at once, lamely explaining to the Baroness that, being dreadfully busy, and being neither a lawyer nor an accountant, I'd felt compelled to trust a trained professional and had seen no evidence of untrustworthiness. But by then it was too late.

Her reply was full of cold anger. Clearly her patience with me was exhausted. It was no longer "Dear Old Joe"—instead it was "Dear Sir Joseph Pope" (my having received in 1911 a knighthood for my years of public service). She implied that I'd shown far more interest in archiving Sir John's papers than in looking after her affairs. She demanded that I transfer her investments to the Royal Trust Company, and her letter concluded: "I also hope and expect that no more correspondence between you and me will be continued by or desired by you."

She was then seventy-seven and more indomitable than ever. For a while I wondered if an old woman's injured and insulted pride would pass. It didn't.

Despite receiving such a letter after twenty-two years of faithful friendship and (unpaid) service toward her, and despite my heightened responsibilities as Canada and the world drifted toward war, and despite my alarm over our son Maurice's enlisting to fight overseas, I found it impossible not to follow the continuing drama of her existence. The Great War caught Lady M. and Mary on holiday in the Swiss Alps, but they managed to return to Italy, where they resourcefully and safely lived out the war years. In the summer of 1916, Lady M. suffered a stroke in San Remo but was soon back at her villa, resting in her garden.

She and Mary remained in Italy long after the war, returning to London only in the summer of 1920. They moved into a flat in the resort town of Eastbourne, where they'd stayed before the war. It was there that Lady M. had her second, fatal stroke, and it was there—not in Ottawa or Kingston, but separated by a vast cold grey ocean from Sir John—where she was buried last year.

Shortly afterwards I received my first letter from Mary. It was neatly typed and correctly spelled, and at first I assumed Miss Coward must have had something to do with that; now I'm not so sure. "Mother's end was quite calm, as she was quite unconscious and therefore did not know anyone," Mary told me. "She was absolutely helpless and had to be carried up and down stairs."

I tried to imbue my reply with all the long-suppressed warmth I had for Mary and her mother. No doubt I sounded more formal than I really felt, but a certain restraint remains the habit of a lifetime: "I received news of your dear Mother's death with great regret. Though of late years an estrangement unfortunately grew between us, I do not forget our long friendship, nor her many kindnesses to me." And more in that vein.

Mary is a woman of fifty-two now. No one, not even Sir John, who loved her with a fierce tenderness, ever dreamt she'd live so long. No one in the days of her youth could have believed she'd achieve so much independence and control over her life. In her capacity to surprise us with her intelligence, charm, strength of character and sheer endurance, Mary is assuredly her father's child.

I speak, I suppose, as a recognized authority. The literary side of my career has been devoted entirely to Sir John: to documenting his achievements, recording his beliefs, clarifying his principles, explaining his character.

From the moment he was interred at Kingston, I was hounded by enterprising, not to say unscrupulous, publishers out to make a quick dollar from the grief Canadians felt over his disappearance. The publishers wanted a book out within the year and made me tempting offers; I told them no, it was too soon. Better to allow some time to elapse and do the job properly, I said. It was all very well for irresponsible scribblers to take advantage of the wave of sympathy and fascination inspired by Sir John's death and get out quick "lives" while his memory was still green, and no fewer than three of them did. For myself, I couldn't approach the subject in any such spirit.

When my *Memoirs of the Right Honourable Sir John Alexander Macdonald* appeared in two volumes in Canada, Great Britain and the United States, over three years had elapsed since his passing. Even then, I stopped the action of the book regrettably short: in 1873, after the so-called Pacific Scandal, a point when much of his life's great work had been accomplished, but much more was still to come.

Ending the narrative there had been Lady M.'s idea. Too many events were still fresh, she'd contended, and too many of the principal actors still alive and likely to be wounded by Sir John's candid and unsparing assessments. As his literary executor, I'd received complete, unrestricted access to his letters, memoranda and other papers; I had plenty of documentation to supplement my personal knowledge of Sir John's opinions, and enough leeway to write what I wanted. But in any case I followed her direction. At that stage I was still a relatively young man and unsure of my own judgment.

Later I doubted I'd been right. I tried to repair the gap by publishing a brief "life" covering Sir John's whole career in the *Chronicles of Canada* series. My other literary endeavours, however, have been of greater scholarly interest.

It was a matter of immense satisfaction and pride to me to work closely for many years with Sir Wilfrid Laurier after he succeeded the four Prime Ministers of the brief Tory interregnum, including John Thompson (may he rest in peace). Prime Minister Laurier continued building the nation on the foundations laid by Sir John. While serving as Sir Wilfrid's Undersecretary of State, I was able to persuade him that the country's public records were in a deplorable and perilous condition; storing our national documents in a variety of leaky Ottawa buildings, ill-sorted, inaccessible and physically unsafe, was a lamentable disgrace. Sir Wilfrid readily agreed. He wholeheartedly supported my proposal to create the Public Archives of Canada after a fine dinner one night at his home on Theodore Street, Minette distracting Madame Laurier in a corner with photographs of the children. Consequently I succeeded in creating a secure, permanent home for Sir John's priceless papers—having already sorted and classified them in every moment I could spare from my official duties.

Flowing from these labours is the volume I'm now about to publish with Oxford University Press: *The Correspondence of Sir John Macdonald*, my annotated selection of my former chief's letters. I've drawn them from the totality of his seventy thousand pieces of correspondence with the great and small stretching back nearly six decades.

Why have I devoted so much of my later years to this huge enterprise? When people ask, I tell them I'm simply acting on my belief that life would be tolerable were it not for its amusements. Instead of attending dinner parties or fishing or playing golf, I'd far rather work, and I couldn't have been happier than editing Sir John's letters for publication in whatever time I could snatch from the daily grind.

I had, of course, a deeper motive.

Twenty-seven years ago I concluded my biography of Sir John by writing that, just as a grand bronze statue had been erected to his memory on Parliament Hill, in time many other cities and towns across Canada would honour our nation's architect. By now it's sadly clear I was wrong. Time rushes by. Prime Ministers, Presidents, sovereigns, wars, loyalties, customs, beliefs succeed each other pell-mell. Fashions in art, literature, politics and morality now care nothing for the masters and precepts of the past. Now the fashion in our political leaders is for the small-minded and the practical, the careful and the colourless—dreary little men like Mr. Meighen and Mr. King, neither with an ounce of the warmth, wit, charm and vision of Sir John or Sir Wilfrid, both of whom inspired us and made us thankful to be Canadians.

Afflicted as they are with historical amnesia, my countrymen now remember Sir John—if they remember him at all—as a caricature: a tippler and schemer, a miscreant and rogue. But if they don't know him as he actually was, or understand what he stood for, how will they ever understand their country? How will they know themselves as civic beings? A nation's existence, after all, resides first in the minds and hearts of its people; it is therefore subject to mortality. And so I've done whatever has lain in my power to make Sir John's true nature clear to all. A few writers and readers of history—too few, to be honest—have thanked me.

Late one night after completing my most recent labour of love, I burned certain of Sir John's papers that I'd set aside. These were pages that will never again see the light of day, either in my book or the Public Archives. Among them were notes of the extraordinary and outlandish dreams he dreamt at the end of his life, which have in part allowed me to construct the present narrative.

I was actually surprised by how few pages required destruction. In sixty years a man can make many enemies, but Sir John, for all his partisanship, left behind relatively little that cannot bear public scrutiny from this day forward.

In consigning the papers to our fireplace after Minette had retired for the night, I burned them—the majority at least—not because their publication would have done Sir John's own memory any great or lasting harm, but out of consideration for the memory of others. I'm entirely confident that this is what he himself would have wished. My action may seem presumptuous, but it was consistent with the paramount, self-imposed mission of my life since Sir John's death. Approaching my own end of days, knowing it can't be far, I take enormous comfort in knowing I serve him still.

"History is not what happened in the past, but the best story we can tell with the available material," writes Joshua Wolf Shenk in *Lincoln's Melancholy*. Even historians tell stories, although we call their writing non-fiction.

Macdonald makes no pretence to being history. It is a work of the imagination, based on stories about Sir John A. Macdonald and his times that have been handed down to us by historians and biographers, memoirists and journalists. A few of the incidents in this novel and most of the conversations are imagined. Scholars of Canadian history will recognize at least three principal scenes where I've chosen to depart from the historical record and let my imagination run. There is more than one avenue to the truth.

Yet *Macdonald* rests on a substructure of recorded fact. Even its inventions are constructed largely from Sir John's written or spoken words, and from anecdotes and *bons mots* attributed to him by people who knew him well—first and foremost his private secretary from 1882 to 1891, Joseph Pope. The parliamentary exchanges are drawn from debates recorded in *Hansard*.

Although the novel is generally true to the sequence of events during the last five months of Macdonald's life, I've taken a small liberty here and there. The first horseless streetcars would not appear on the streets of Ottawa until June 1891, but I've put them there in March; Macdonald's Minister of Justice, Sir John Thompson, was knighted before 1891, but I've omitted Thompson's title because two Sir Johns would have been confusing. On the other hand, details of Macdonald's medical treatment during his final days are as accurate as I could make them, based on the recollections of his personal physician, Robert Wynyard Powell, on deposit in Library and Archives Canada, an institution that Joseph Pope was instrumental in founding; physical and meteorological details of Macdonald's death watch and funeral are drawn from eyewitness reports in newspapers and books.

I felt moved to write this novel on reading Donald Creighton's great two-volume biography, *John A. Macdonald: The Young Politician* (1952) and *John A. Macdonald: The Old Chieftain* (1955). These books had belonged to my late father, William T. MacSkimming, a Scottish immigrant to Canada like Sir John himself; reading them became a search for the father, in both a personal and national sense.

The literature on Macdonald is scarcely as voluminous as that on Washington or Lincoln, but readers curious to delve further into the historical record will find the following works also enlightening and even inspiring:

E. B. Biggar, *Anecdotal Life of Sir John Macdonald*

Sandra Gwyn, *The Private Capital: Ambition and Love in the Age of Macdonald and Laurier*

J. K. Johnson, ed., *Affectionately Yours: The Letters of Sir John A. Macdonald and His Family*

Lawrence Martin, *The Presidents and the Prime Ministers: Washington and Ottawa Face to Face, the Myth of Bilateral Bliss, 1867–1982*

Lena Newman, *The John A. Macdonald Album*

Joseph Pope, *Memoirs of the Right Honourable Sir John Alexander Macdonald, G.C.B., First Prime Minister of the Dominion of Canada*, vols. 1 and 2

[my copies of the original 1894 edition belonged to Joseph-Israël
Tarte and are signed by him]
Maurice Pope, ed., *Public Servant: The Memoirs of Sir Joseph Pope*
Louise Reynolds, *Agnes: The Biography of Lady Macdonald*
Maggie Siggins, *Riel: A Life of Revolution*
Cynthia M. Smith and Jack McLeod, eds., *Sir John A.: An Anecdotal Life
of John A. Macdonald*
P. B. Waite, *Canada 1874–1896: Arduous Destiny*

For their invaluable encouragement and faith in this novel, I'm
deeply grateful to my first reader, Suzette DeLey MacSkimming;
my literary agent, Dean Cooke; and my publisher and editor,
Patrick Crean. I also wish to thank Jim Allen of Thomas Allen
Publishers, John Bemrose, Bill Hawkins, Chris Wells and Helga
Zimmerly, all of whom read an early draft, and the Canada Council for the Arts. The seed of this novel was planted in my subcon-
scious over two decades ago when I edited Heather Robertson's
fictional trilogy based on Prime Minister Mackenzie King, starting with *Willie: A Romance*.

R. M.